INNSMOUTH

The Weird of Hali

Novels by John Michael Greer

The Weird of Hali:

I – *Innsmouth*

II – *Kingsport*

III – *Chorazin*

IV – *Dreamlands*

V – *Providence*

VI – *Red Hook*

VII – *Arkham*

Others:

The Fires of Shalsha

Star's Reach

Twilight's Last Gleaming

Retrotopia

The Shoggoth Concerto

The Nyogtha Variations

A Voyage to Hyperborea

The Seal of Yueh Lao

Journey Star

The Witch of Criswell

INNSMOUTH

The Weird of Hali

Book One

John Michael Greer

Published in 2023 by
Sphinx Books
London

British Library Cataloguing in Publication Data

A C.I.P. for this book is available from the British Library

ISBN-13: 978-1-91257-387-5

Typeset by Medlar Publishing Solutions Pvt Ltd, India

www.aeonbooks.co.uk/sphinx

The prophet's blood pools scarlet on the stone.
His eyes, that knew futurity and fate,
Stare blind and bleeding through a broken gate
Into a burning fane, where he alone
Once heard the inmost whispers of the Earth.
Did they forewarn him of the cold command,
The pounding hooves, the weapon in the hand
That struck him down, the laugh of brutal mirth?
Now muffled figures murmur in the night
His final words; now others gaze aghast
At fell shapes rising from the sleepless past.
The age that dawned there, in the flame's red light,
Shall end in flame when, as he prophesied,
Four join their hands where gray rock meets gray tide.
　　　　　　　　　　—"Hali" by Justin Geoffrey

CONTENTS

CHAPTER 1

THE HOUSE ON HALSEY STREET

The door closed with a bang, shutting out the raw September evening and the Arkham streetscape outside. Owen Merrill swung his backpack off one broad shoulder and plopped it on the floor of the entry, got his wet coat hung on a peg on the wall, then scooped up the pack again and went through the door into the living room.

One of his housemates, Jenny Parrish, was curled up on the battered old couch with a brown nineteenth-century volume open in front of her, her thin pale face just visible through a mop of mouse-colored hair. She gave him an owlish look. "Hi, Owen."

"Hi." Indistinct sounds came from the dining room, and a moment later voices followed them—one belonged to Barry Holzer, another housemate; the other to Kenji Takamura, Barry's friend and perennial study partner. Owen dropped his pack on the overstuffed chair he liked best and went into the dining room, where Barry and Kenji were huddled over a couple of laptops, working on a class assignment.

"Hey, it's our historian of ideas," Barry said, looking at Owen over the top of his glasses. His blond hair and the brown beard on his chin both looked dyed, though Owen knew better. "Those ideas getting any more hysterical?"

1

The joke hadn't improved any with age, Owen decided. "Laugh a minute," he said. "That program you're writing's going to take your next two jobs away from you, you know."

"I for one welcome our new cybernetic overlords," Barry said, grinning. Kenji laughed and rolled his eyes.

Owen went on into the kitchen, got water heating in a saucepan and found a packet of dollar store ramen in his end of the cupboard. That went into the water as soon as it boiled, along with half a packet of mixed frozen vegetables and a vaguely grayish hot dog from a plastic bag in the fridge. Ten minutes, a pat of margarine, and a splash of cheap soy sauce later, dinner was ready. He poured it into a big bowl, fetched a fork, soaked the saucepan in the sink, and headed back through the dining room.

"Still chasing down stuff in the basement spooky section?" Barry asked.

"Of course," said Owen.

"You gotta lay off the tentacles, man," Barry told him. Kenji gave him a puzzled look and Barry turned to him. "Owen's doing his thesis on Lovecraft."

"Oh my God," said Kenji. "Say it isn't so."

"'Rhetorics of Otherness in the Horror Fiction of H.P. Lovecraft,'" Owen quoted himself. "Miskatonic's got one of the two best Lovecraft archives in the country, and a couple of the best Lovecraft scholars anywhere, so why not?"

Kenji dropped his face into his hands in mock despair. "Why not, he says. Look, I know Lovecraft is Arkham's one feeble claim to fame. I know the town would go belly up in fifteen minutes without the Lovecraft Museum, the festival, all that crap—but for the love of God, do you have to encourage them? And now there's that new deejay on WMSK—"

"The one who calls himself the Fun Guy from Yuggoth?" Barry asked, with a wicked grin. "He's pretty good. Have you listened to his show?"

Kenji shuddered. "No. I don't want my brain to dribble out my ears."

"I'm not actually much of a Lovecraft fan," said Owen, "but from a history of ideas standpoint, the guy's really interesting."

"I'll take your word for it," said Kenji. "You want to spend your time with Cthulhu, Nyarlathotep, Yog-Sothoth, and the rest of that crew—"

"Iâ Shub-Niggurath!" Barry belted out with revival-meeting enthusiasm. "Black Goat of the Woods with a Thousand Young?"

"—see what I mean?" Kenji said. "They've already eaten Barry's brain. Yours is next."

Owen laughed and went back out into the living room, displaced his pack from the chair, slumped back into it and attacked the ramen. He was halfway through it when the door slammed again, and "Hey, all" sounded from the entry.

"Hi, Tish," Jenny and Owen both said.

Tish Martin sailed into the living room and dumped a brightly colored shoulderbag of books on the end of the couch Jenny wasn't occupying. She untied the red scarf around her head and shook loose a torrent of long braids with a sigh of relief. "Oh man," she said. "I thought today wasn't *ever* going to be over." She headed for the kitchen, and her voice, Barry's, and Kenji's tumbled over each other.

Owen finished his ramen, ducked past the conversation into the kitchen to soak the bowl, came back out, grabbed his backpack and headed for the stair. Two flights up he turned down a mostly unlit hall, unlocked a door, stepped through. Inside was a cramped L-shaped room with cracked plaster on the walls, and five mismatched pieces of furniture—bed, dresser, bookcase, desk and desk chair—that had been handed down to him from decades of Miskatonic grad students and would doubtless be passed on to decades more. The landlord didn't allow anything to be hung on the walls, so there weren't many personal touches, just the books, a scattering of notebooks and papers on the desk, and a photo in a cheap standing frame on the dresser: half a dozen young men in desert fatigues, arms around each other's shoulders, standing in front of the Air

Force plane that was about to take them home. A younger Owen was on the left, sandy hair in an Army buzzcut, an uncommon grin across his square solemn face.

He went to the room's one window. It faced north, looking down on the gambrel-roofed houses on that side of Halsey Street, a stretch of rain-soaked sidewalk that had seen many better days, and a narrow slice of street. Further off, a line of leafless trees clawed at the clouds, and beyond them the cyclopean masses of Miskatonic University's main buildings rose stark and angular against a darkening gray sky. He had something like a thousand pages of reading to get through in the next week and a dozen pages to write to keep his thesis on schedule, but he stood at the window for a moment longer, staring down moodily at the sidewalk.

Kenji was right, he thought: there really was no getting away from H.P. Lovecraft in Arkham. Though the man himself spent most of his life down in Providence, and visited Arkham all of three times, he'd set so many of his most famous stories in and around the town that the local chamber of commerce started seeing dollar signs once his stories came back into fashion. They'd turned Lovecraft into the same sort of combination patron saint and cash cow that Salem made out of the old witch trials.

These days there was the Lovecraft Museum to bring in the tourists, and a Lovecraft Days festival every August, complete with vendors selling "What Part of Cthulhu Fhtagn Don't You Understand?" bumper stickers and a costume parade for eldritch horrors of all ages. The park between Federal Street and Peabody Avenue, Washington Park until then, had been renamed Lovecraft Park, and had a bronze statue of the man himself in the middle of it, standing there looking off vaguely westwards while three bronze tentacles writhed around his feet and an eye on a stalk peered up at him from under the pedestal. You couldn't walk three blocks anywhere north of the Miskatonic without seeing something Lovecraft-themed perched in a shop window or dangling from the rearview mirror of a passing car.

He shook his head, tried to focus. Crows circled over the Miskatonic campus, cars on Derby Street grumbled to themselves and moved on, the distant hills north of town rose up somber to rounded peaks marked here and there with circles of standing stones: a normal fall evening in Arkham. The day's classes had been fine, and the next section of his thesis wasn't going to be any kind of a problem, he knew. Still, something had his nerves on edge.

He opened the backpack and hauled out a stack of books with Orne Library call numbers on the spines, then popped his laptop open and clicked on the folder where he kept his music downloads. A tap on the mousepad brought the first chords of an old Muddy Waters blues piece belting out of the speakers. The sonic environment settled, he got to work on his thesis.

Below, a tall figure in a long black coat and a broad-brimmed black hat came striding along the sidewalk, glanced up at the window, walked on.

* * *

The next morning Owen was dressed in his usual sweatshirt and jeans and ready to head out the door while most of his housemates were puttering around in bathrobes and pajamas. Two sliced bagels and a cup of tea the color of road tar did for breakfast; he washed his dishes from the previous night, left them in the drying rack, scooped up his backpack and headed for campus. The last drops of another rainstorm came splashing down from a ragged sky as the door closed behind him. He dodged puddles on the sidewalk—his shoes were worn enough that stepping in one meant wet socks all day—up to Derby Street, trotted across it when the traffic gapped open, then waited for the light to get across Federal Street, which cut straight through campus on its way out of town to Innsmouth and Newburyport.

On the far side of the street was a big bronze statue of Cthulhu, the tentacle-faced Great Old One whose obscure legends Lovecraft made famous in his fiction, perched atop a pedestal with the words LOVECRAFT MUSEUM in faux-spooky letters below it. Behind it was a parking lot, and behind that was the museum itself, housed in the old gray Arkham Sanitarium building. Some prankster had stuffed a beer can into the Great Old One's outstretched hand, which was mild by Miskatonic standards. Come winter break, if campus tradition was any guide, Cthulhu would be wearing a Santa Claus hat.

The light finally changed, and he and the dozen other students who'd piled up at the crosswalk surged across. Alongside the parking lot ran the huge brick mass of Orne Library, and beyond that was the Armitage Union, with the delirious angles of Wilmarth Hall just visible over its roof. Owen cut across the parking lot, started up the walk between the student union and the library, then veered over to the Armitage Union's south entrance to check out the bulletin boards.

Somebody had stapled a solid line of flyers across the top of every one of the boards, with EXPERIMENTAL SUBJECTS WANTED across the top, a bunch of small print below that, and a ninth floor room number in Belbury Hall, the psychology building, on the bottom. Somebody else had plastered big posters about a lecture on Man's Future in Space here and there over the top of everything else. Owen ignored them both. Further down, in among the rooms for rent, lost pets, things for sale, and housemates wanted, were the posters he was looking for, announcing music gigs. Mostly Arkham got local garage bands with names like Squidface and Hatheg-Kla, but every so often something better showed up.

That day Owen was in luck. A poster down toward the bottom of one board yelled ISAAC JAX AND HIS COTTON-MOUTHS—DELTA STYLE BLUES, with the date and a few other details below it. The rest of the poster showed a crossroads under a crescent moon, with a tall figure in a broad-brimmed hat and a long coat standing there, backlit by the moonlight. Owen fished a pen and a little spiral notebook from his jacket pocket and noted down the details. He didn't know the band, but a few minutes online would fix that, and if they were any good he'd want to try to make time to go see them.

From there he crossed the quad to Morgan Hall and found his way through mostly empty halls to his morning class, a critical-theory seminar. It was as bland as cold oatmeal and a good deal less substantial, but he took notes dutifully, tried not to watch the clock too obviously while the minutes ticked away. When it was over, he extracted himself from the class-room, took the stairs down to the entrance two at a time, and crossed the quad again to Orne Library.

He went in the big main entrance and turned immediately to the right, heading straight for an inconspicuous door over in an angle. Beyond the door was a bare concrete stair, dimly lit, leading down into the basement of the library. He trotted down the stair, came to an unmarked metal door at the bot-tom, opened it onto a bare corridor that led to another, identi-cal door. Beyond that was a little office with a desk in it and another blank door beyond it. Nobody was in the office, so Owen went to the door and pushed the buzzer next to it.

A minute later the lock clicked, the door opened, and a wrin-kled face framed in flyaway white hair peered out through it. "Owen? Yes, I thought that would be you. Come in, come in."

The door opened the rest of the way to let Owen through, clicked shut behind him as the old man waved him through. Beyond was a bare windowless room with concrete walls and rows of steel bookshelves under the glare of long rows of fluorescent lamps. Another desk was just inside the door; further in were two steel tables with a scattering of chairs, and that was all.

Owen put his pack on the desk, pulled his laptop out of it, set it on one of the tables and fetched two cotton gloves from a box nearby.

"What will it be this time?" the old man asked him, regarding him with disconcertingly bright blue eyes. "Von Junzt again, I suppose."

Owen nodded. "He's not quick reading."

The old man made a sound halfway between a laugh and cough. "No. You really do need to work on your German, you know. The Bridewell translation's riddled with errors, and you miss far too much that's in the original."

"Oh, I know," said Owen. "But then I'd also have to learn Arabic for *Al Azif*, Latin for Prinn and the *Liber Ivonis*, Greek *koine* for the Pnakotica—"

"Well, of course," the old man said, as though that was the most obvious thing in the world. "But you'd also want a grounding in Old Lomarian for that last one, of course. The Greek text is by no means wholly reliable, you know, and the surviving Lomarian fragments really do need to be consulted if you want to be properly thorough about it."

Owen laughed, said nothing, and followed the old man back into the stacks.

"Here you are," said the old man. The book he handed Owen was a stout nineteenth-century volume with *The Book of Nameless Cults* in ornate script on the spine. Owen took it carefully in both hands, carried it back to the table. The old man went back to his desk, sat there with one eye on Owen and one on some project of his own. The sound of his pencil scratching over the paper and the ticking of the clock high on the wall were the only sounds in the room.

Owen didn't mind any of it. Dr. Abelard Whipple was the restricted-collection librarian at Orne Library; his eccentricities were a reliable topic of Miskatonic gossip, but Owen had spent enough time in the restricted stacks to be comfortable with the old man's habits. He booted up his laptop, then paged through the book until he got to the place he'd stopped reading two days before, and launched into another of von Junzt's lurid accounts of lost continents, vanished civilizations, prehuman races, and forgotten beliefs. The chapter before him was an account of the dealings of the ancient prophet Hali with Nyarlathotep the Crawling Chaos, the messenger of the Great Old Ones, and Owen soon lost the thread of the story amid the tangled thickets of nineteenth-century prose.

All of it was thesis fodder, though. Lovecraft had borrowed heavily from von Junzt and half a dozen other volumes of occult literature from ancient and medieval times, taking colorful details and sometimes entire plots out of them for his stories. Showing how those borrowings had shaped Lovecraft's sense of the Other was central to the argument Owen was making in his thesis. He spent most of three hours taking notes, before sitting back and closing the book.

At the sound, the old man looked up from his work. "Enough for the day?"

"I've got a class at one," Owen said.

"Too many classes and not enough time for real scholarship, that's the problem with today's university," said Dr. Whipple. "I grant you this, you apply yourself. I wish that could be said of others. Why, I had someone here yesterday afternoon who couldn't be bothered to spend a quarter hour on anything. Get a book, page through it, scribble something down, and then it was on to the next book. How anyone can expect to learn anything that way, I'm sure I have no idea."

Owen shut his laptop, stood up. "Don't worry about the book," the old man said to him. "I'll get it put back in a moment."

"Thanks. See you Sunday, Dr. Whipple."

"Of course, of course. See you then, Owen."

* * *

Lunch at the Armitage Union was two slices of greasy pizza and a cup of tea downed while checking email and looking up Isaac Jax and His Cottonmouths. Then it was out the door and back across the quad to Morgan Hall, and down a narrow inconvenient stair to his afternoon class. That was History of Ideas 488, American Popular Culture 1919–1941, one of a half dozen classes on the odd corners of the past that only got onto the schedule because the professors who liked to teach them had enough clout to get them there or were close enough to retirement not to care about campus politics. HID 488 was one of Dr. Miriam Akeley's pet classes, and even though she rarely got thirty students for it and had to teach it in a dismal basement classroom, word in the department was that she'd made it plain that she planned on teaching it every few years until they carried her off campus feet first.

When Owen arrived, Professor Akeley was perched on the edge of her chair, silver-haired and lean as a heron, dressed in her usual black dress and white sweater. Owen took a seat in the back row. Strictly speaking, he was auditing the class as one of Akeley's grad students, though she didn't pay much attention to such technicalities. The moment the clock said one, she stood up, walked to the podium in front, and launched into the lecture.

"Degeneration," she said. "Americans between the wars were terrified of it—terrified that all the progress of the previous century would turn out to be temporary. It wasn't just political or economic or cultural decline that scared them, but raw biological decadence. Nowadays we barely recognize the concept. Back then it was front page stuff."

She started pacing across the front of the room. "Was there a racial subtext to it? Of course. There was a racial subtext to everything in American popular culture between the wars. We'll be talking more about that next week. What I want to focus on right now is the way that the people who thought of themselves as the cultural and ethnic American mainstream felt beseiged by biology, dragged down by their own bodies toward the primordial slime."

At the far side of the room, she turned suddenly. "Owen, you're our Lovecraft scholar. Give us a description of a common or garden variety Great Old One."

"Sure," said Owen. "Here's a quote. 'Gigantic—tentacled—proboscidian—octopus-eyed—semi-amorphous—plastic—partly squamous and partly rugose—ugh!'"

The "ugh" got a general laugh. When it died down, Professor Akeley went on. "That is to say, alive. Biological. Not clean and cerebral and linear and abstract. Let's follow that same thread elsewhere." Then she was off, pacing back and forth, making sharp gestures with her hands to punctuate her words, quoting at length from a dozen different American writers of the era, trying to get her students to think their way into a world of ideas their great-grandparents had inhabited. It was classic Miriam Akeley, entirely extempore and so full of citations and facts that those students who weren't simply watching open-mouthed were taking notes as fast as they could and still struggling to keep up.

"It's easy to laugh at these ideas," she said as the clock showed ten to two. "The thing is, we've still got many of the same attitudes today. Most of us still think that reason trumps everything else, that the mind is superior to the body, that the artificial is always an improvement on the natural—we glorify the sterile and mechanical, and our reaction to living matter is still Lovecraft's 'Ugh.'" She sat down, waved her hand. "That's it for now. See you all Monday."

Most of the students headed for the door. A few went forward instead with questions or comments, and after the crowd thinned out, Owen unfolded himself from his chair and went up to join them. He stood back, waited for the conversations to wind down.

Finally the last of the students made off. Professor Akeley looked up at Owen from her chair, and said, "Ugh."

"Ugh," he replied cheerfully.

She pulled herself out of the chair, started for the door. "I hope that lecture wasn't too erratic. I was more than a little distracted. Shelby told me this morning that she won't be continuing her assistantship in the spring semester."

"She—what?"

"Yes, that's more or less what I said, too." They left the class-room, crossed the hallway outside and started up the inconve-nient stair.

"Some kind of personal thing?"

"No, that's just it. She's changing departments. The new program over in Belbury Hall—I don't know if you've heard about it yet—she's dropped out of history of ideas to take her degree there, and gotten an assistantship for spring semester."

The door at the top of the stair opened onto the main entrance of Morgan Hall, which was crowded with students, so neither of them spoke until they were outside and angling across the quad toward the sprawling concrete hallucination of Wilmarth Hall.

"I don't know why she's throwing away everything she's done so far in our department," Professor Akeley went on once they were out of anyone else's earshot. "I can't think of any-thing I did or said that might have upset her, but this morning she was rather—brusque, I think, would be the right word. Not like her at all."

"I'll ask her," Owen said. "We talk fairly often."

"Thank you." She shook her head. "How's the thesis coming?"

"It's plodding along. I was sitting there for the last hour taking down the names of books—I had no idea how heavily Lovecraft drew on the whole racial decline thing."

"Oh, yes, in his own way he was quite the heir of the fin-de-siècle Decadents. Have you read Max Nordau's *Degeneration*?"

"Not yet."

"I don't think Orne Library still has it, not the way they've been purging the collection, but I've got a secondhand copy of the English translation at home—very popular in Lovecraft's time. You can borrow it, if you like."

"Thank you."

"You're welcome." They reached the bulbous main door of Wilmarth Hall, and Professor Akeley turned to face him. "You're still available tomorrow, I hope."

"Of course."

"Good. We've just gotten another three boxes from Milwaukee, from the Harriet Blake estate. Bron emailed that he's pretty sure a couple of the letters are in Lovecraft's handwriting."

"No kidding."

"That's what he says. Well, we'll see."

* * *

The next day was a Saturday. Owen got up early anyway—though he'd been out of the Army more than six years, he still had trouble sleeping much past dawn most mornings—and had the downstairs to himself for hours. By the time Tish came down the stairs in pajamas and a garish plaid bathrobe, in search of the day's first cup of coffee, he'd had breakfast, done his share of the dishes, and put two hours of hard work into his thesis, turning the citations he'd found in von Junzt into a good quarter or so of the section on Lovecraft's use of magical literature.

"It's way too early," Tish told him as she came back from the kitchen with a cup in her hand. "Don't you dare look that cheerful."

Owen laughed and shut his laptop. "You'll feel better after the second cup."

"The second pot, maybe." She flopped onto the couch, pushed her braids out of her face. "Tell me again why I thought med school was a good idea. Another semester like this and they'll just about have to haul me down to West Annex and flop me on the slab with the other cadavers."

"Beats flipping burgers."

She grinned. "You know perfectly well I used to be an assistant hotel manager."

"I hope I get that lucky." Owen shouldered his backpack. "You know what the liberal arts grad student says on his first job."

"Yeah. 'Would you like fries with that?'" Tish shook her head. "Owen, you'll do better than that, you know you will."

"I don't know. Some days, assistant hotel manager sounds like a good idea." He went into the entry. "See you later."

Outside the wind was blowing brisk and raw out of the west, sending dead leaves scurrying across the pavement. Owen tried to shove his worries out of his mind as he took his usual route to campus, past the Cthulhu statue and Orne Library, and then across the quad to Wilmarth Hall.

Back in his undergraduate years at Purdue, Owen had taken a survey class on the history of architecture, and the professor who taught it livened up the last day of class by showing the weirdest examples of American campus architecture he could find. Owen hadn't so much as heard of Miskatonic University when Wilmarth Hall appeared on the screen during that class session, and he'd laughed, along with most of the other students in the lecture hall, at the bulbous, wrinkled shapes of concrete and steel that formed its walls and the dizzy profusion of spires and cupolas that made up its roofline. He'd laughed even harder when, after months of correspondence, he'd come to Arkham for the first time and realized that he was going to be doing much of the work for his master's program in that very building.

The main doors were out of order again—they had some kind of innovative-for-the-1960s mechanical hardware that never worked for long—so he ducked through one of the smaller doors that flanked it, headed for the stairway that wandered up the middle of the building, climbed to the seventh floor, went down the hall to the seventh door. Above the door was a century-old sign in ornate Old English letters:

Program in Medieval Metaphysics

That short-lived project from the 1920s had been the seed from which, through more than a dozen departmental reorganizations, Miskatonic's History of Ideas program had sprouted, and the sign had accompanied the program on its journey from the old campus downtown to the eldritch spires of Wilmarth Hall. The door beneath the sign was unlocked; Owen pushed it open.

"Owen? Oh, good," said Professor Akeley. With no classes to teach that day, she was wearing slacks and a half-illegible sweatshirt from some West Coast tourist attraction, and her silver hair was tied back in a ponytail. "Could you give me a hand with this?" She was trying to lift a carboard box that probably weighed half as much as she did.

Owen dropped his backpack on an office chair and went to help. The box was as heavy as it looked, and it shifted threateningly as they hauled it up onto a table. There were two other boxes on the floor that looked no lighter, but she waved him off when he went to pick one of them up. "We'll get one at a time. I'm pretty sure this one's full of books, but we'll see."

She went to her desk, got a box cutter from one of the drawers, attacked the strapping tape that sealed the box and got it to surrender after several tries. The flaps came open, the packing materials found their way into an undignified heap on the floor, and she started lifting out magazines with brown pages and covers that were a faded ghost of their once-gaudy selves.

"Pulps," Professor Akeley said disconsolately. "There might be something in there for the Upham Collection, but it's mostly *Weird Tales* and *Amazing Stories*, and they had every issue of those when I was still at UCLA." More magazines followed the first stack onto the table. "Here's something else," she said then, and a book with a dust jacket in fine art-deco style joined the magazines: *The People of the Monolith and Other Poems* by Justin Geoffrey.

"That's pretty rare, isn't it?" Owen asked.

"These days? Yes, though it had quite a run of popularity in its time. Lovecraft's copy is in the Orne—it's got dozens of his annotations in pencil." She gave him a sidelong look and a smile. "Those might make a good dissertation topic for somebody."

Owen laughed. "Let me get the thesis done and we'll talk."

He got the second box up on the table, started piling the packing material into the empty box while Professor Akeley cut more strapping tape and added to the heap. The second box held more magazines and a bundle of letters tied up in string, most of them from science fiction and fantasy authors of the Twenties and Thirties. Professor Akeley cut the string, sorted through the letters, and said, "Here you are. Two—no, three, from Lovecraft. No, here's another one. They look pretty ordinary, but you never know."

Once the second box had given up its treasures, the third box went on the table, and yielded more bundles: business letters to and from art galleries, this time, along with carbon copies of hand-typed manuscripts and responses from publishers. "Oh, my," said Professor Akeley, after sorting through a few of them. "This is going to interest quite a few people. These are Robert Blake's own copies of his work, and it's not just the stories he published before he died; this one looks like a sequel to "Shaggai," and this is longer—I think it's actually a short novel. I'll have to email Jim Willett at Brown and ask him if anybody knows about these."

She fished around in the packing material at the bottom of the box, then went to her desk. Owen glanced over the four letters; the handwriting was Lovecraft's typical half-legible scrawl, but he was able to pick out enough of it at a glance to follow the ordinary chitchat of one pulp magazine author to another. After a moment, he idly picked up the Justin Geoffrey book, opened it, read a few lines:

```
To pass that Gate, to wake the waiting shapes
That twist and writhe in their unhallowed
sleep:
Have I the strength? Or having come thus far,
Dare I draw back?
```

No wonder all the authors in Lovecraft's circle liked Geoffrey, he decided. He leafed further, and then the book fell open to a loose sheet of paper stuck between pages, covered with writing in a familiar hand. He lifted it out from between the pages, set the book down. "Five Lovecraft letters," he said.

"Anything interesting?"

For answer he walked over to the window and held the yellowing paper angled to catch the light. This is what it said:

April 18 1934

Dear Bob,

I hope you won't take it amiss if I revert to the points I tried to make in our conversation last night. I was taken aback by yr comments & don't think I stated things as strongly as I should. You're right, of course, that I once dabbled (and more than dabbled) in the old lore, but I've had reason to regret that ever since—whatever my stories might have gained from the experience, I assure you, was not worth the cost. I cannot be too emphatic in cautioning you not to follow my example. These things belong to an older time and should stay buried.

You mentioned my Innsmouth tale—many thanks for the praise! The story itself is of course merely a story, but I made free use of things I saw there in 1929 & also of the teachings I once studied. I didn't invent the Esoteric Order of Dagon, nor the city of Y'ha-nthlei. Nor, I'm sorry to say, the monstrous crossbreeds. That's bad enough when it takes place between races that are entirely human—but I'll write no more on that subject.

Use the lore in yr weird tales if you like, for the old dark superstitious beliefs build the right mood and atmosphere like nothing else. Mention a god here & a book there—name-dropping is as necessary to the author of supernatural horror as to the social climber—but I beg you most earnestly to leave the matter at that. There are real dangers in such things. I had much trouble escaping those dangers myself, and would feel I'd failed in the first duty of friendship if I didn't warn you off them.

But let us speak of better things! I was delighted to hear that Wright has agreed to publish "The Burrower Beneath"—may he be similarly inspired regarding yr other tales. I look forward to further daemonic blasphemies from yr pen.

Yr Obt.,
HPL

"That's—really strange," Owen said at last. He crossed to Professor Akeley's desk, handed her the letter. She read it, glanced at him with an oddly wary look, set it down on the desk, and swiveled in the chair to face him.

"True," she said. "I'd tend to question its authenticity. Everyone knows Lovecraft didn't have any interest in—" She glanced at the letter again. "—'the old dark superstitious beliefs' except as raw material for his stories. Do the other letters say anything odd?"

Owen went to the other four letters, read through them one at a time. "No," he said then. "There's some interesting stuff on some of Blake's stories, though."

The professor nodded, then indicated the letter from the book of poetry. "I'll have somebody look at this and see if the handwriting's genuine. Probably just someone's idea of a prank." She got up, went over to the table. "Let's see if we can get the rest of this sorted out."

CHAPTER 2

THE DEVIL AT THE CROSSROADS

O wen put that afternoon and evening into working on his thesis. More precisely, he tried to do so, between long periods spent staring out the window at the wet street below, thinking about things that had nothing to do with the transformations of Victorian horror fiction in Lovecraft's image of the Other. His thoughts kept circling back to other things: to the letter of Lovecraft's—if it was his at all, and not a forgery, as Professor Akeley seemed to think—but more often to the news about Shelby.

It made no sense. Shelby Adams was the rising star of Miskatonic's history of ideas department, guaranteed an assistantship for her doctorate program there if she didn't decide that Harvard would be a better career move. She'd already started attending conferences and had a paper published by one of the important journals, with another on the way, building the sort of reputation that would land her a top-notch position and a fast track to tenure once she got her Ph.D. and started teaching. You didn't chuck that kind of preparation, burn your bridges with your previous department, waste a couple of semesters worth of classes and jump into some other graduate program in—what had Miriam Akeley said? Some brand new program. At least, Owen told himself, you didn't do that if you were as ambitious as Shelby was.

That got him thinking of his own career prospects, a subject he'd tried to avoid of late. With each year's budget cuts landing first and hardest on the humanities, his chances of getting an assistantship in the doctorate program at Miskatonic or anywhere else were not looking good, and even if he managed to get his Ph.D., job openings at universities were scarce and those with a shot at tenure were scarcer still. He shook his head, tried to drag his thoughts back to the paper. You made your choice six years ago, he told himself, stick with it.

Rain pattered against the window. It sounded uncomfortably as though someone or something was laughing at him. True enough, he'd made his choice; he'd taken his G.I. Bill benefits straight out of the Army into Purdue, and come out four years later with a cum laude degree and two assistantship offers from grad schools; a doctorate and a teaching position were the next stations on the line. All the way along, though, he'd felt out of place, and more so since he'd come to Miskatonic. Maybe it was just that he was older than his classmates, and come to the university from a school of hard knocks in which firefights and roadside bombs were the required courses. Maybe.

Only after the sky was dark, and he'd downed another dinner of dollar-store ramen fancied up with whatever had been cheapest at the grocery the week before, did he finally manage to push aside worries about Shelby and his career, and concentrate on his work. The words finally started to flow, and he typed late into the night, finally turning in when the screen began to blur into meaninglessness before his eyes and only the very occasional car engine made itself heard past the muttering of the night wind.

The first church bells finally woke him—he'd managed to sleep past dawn for once—and Orne Library wasn't open till noon anyway, so he put the morning into his reading. At ten to noon, extracting himself from a stack of books, Owen threw on his coat and headed for campus. Someone had chalked GO SHOGS on the pedestal of the Cthulhu statue—the Miskatonic administration and the national media insisted on referring to the college team as the Mariners, but everyone in Arkham called them the Shoggoths, after another of the legendary critters Lovecraft had made famous—and stuffed a Miskatonic pennant on a stick into the tentacled god's outstretched hand. He recalled after a moment that the football team was playing a home game that night, and made a mental note to try to get home before the game let out and the bars filled up.

He'd almost reached the entrance to Orne Library when one of the doors opened and a familiar figure came out. "Shelby!" he said. "Hey."

"Hi, Owen." She stopped as he walked over to her.

"You got a moment?"

"About that." White-blonde hair whipped around her face in the wind.

"I heard about you leaving History of Ideas."

"Yes." She smiled. "Have you heard about the Noology Program?"

The phrase wasn't familiar to him. "No."

"You should check it out. It's *the* cutting edge, and ten years from now it's going to be the only game in town. Here." She dug in her purse, pulled out a flyer folded in thirds, handed it to him. "Ninth floor, Belbury Hall—ask for Dr. Noyes. You really should look into it." She started walking. "Got to run. Bye!"

"Take care," he called after her, then glanced at the flyer, stuffed it in his pocket, and went into the library.

Down in the restricted stacks, he greeted Dr. Whipple, settled down with von Junzt, and spent a good five hours in the notional company of Cthulhu and his eldritch kin. The last two chapters of the book were full of material Lovecraft had cribbed: a long passage about the god Yog-Sothoth, who was both the Gate and the Guardian of the Gate—whatever that meant—and appeared in the form of iridescent spheres of light; two confused legends of the fertility goddess Lovecraft called Shub-Niggurath, though von Junzt spelled the name differently; some cryptic passages about the King in Yellow and the Yellow Sign; more about black-clad Nyarlathotep, who roamed the earth in the service of his eldritch masters; and then, just before the end of the book, a long and ornate account of Cthulhu himself, dead yet dreaming in the drowned city of R'lyeh, until the stars came round right again and released him from his long imprisonment.

Owen didn't get up from his chair until he'd finished with von Junzt. The old man nodded approvingly, told Owen not to worry about returning the book to the stacks, grumbled about impatient people who couldn't be bothered to take the time to make sense of the old books, and settled back at his desk as Owen left. Once he was back in the main stacks, Owen spent another hour chasing down books Miriam Akeley had named in her lecture the day before, and went back to the house on Halsey Street feeling good about the day's work.

He was up in his room, pulling books out of his backpack, when he remembered the flyer Shelby had given him. After the books were piled on his desk, he pulled the thing from his pocket and unfolded it. Across the front was:

NOOLOGY
Toward a Final Synthesis
of Science and Culture

He opened the flyer, read the three columns of text inside, and then went back and read them over again. It was curiously vague. It went on at length about interdisciplinary perspectives and using the methods of science on the problems of the humanities, without giving Owen any sense of which disciplines, methods and problems the author had in mind; it suggested a link between noology and the march of human progress without ever quite saying anything specific about how those two things were connected; it promised, or seemed to promise, imminent breakthroughs without taking the trouble to mention what was going to get broken in the process. Owen read it a third time, to see if it would make any more sense. It didn't, and something about the text left a bad taste in his mind. After a moment, he tossed the flyer onto the top of his bookcase and went back downstairs.

* * *

Five-Ninety-Five—officially HID 595, Graduate Seminar in the History of Ideas—was one of the few programs that had survived more or less intact from the days when Miskatonic still had a program in medieval metaphysics. Every Monday, under the genial and eccentric guidance of Professor Michael Peaslee, two dozen or so grad students gathered in a cluttered upper room in Wilmarth Hall for no-holds-barred discussion of some topic drawn from the history of ideas. That semester, the topics came from ancient Greek literature; the semester before, it had been the history of the scientific revolution, and there was a lively betting pool among the grad students about what the next semester's theme would be. Five-Ninety-Five was an anachronism in an era that had largely reduced university education to job training, but Owen rarely missed a session.

Around half of the other class members had already arrived when he came through the door. Most of them nodded or waved, and he greeted all with a lazy wave of one hand, went to his preferred spot over next to the room's one big window, shed his backpack and settled into the seat. By the time he had his cell phone off, the room was nearly full; the last burst of students through the door included Shelby Adams, who looked preoccupied.

At five seconds to one, the familiar beat of heavy footfalls sounded in the hall outside. At one o'clock exactly, Professor Peaslee came in: dumpling-shaped and fussily dressed, his gray hair an unmanageable mane flopping around his pink and flustered face. He clumped over to his chair, plopped down into it, blinked at the class as though he was surprised to find anyone there, then cleared his throat and pulled a stack of half-crumpled papers from his briefcase.

"Plutarch, *On the Silence of the Oracles*. You've all read it, right? Okay, good. Let's cut to the chase. Plutarch says that the Greek oracles used to hand out messages from the gods, and now they don't any more. The characters in his dialogue offer various reasons on offer as to why that happened. Is Plutarch right about the oracles? Who's right about what happened?" He waved a hand. "Discuss."

Jim Malkowski, a big blocky guy with a thatch of blond hair who was doing a degree in philosophy, raised a finger and got Peaslee's nod. "My take is that Plutach's engaged in common or garden variety nostalgia for the good old days," he said. "It's a common bit of religious rhetoric: miracles always happen in the distant past or the imagined future, never here and now."

Shelby got the nod next. "I'm inclined to agree. Do we have any evidence that the oracles ever made sense in the first place?"

Three other students leapt to the attack, reeling off citations from ancient Greek writers about oracular pronouncements. Once the issue had been hammered into place in a flurry of quotes and counterquotes, Luellen Blair, a middle-aged minister in training who was getting a degree in comparative religion, got the professor's attention. "I'm sure the rest of you have already thought of this," she said, "but Plutarch fits into a broader context in the history of religions. He's a transitional figure, right on the cusp between the old robust Pagan faiths and the abstract philosophical religion that replaced them in classical Greek culture. The oracles belonged to the older tradition, which had a much more practical side to it."

"Good point," said Maria Sanchez, one of the Greek-quoters. "The later tradition focused on individual salvation on the far side of death—like some other religions we could all probably name. The older religion didn't have that focus at all. Zeus, Demeter, Hermes—they were expected to do things for their worshippers."

"You're saying," said one of the other Greek-quoters, a mousy guy with a pale face and horn-rimmed glasses, "they orter git better gods like some o' the folks in the Injies—gods as ud bring 'em good fishin' in return for their sacrifices, and ud really answer folks's prayers."

"Howard!" Owen and two other students called out. It was a Five-Ninety-Five tradition that no class session was complete without at least one Lovecraft quote or reference, and another tradition for seminar members who caught the reference to respond accordingly.

"Nice," said Professor Peaslee. "'Shadow over Innsmouth,' right?"

"Spot on," said the quoter.

"It's a valid point, though," Maria went on. "The Greek gods were active in the world. It wasn't just a matter of accepting whatever happened and hoping you'd go to heaven—the gods and goddesses were supposed to do things here and now. All of the earliest strata of Greek literature presupposes that."

"Inadequate knowledge of cause and effect," said Shelby. "Typical of premodern times."

"We're talking about the people who invented logic," Maria reminded her.

"It's not just Greek religion," said one of the historians. "All the old polytheistic religions have gods and goddesses who are right here in the world, doing things."

"So do the older books of the Old Testament," Luellen Blair noted, "and the Gospels."

"According to Christian theology," Owen asked her, "when did that stop?"

"There's a lot of debate on that," she said, "but the most common view is that the really major miracles—the direct outpourings of the Holy Spirit, as we'd say—stopped with the death of the last of the apostles called by Jesus himself, say between 75 and 100 AD."

"So right about the time Plutarch says the oracles stopped making any kind of sense," said Jim Malkowski.

The room got very quiet for a moment, and then everyone piled in at once, tossing out quotes, arguments, speculations about what might have happened to change the way people thought about the gods. It was a good Five-Ninety-Five session, with shouts of "Howard!" greeting two more Lovecraft references. When the hour was over, though, Owen stood by his chair for a long moment while most of the others piled out the door, Shelby among them.

"Interesting stuff, eh?" Professor Peaslee asked him.

"Yeah. It's as though something actually did change." Owen shook his head. "Spooky." *These things belong to an older time*, the letter had said; he tried not to think of that as he left the classroom and headed out the door.

Unexpectedly, Shelby was waiting there. "Hi, Owen. Got an hour or so?"

"Why?"

"I was wondering if you wanted to go over to Belbury Hall. I've mentioned you to Dr. Noyes, and he says he'd be interested in talking with you."

"I'll have to take a rain check," he said. "Akeley's expecting me in five minutes."

She nodded. "Okay. See you soon."

* * *

That evening, he came downstairs to make dinner to find Barry and Kenji huddled over their laptops on the dining room table. "Hey, Owen," Barry said. "Those ideas—"

"Nope," said Owen, forestalling him. "No more hysterical than that joke."

"You gotta pardon Barry," said Kenji. "The tentacled horrors ate his brain." He put one hand on top of his own head and made a brain-sucking motion in among the spikes of black hair.

"And starved to death," Owen snapped back.

"Ouch," Barry said, laughing. "I'm crushed."

Kenji shook his head. "By a squamous, rugose tentacle." He looked up from the screen to Owen. "You probably even know what those words mean."

Owen laughed, went into the kitchen. "Of course," he said over his shoulder, while he got his ramen going. "Squamous means scaly, and rugose means wrinkled."

"Well then, for God's sake, why didn't Lovecraft just say so?" Kenji said, throwing up his hands in mock despair. "Whole generations of students at this tentacle-ridden university have been pounding their heads against the nearest wall trying to figure that out."

Owen chopped up another grayish hot dog. "Hey, it's not my fault that nobody told them to look it up in the dictionary."

"Isn't that one of the books they keep in the basement of Orne Library, the ones that are supposed to drive you crazy if you read them?"

"Just about," Owen said.

"As though," Barry said, "we don't have enough to worry about in this world without outfitting horrible creatures with horrible adjectives."

"They're supposed to be horrible," said Jenny Parrish, walking in just then from the living room. "Lovecraft was a horror writer, right?"

"Sure, but why make the vocabulary even more hideous than the monsters?"

"Listen to the words," Jenny said. "Rugose, wrinkly. Squamous, scaly. They may mean the same but they don't sound or feel the same, and the sound and the feeling matter."

"English department?" Kenji asked her pointblank.

"I'm doing a year of postgrad in French literature," she said, "but yes, I majored in English lit. I'm trying for an assistantship in History of Ideas for next year."

"Two of 'em," Barry said, letting his head sink into his hands. "Cthulhu spare us."

Owen looked up as Jenny came into the kitchen. "You should talk to Dr. Akeley," he said to her. "She just had one of her grad students bail on her, so there's a spot open."

Jenny's plain thin face lit up. "Seriously? Thanks." Then, considering the mix of ramen, hot dog slices, and formerly frozen vegetables in the saucepan: "You're going to eat that?"

"No, he's going to offer it to Great Cthulhu," Barry said from the dining room. Owen laughed and kept stirring.

* * *

Tuesday was Owen's one day without classes that semester, so he'd made it laundry day to miss the weekend rush. After downing breakfast, he got everything that needed washing into a shapeless orange and black Miskatonic duffel, and then holed up in his room until the clock showed ten AM, taking notes for his thesis when he wasn't staring out the window at the gray morning. At ten sharp he shrugged on a coat, shouldered the duffel and headed out the door.

Outside the wind was raw and wet under a low flat ceiling of cloud. The trees lining the streets of Arkham, still clutching the rags of autumn leaves, bent inward like beggars muttering to one another. As Owen waited for the light to change at one intersection, a county bus pulled out of the Dyer Street station and turned past him; the route sign above the front window read 18 TO NEWBURYPORT VIA INNSMOUTH. Owen watched it go and then shook his head, thinking about the fifth Lovecraft letter with its strange message.

The laundromat was a narrow little hole-in-the-wall place with machines down one side and chairs and a sorting table on the other. Owen had a book with him, one of the titles Professor Akeley had mentioned, but the letter was still bothering him. Once he'd given the machine its weekly ration of clothes and quarters, and waited long enough to hear water gurgle and hiss inside, he tossed the duffel on a shelf above the sorting table and went back out.

Around the corner on Hyde Street was the North Side Branch of the Arkham Public Library, a bleak little brick building of Eighties vintage. Owen ducked inside just as the first raindrops drummed on the sidewalk. There was a mural in the entry; inevitably, it included an image of Arkham's patron saint, with a lumpy, bright green Cthulhu on one side and a blobby black shape that was probably supposed to be a shoggoth on the other.

The librarian, a sad-faced old man with a little mustache, said something vaguely welcoming. Owen mumbled a response, and buried himself in the shelves. There were three books on H.P. Lovecraft in the biography section; he chose the thickest, took it to the librarian's desk, had to fumble in his wallet to find the library card, and finally headed back out into the rain, tucking the book under his coat to keep it dry.

Back at the laundromat, he made sure his washer was still turning, and flopped down in one of the chairs. A few seats away, a man in a long black coat, a loosely looped gray scarf, and a broad-brimmed hat leaned back in one of the postures of patient boredom that laundromats, bus stations, and other places of waiting inevitably put up for display. Owen pulled the book out from under his coat, opened it, and started leafing through the index for references to Lovecraft's attitudes toward magic and occultism. Finding one, he paged forward and read:

Lovecraft's own attitudes toward the occult, on the other hand, are well documented. While a few of his friends, notably William Lumley and fellow author Robert

Blake, claimed he dabbled in occultism during his New York years, nothing in Lovecraft's own writings or letters supports
their claim, nor have researchers turned
up any trace of his involvement in the New
York occult scene of the late 1920s.

"I couldn't help but notice what you're reading," the man in the long coat said then. He had a deep voice, with a trace of an accent Owen didn't recognize.

"Yeah," said Owen, without looking up.

"His work has some remarkable points of contact with the dark superstitious beliefs of the past, wouldn't you say?"

Startled, Owen looked up then. The man was considering him with a slight smile. Lean face, dark brown skin, and a nose arched like a hawk's beak gave him a Middle Eastern look, though not one Owen could place. He knew all of Miskatonic's liberal arts faculty by sight, and this wasn't one of them; a researcher or visiting faculty from another university, maybe? Something about the man made that seem unlikely.

"I suppose so." Owen managed to say.

The man got up and went to the door. With the same slight smile: "No doubt it depends on which of his letters you've read."

It took just a moment for the comment to sink in, and by the time it did, the door had swung open and shut. Owen jumped to his feet and went out the door after him.

He was gone. There was no one on the sidewalk for a block in either direction, and no one on the other side of the street.

Owen stood there in the rain for a long moment, looking this way and that, and finally went back inside. It was only then that he realized that the washer with his clothes in it was the only machine running in the laundromat.

* * *

Wednesday he pelted out of the house on Halsey Street as soon as he'd downed breakfast, took in another session of the critical-theory seminar, then buried himself in the restricted stacks of Orne Library for three hours, where a ponderous Victorian tome on the excavation and interpretation of the Eltdown Shards kept him busy enough to chase troubling thoughts out of his mind. Once or twice, as he turned the crisp yellow pages, he found himself wondering whether the letter was right and Lovecraft had actually studied and practiced the lore of the Shards, but each time he was able to force his mind back to the work at hand.

Then it was back across the quad to Morgan Hall. Professor Akeley was perched on her chair in the little basement classroom as usual. At one o'clock exactly, she got up and started into the day's lecture. "It's not often that you can point to a single month when a given set of ideas dropped right out of popular culture, but today's topic is an exception. The month was April 1945. That's when the first ugly news reports and photos started coming out of the concentration camps at Dachau and Bergen-Belsen, and people across the United States and the rest of the world had to face the consequences of the racial pseudoscience that was all over American popular culture straight through the years between the wars."

She went on, sketching out an entire landscape of popular thought that had been swept out of sight in a hurry once the Holocaust showed where it led. She talked about how every ethnic group was assigned a place in an imaginary sequence spanning the distance from ape to Englishman, how ideas of sterilizing the supposedly unfit in order to accelerate human progress were perfectly acceptable in polite society, and how sex between people of different ethnic groups was shrouded in a language of pious horror that very imperfectly hid the outlines of an entire culture's unacknowledged desires. It was another brilliant lecture, and once again Owen ended up with pages of hastily scrawled notes pointing to sources and perspectives he hadn't yet included in his thesis. When it was over, he went up to the front of the class, and waited while the undergrads pelted her with questions and argued with the answers.

Finally they were alone in the classroom. "Well, that wasn't too bad," Professor Akeley said in a tired voice. "The last time I taught this class I had two white supremacists in the back row and the class nearly ended in a riot." She shook her head, then got out of the chair and started for the door. "You look unusually thoughtful today. What's on your mind?"

"I wanted to talk to you about that fifth Lovecraft letter," he admitted.

She went to the door, closed it, turned to face him. "I was afraid of that. Owen, you haven't been following Lovecraft studies that long, have you? You have no idea how poisonous the debates about Lovecraft and occultism tend to get. It's the kind of thing that wrecks academic careers—the kind of thing you don't want to get anywhere near."

"Even if there's conclusive evidence."

"Especially if there's conclusive evidence." She considered him for a moment, and went on. "This is to go no further."

"Okay," he said, wondering what he'd gotten himself into.

"It doesn't really matter whether Lovecraft took occultism seriously. It matters even less whether you or I do. What matters—" Her voice dropped. "—is that there are other people who do take it seriously. Seriously enough that it really isn't safe to attract their attention. As Lovecraft said, there are real dangers in such things."

Owen took this in, and slowly nodded. "Got it."

"Thank you," she said with evident relief. "It's simply one of those things." She went to the door, opened it. "You haven't heard yet—I got an email this morning from Jim Willett. He's absolutely over the moon about the new Robert Blake stories." They crossed the hall to the inconvenient stair, started climbing.

* * *

Later that afternoon, Owen went back to the house on Halsey
Street and tried to get to work on his thesis, tackling the way
Lovecraft used the old legends of Yog-Sothoth to relativize the
concepts of space and time and relating them to the popular
impact of Einstein's physics. His mind kept wandering to other
things, though. After a while, he noticed the flyer Shelby had
given him, sitting neglected on top of his bookcase, and picked
it up. The text made no more sense on another reading than it
had when he first tried to decipher it, and left just as uneasy a
feeling in him. After a moment, he got onto the internet and
went looking for information on noology.

There wasn't much. The obvious domain names had been
purchased but didn't yet have websites; there were a couple of
mentions of the Miskatonic University Noology Program in the
campus site, all mentioning the same office on the ninth floor of
Belbury Hall; there were a few other references here and there.
Finally he found an article tucked away in an abstruse online
journal he'd never encountered before. It wasn't much clearer
than the flyer: it claimed that noology was destined to replace
philosophy the way that astronomy had replaced astrology,
and approvingly quoted several media figures on the militant
atheist side of the current round of culture wars. The humanities, it suggested, were a mere waste of time in an age in which
the human race needed to unite all its efforts in the cause of
reason and progress.

Sounds great, he thought sourly. But what did they mean by
those fine slogans? The article never quite got around to saying, and the raw evasiveness of it all did nothing to make him
less wary. He closed the browser, tossed the flyer in the waste-
paper basket and buried himself in his thesis, hammering out
a workable first draft of his discussion of the influence of the
theory of relativity on Lovecraft's thought. He kept at it until
Jenny's tentative knock at the door reminded him of the blues
concert that night.

Arkham didn't have much night life, aside from local garage
bands and whatever students at the university managed

to cook up for themselves, but J.J.'s was an exception worth noticing. It was a drafty barn of a place on Fish Street, close to the railroad tracks, that got remodeled into a music venue in the Sixties and managed to keep going straight through the decades that followed. Wednesday was blues night at J.J.'s; top groups came through now and then, playing Arkham Wednesday night and Newburyport Thursday, and then rolling on to bigger markets like Portland or Manchester for the more lucrative Friday and Saturday night shows.

The cold damp air slapped Owen across the face like a wet towel as he headed out the door after Jenny and Tish. The last red glow of sunset was bleeding to death in the hills off to the west as they walked through Arkham's university ghetto: lines of old gambrel-roofed houses cut up into apartments or disfigured with big, blocky, cheaply built additions, with here and there a hole-in-the-wall place selling pizza or liquor or Chinese takeout. As they walked, Jenny and Tish chatted animatedly about some bit of campus politics that had blown up the previous weekend, yet another scandal in the troubled English department. Owen tried to get interested in it, and failed completely. The conversation he'd had with Professor Akeley replayed in his head over and over again.

As they got closer to J.J.'s, the mostly empty sidewalks started to come alive. Alone or in little clusters, people headed toward Fish Street from the student neighborhoods. Friends waved to one another, conversations sprang up, and Owen had to step into the street more than once to get around a knot of people standing there talking on the sidewalk. Finally, the front door of J.J's beckoned. Owen paid the cover charge and followed the others inside.

There were cheap round tables around three sides of the room and a space for dancing in the middle; the stage jutted out from the fourth side, and Isaac Jax and His Cottonmouths were up there already, shooting the breeze with each other and the management and tipping back a beer or two. Owen and his housemates settled at a table over on one side. Faking an enthusiasm he didn't feel, Owen flagged down a server and treated the others to the evening's first beer.

The two women ordered something yellow and bland. Owen asked the server to bring him the darkest beer they had, and left it at that. What came back from the bar was something called Puritan Black Stout, from a Danvers microbrewery. The bottle had a frowning Pilgrim on the label in the signature black buckle-fronted hat, arms folded, glaring defiance at every sin Owen cared to imagine and some he didn't. He sipped, then downed a slug. It was good and bitter, and it did much to improve his mood. The moment he put the bottle down, of course, Tish chaffed him for drinking used motor oil, he offered a speculation about which of Lovecraft's eldritch deities had produced her beverage via its kidneys and bladder, and the evening finally got off to a decent start.

The show was better than the beer, which was saying something. Delta style blues, the poster had claimed, and Isaac Jax lived up to it, belting out a mix of old standards and new pieces that sounded as though they could have been penned by Robert Johnson or Son House. His slide guitar playing and the string-band sound of the Cottonmouths made the mix perfect. Toward the end of the first set, Jax launched into "Cross Road Blues," and Owen leaned back, remembering the old stories of the black-clothed, black-hatted devil who supposedly met some of the old bluesmen at a crossroads by midnight and taught them their chops.

Then he happened to glance to his left.

The man in the long black coat he'd seen at the laundromat was sitting three tables away, leaning back in his chair much as Owen was. Rings glittered on the hand that wrapped around his chin. He was enjoying the music, or so the smile that creased his lean dark face suggested. After a moment, he glanced toward Owen, nodded a greeting, and turned back to Isaac Jax and His Cottonmouths.

Owen turned sharply away, tried to lose himself in the music again. It didn't work. After a few minutes, admitting defeat, he glanced back to his left.

The man was gone, and there was no chair in the place where he'd been sitting.

Owen stared, then turned away again. A server went past, and he flagged her down, ordered another beer. When that was gone, he repeated the operation and got another. You could get food at J.J.'s between sets, though Owen usually didn't. This time, he splurged on chicken and french fries, and between a full stomach and enough beer, managed to get his nerves calmed down enough to enjoy the rest of the show.

* * *

"Fair enough," said Professor Akeley. She and Owen were in her office in Wilmarth Hall, where they'd just spent a good portion of Thursday morning discussing his thesis. Rain drummed against the window; through the blurred glass, the gray mass of the East Campus Parking Garage could just be made out, looming up against the green whaleback shape of Meadow Hill. "I'd like to see you expand the section on the historical origins of Lovecraft's image of the nonhuman Other, as I said. Aside from that, it looks as though you're pretty much on track."

"Thank you."

She nodded. Then, after a moment: "Did you ever have a chance to talk to Shelby?"

"Not really. Every time I've tried to bring up the subject, she's turned it into an excuse to try to get me to go to Belbury Hall and talk to the people in the Noology Program."

Akeley looked away. "I hope you don't do that."

Owen gave her a startled look.

"Over the last two weeks," she said, "six other grad students have walked away from their programs and started over again there. The other professors are just as baffled as I am. Everything was going fine, as far as they knew, and then—" She shook her head.

"That's spooky," Owen said. Professor Akeley didn't respond, and after a moment he went on. "Shelby gave me a flyer about the Noology Program. It was basically doubletalk."

"I've seen it."

"I looked noology up online, and didn't have any more luck figuring out what it's supposed to be—a lot of vague hand-waving about progress and reason. Do you have any idea what it's about?"

"I don't know," Professor Akeley said. She turned to face him. "When I first heard about noology last April, when it was still supposed to be under the interdisciplinary studies program, I figured it was one more academic fad like postmodernism or critical theory, with some cognitive psychology thrown in to make it look more cutting-edge. You're right that the publications on the subject are gibberish, but that's nothing new in the academy these days. But there's this business with Shelby and the others, and…" She let the sentence trail off and looked back out the window.

Owen thought about that for a time, and then said, "Does this have anything to do with what you told me yesterday?"

"Forget about what I said yesterday," she replied, her voice low and tense. "That isn't a question you should even be thinking about."

It was as much answer as he needed. He changed the subject immediately and asked her about the Robert Blake stories, and they spent the next quarter hour chatting about the reactions of the dozen or so Robert Blake scholars who'd already responded to her emails. Everything seemed fine between them when he left the office, but he noticed the worried glance she sent after him as he headed for the stairs.

Outside, he started across the quad, then on an impulse veered and went north between Wilmarth Hall and Morgan Hall. Beyond them was another grassy square edged by bare trees, with an abstract sculpture of rust-colored metal in the middle of it. Beyond the sculpture, the pale mass of Belbury Hall climbed a dozen stories toward the clouds. Despite what Professor Akeley had said, the thought of going in through the big glass doors of the hall and taking the elevator up to the ninth floor kept circling through his mind.

Each time he came close to taking that first step toward the doors, though, something stopped him, and after a few moments he realized what it was. He'd learned in Iraq to trust the gut feeling that warned of impending danger, and though he couldn't tell why, the thought of going any closer to the Noology Program, whatever it was, set that reaction going in him. He turned abruptly and walked back between the two buildings, heading away from Belbury Hall.

* * *

Restless and uneasy, he left campus and plunged into Arkham's gritty heart, hoping to walk his way to some kind of clarity. The rain had stopped but great ragged masses of cloud hurried by overhead on their way to soak Boston and points further south. WITCHES BANISH PHANTOMS, the front page of the Arkham Advertiser read; Owen gathered that Arkham High School's football team had lost the annual grudge match with its perennial rivals from Salem. He laughed sourly, wondering if a witch could banish the phantoms that haunted him just then.

He crossed Lovecraft Park, trying not to notice the gaunt puzzled bronze face looming above him, and headed down Hyde Street, where the steeple of the Asbury Methodist Episcopal Church stabbed ineffectually up at the sky. The church had an old-fashioned reader board in front of it, white letters clinging none too securely to a black background. The side facing him said JESUS LOVES YOU; he passed it and glanced over his shoulder, then stopped and read it: SUNDAY'S SERMON: MYSTERIES HIDDEN FROM THE FOUNDATION OF THE WORLD. He gave it a long bleak look, then walked on by and turned south on Garrison. The street went past the boarded-up train station, over the railroad tracks on one bridge, over the churning brown waters of the Miskatonic River on another.

South of the river was the old downtown district, where long-abandoned stores and empty office buildings clustered around the original Miskatonic University quad. That had once been the part of town that mattered, but the end of the postwar boom and the construction of the new campus north of town had changed that. These days the old quad was office space for the alumni association and the financial aid department, and the streets around it were as fine a specimen of urban blight as could be found anywhere in New England. Owen paced down cracked and crumbling sidewalks past one boarded-up storefront after another. High overhead, empty windows with or without benefit of glass stared like blind eyes at the dark hills around the town.

Finally, walking more or less at random, he came to one of the bridges over Hangman's Brook and stopped there, leaning on the railing, staring at the stream. The dark tree-covered mass of Hangman's Hill crouched against the skyline in front of him, and the black waters of the brook went splashing past below. Off to the west, the hills rose up in dark rumpled shapes thick with trees. He stared at the water for what seemed like a long time.

Eventually, he noticed that someone was standing beside him.

He stared resolutely down at the water, but could not help seeing the brown fingers that grasped the railing, bright with ornate rings, and the long black coat fluttering and flapping in the wind. Finally, Owen glanced up, saw the dark hawk-nosed face, the gray scarf and broad-brimmed black hat of the man he'd met in the laundromat.

"You know something about me," Owen said, "and something about—" He stopped, catching himself.

"About the Lovecraft letter you read," said the man. "Yes."

Owen drew in a breath, but before he could speak the man went on. "Hear me out. I'm guessing that you've finally figured out that you're on the edge of something serious and dangerous. Am I right?"

"Yeah," Owen admitted. "I'm wondering how you know."

"That's irrelevant now," the man said. "What matters is that you've got a choice to make, and not much time left to make it. You can back away from all of this, forget about the letter you read, put as much distance as possible between yourself and everything connected to it. Just finish your thesis, take your doctorate at some other university, and act as though you've never even heard of Howard Phillips Lovecraft. That might just possibly get you out of this business before you've gotten in too deep."

Owen considered that for a long moment. "And the other choice?"

"Go deeper. Ask the questions you're not supposed to ask, look past the obvious to what's actually going on. If you do that, though, there'll be no way back." The man glanced at him. "And if you do that, sooner or later, you'll have to take sides. Nobody's neutral in this business." He paused, then went on: "All things considered, I'd advise you to leave it alone."

"I'm not sure I can," Owen said. "I'm really not."

"Understood." The man paused again, as the wind whipped past them. "If you've gone too far already, or if you choose to keep on going, you may have to run for it at some point. Do you know the ravine north of town?"

"The one past campus on the east side?"

"Exactly. On the far side of the ravine is an old white stone; you might have heard of it. Go there if you're in danger. You'll find protection, and guidance."

Owen stared down at the water for a time. "Thank you," he said finally.

Then, all at once, the man was gone, as if he'd never been there at all.

Owen drew in a long ragged breath, clenched his hands on the bridge railing, and considered the possibility that he was going insane. The alternative—

The alternative was, if anything, less palatable still.

The splashing creek and the wind offered him no answers. After a while, he turned away from the bridge, started back toward Halsey Street.

* * *

Friday he went through his usual routine: critical-theory seminar first thing in the morning, three hours down in the Orne Library basement, Miriam Akeley's class after that, and then home. The whole time he was distracted and edgy, wrestling with the questions that haunted him. During his stint in the restricted stacks, chasing down references to the nature goddess Shub-Niggurath in the commentary on the Eltdown Shards, he considered mentioning the letter to Dr. Whipple, who didn't seem to care about anything other than the ancient books he guarded and his own obscure work with them, but decided against it. The man in black had talked about taking sides, but Owen had no idea what the sides were or what the conflict between them might involve. How could he even begin to guess where the librarian stood?

That afternoon's class on popular culture returned to racial ideologies in the years between the wars. "The medieval Christian church claimed that Jews sacrificed Christian babies, engaged in every imaginable sort of sexual depravity, and were plotting to conquer the world," said Professor Akeley, pacing back and forth in front of the class. "Those same claims got dusted off, decked out in pseudoscientific drag between the wars, and splashed around freely wherever status panic had an ethnic dimension.

"The Jews got more than their share of it, of course, but here in America, so did people whose ancestors came from Africa, east Asia, south Asia, the Slavic countries, you name it—just about everyone who wasn't from western Europe was supposed to be into human sacrifice, deviant sex, and conspiring to destroy the world. Dig into the popular fiction of the era, and if you find someone who's assigned the role of being evilly evil for the sake of sheer unadulterated evilness, that's what they're up to. Here in Arkham, of course, the obvious example is H.P. Lovecraft; the worshippers of Cthulhu and the fish-people from Innsmouth are cut from exactly the same sex-crazed, baby-slaughtering, world-destroying cloth as the imaginary Jewish world conspirators of *The Protocols of the Elders of Zion*."

Even though he'd seen it coming, that last sentence hit Owen like a fist. If there actually were worshippers of Cthulhu...

When he left Morgan Hall, Shelby was waiting for him. "Dr. Noyes has office hours today," she told him. "Let's go."

"I'm not interested," he told her.

"What?"

"I'm not interested. I'm perfectly happy with the program I'm in, and I don't see a point to looking at other options."

"That's because you don't know what we can offer you."

We? The word startled Owen, but he managed to keep the reaction off his face. "I read the flyer you gave me, and I looked up noology online. If that's what turns your crank, hey, great—it's not what I want to do."

She faced him squarely. "Owen, ten years from now noology is going to be the only game in town. Not just here at Miskatonic—everywhere."

"The postmodernists used to say that."

She laughed. It was not a pleasant laugh, and he couldn't remember ever hearing a laugh like that from her. "This is much bigger than postmodernism. Much, *much* bigger."

Owen rolled his eyes. "Right. I'm still not interested. Bye." He turned and walked away before she could say anything else.

THE DEVIL AT THE CROSSROADS

That night he sat in his room until late, chin propped on his hands, staring out the window at a darkness that held no answers he could see. All his housemates were buried in their books, but the silence of the old house did nothing to settle his thoughts. He recalled the warnings he'd been given, by Professor Akeley, by the nameless man in black he'd met in the laundromat and on the bridge over Hangman's Brook, and weighed them against—what? A scrap of paper from a dead author of pulp horror fiction. Maybe the professor was right, he told himself. Maybe it was just a forgery.

No. The response came hard and fast, from the gut. No. The man in black was right: whatever he'd stumbled across was far more serious and dangerous than that.

"I can't," he said aloud, suddenly feeling desperate. "I can't." At that moment, he couldn't have said whether he meant that he couldn't go any further into the mystery that had opened up in front of him, or that he couldn't do anything else.

Finally, feeling crumpled and miserable, he got undressed, turned off the light and crawled into his bed. He didn't expect to sleep, not for hours, but somehow sleep took him within moments, plunged him into a welcome darkness that left no room for worries or dreams. Only once, toward morning, he dreamed that someone or something was perched on the foot of his bed, motionless, watching him with pricked ears and pale unblinking eyes. Was it threatening him, or protecting him? He couldn't tell.

He blinked awake to find daylight pouring in through the window. The uncertainties had vanished with the night; he knew the moment he woke what he had to do.

He rolled out of bed, woke up his laptop, got a search engine and typed something into it. The information he needed was two screens down. His cell phone beeped as he punched buttons, relayed a distant ring in scratchy tones. "Hello?" he said into it. "Yes, I'd like to make a reservation for tonight. Yes. Just one. Yes." He fumbled with his wallet, got out his one and only credit card, read the number and expiration date. "Yes. Thank you. Have a great day."

Once that was done, he dressed, packed his laptop, some books, and a change of clothing in a backpack, added his comb and toothbrush from the bathroom once he'd finished using them, and went downstairs. Jenny Parrish was up, sitting at the table in the dining room with a bowl of cereal in front of her; nobody else was awake.

Jenny gave him a worried look. "Are you okay?"

"Yeah, I think so." He went into the kitchen, pulled two bagels out of the bag, popped them into the backpack along with a bottle of water. "I just need to get out of town for a bit. I'll be back Sunday night."

"I'll tell everybody," she said. "Have a good weekend."

"You too."

He was out the door before she could say anything else. The morning was bright, as though the rains of the days just past had scrubbed it clean, but there were clouds piling up in the northeast sky and the wind blew raw. He walked fast, knowing that he didn't have much time if he was going to make the trip that day.

The Dyer Street bus station had a little lobby lined with schedules and a big outside shelter where the buses pulled up. Owen ducked into the lobby just long enough to check the schedule he needed, and then went back out into the blustery air. His waking had been well timed; not ten minutes later, the number 18 bus pulled up to the stop and the door hissed open.

"How much to Innsmouth?" he asked the driver.

"Five-fifty one way, eight round trip."

Owen pulled some bills out of his wallet, and pushed them down into the fare box. The driver nodded, as though that settled something, and handed him the round trip ticket. Owen pocketed it, went halfway back, slid into an empty seat, and closed his eyes, as the bus pulled out of the station and headed toward the Federal Pike and Innsmouth.

CHAPTER 3

THE SPIRES OF Y'HA-NTHLEI

At first glance, Innsmouth could have been any of a hundred other decayed fishing towns along the New England seaboard, more than a century past its best days and showing it all over. The bus turned off the pike and rattled along what the signs said was Federal Street, past long-abandoned shops and clapboard-covered houses with peeling paint and tattered curtains. Off to the right, each cross street let through a glimpse of the harbor and the old breakwater past it. Owen watched the houses roll by, and wondered for the tenth time why he'd come there at all.

The trip really made no sense, when he thought about it, and the more he thought about it the less sense it made. Even if the letter from Lovecraft was telling the unvarnished truth about things he'd seen at Innsmouth, the Esoteric Order of Dagon, the undersea city of Y'ha-nthlei, and the "monstrous cross-breeds," whatever they were, wouldn't be right out there waiting to be spotted by a stray grad student from Miskatonic on an overnight trip. If there was anything to the local legends he'd used in his story, Owen guessed, Lovecraft must have learned about it from some occultist he'd known in New York. It was all perfectly obvious, but none of it did anything to dispel the cold clear feeling down at the core of his mind that somehow coming to Innsmouth had been the right choice to make.

Graying clapboard gave way to discolored brick as the bus reached Innsmouth's business district, where the air of decay and neglect was even stronger than it had been further south. Two blocks in, the bus swung left and pulled over to the sidewalk, and the driver turned around in his seat. "Here you go. I'll be out of here southbound four o'clock sharp tomorrow."

Owen shouldered his pack and went forward to the door. "Thanks."

The driver reached over and hauled on the handle, and the door hissed open. Owen went down the steps onto cracked concrete. Behind him, the door wheezed shut again, and the bus grumbled to life and rolled away.

He was standing on one side of the town square. Like most New England town squares, this one had no resemblance to the geometrical figure; it was a rough half-circle with the flat side against the shallow gorge of the Manuxet River, which tumbled over three small waterfalls on its way to the sea. A bridge over the gorge carried Federal Street across the river into the northern half of the city. Past the bridge, on the far side of the river and a block or so downstream, a tall brick building with belfries on it had MARSH REFINERY painted on it in peeling white letters.

As the sound of the bus faded out, a hush seemed to settle over the battered old town. Salt-scented wind off the sea keened among the buildings, the Manuxet splashed and muttered over its falls, but the streets were deserted. When a car suddenly started up a few blocks away to the south, the noise was loud enough to make Owen jump.

He turned. Most of the buildings on the square were boarded up, with more than the usual flavor of urban blight about them. When he looked at them, something he couldn't identify made his skin crawl. Only a few businesses on the square seemed to be open. On the other side of Federal Street, a restaurant had a chalk sandwich board out in front announcing daily specials, and the lights were on in a battered-looking Rexall drugstore just past it. Then there was the Gilman House Hotel in front of him. It had been remodeled sometime in the Fifties, from the style of the windows and the big sign over the door, where red neon blared NO VACANCY. After a moment, he walked up the steps and pushed open the glass door.

The lobby looked even older than the sign out front, a tawdry little space with a handful of chairs that had seen many better days and pale blue wallpaper dotted with fishes and shells. The scent of the sea air was somehow even stronger in the lobby than it was outside. The main desk filled one side of the room, and behind it sat a young woman; she had brown curly hair, brown eyes, skin somewhere between brown and olive, and a cast of facial features that wasn't quite any ethnic group Owen recognized. "Can I help you?" she asked.

"I have a reservation," Owen said. "The name's Merrill, Owen Merrill."

She gave him a look he couldn't read, pulled out a notebook from under the desk, found the reservation. "One night, Mr. Merrill?"

"That's right."

She gave him a form to fill out. He scribbled on it and handed over his credit card, then watched in bemusement as she ran it through an old-fashioned card machine and had him sign the carbon-paper form. Keys rattled as she reached under the desk again. "Room 402. The elevator's that way." Then, with the same unreadable look: "The front door's locked at ten. Your key'll open it, but there's not much going on in town after nine or so, and it's not always safe to be out late at night."

"Okay, thanks."

"Enjoy your stay, Mr. Merrill. Checkout time tomorrow is eleven AM."

Room 402 was shabby but clean, with the bleach-smell of newly laundered sheets. There was one window, looking west over rooftops toward the brown marshes inland. He stowed most of his things in the dresser, put his backpack with the laptop in it back over one shoulder, and headed back down to the lobby. The young woman was still behind the desk.

"Excuse me," Owen said. "Is there a public library here in town, or a historical society?"

"One of each. Fortunately they're right next to each other." She pointed out the door. "Three blocks north of the river on Federal; stay on the west side, and they'll be there on your left when the street takes you around New Church Green." Then, considering him: "Looking into local history?"

"Well, more or less." He'd decided that research for his thesis would make a good cover story, but he felt a sudden reluctance to say anything at all about his search. Still, she was smiling and waiting for him to speak. "I'm sure you know all about H.P. Lovecraft here," he said finally.

"Yes." Her nose wrinkled in distaste. "He's not very popular in Innsmouth."

"I bet. He had his issues, didn't he?"

That earned him another of her unreadable looks. "That's one way of putting it."

"He's supposed to have taken a bus trip through here in 1929. I'm looking for anything that could explain why he got so bent out of shape about the place."

"Mrs. Marsh at the historical society can tell you all about that," she said. "She's had papers published in historical journals."

"No kidding. Okay, that's my first stop, then."

"Glad to be of help, Mr. Merrill."

He thanked her and headed out the door.

The day had turned cloudy, and the sea wind still whipped through the streets. Owen turned and went along the sidewalk to where worn paint on the street marked a crossing. He looked back the way he'd come. The glass door of the hotel was in just the right position to give him a view of the hotel desk and the young woman behind it. She was on the phone, talking to someone, with an intent look on her face.

* * *

The Innsmouth Historical Society building was a brick Federal-style house wedged between an abandoned sandwich shop with boarded windows and the bland stucco face of the public library. A well-weathered sign on the door said OPEN THURS-SAT 10-5, but the entire neighborhood had such an air of malign neglect that Owen wasn't sure the door would actually open when he turned the knob.

Despite his suspicions, the door creaked open. Inside was a short entry hall, and then what had probably been the parlor a century before. Now it looked like an office and had a steel desk with an old electric lamp on it to one side. A middle-aged African-American woman in a blue dress decades out of fashion was sitting behind it, reading a big leatherbound book. She looked up with a polite smile as Owen came into the room. "Can I help you?"

"Are you Mrs. Marsh?"

She set the book aside, stood up. "That's me," she said, shaking his hand.

Owen introduced himself. "My thesis is on H.P. Lovecraft, and the desk clerk at the Gilman Hotel told me that you're the person to talk to about his trip here in 1929."

"Yes, I've studied that a bit," Mrs. Marsh said. "If you'd like to pull up a chair?"

Owen found one that didn't look too fragile, brought it over to the desk as she settled back in her chair. "First things first," Mrs. Marsh said, pulling open one of the desk drawers. "You'll want these." She took two staplebound pamphlets out of the drawer, handed them to Owen. "You can keep them; I've got dozens of copies."

They turned out to be photocopies of a pair of articles from something called the Essex County Historical Bulletin, dated most of twenty years back. The titles were "Notes on H.P. Lovecraft's Visit to Innsmouth" and "More Notes on H.P. Lovecraft's Visit to Innsmouth," by Annabelle Marsh; a little note identified her as president of the Innsmouth Historical

Society. He flipped through the articles, glanced up at her. "Thank you. These look really thorough."

"Thank you. Yes, I spent quite a few hours chasing down the details."

"The thing I wonder," said Owen, "is why he took such a dislike to the place."

"Well, that's another matter." Mrs. Marsh sat back in her chair. "You know his attitudes about race, of course." Owen nodded ruefully, and she went on. "Innsmouth was a difficult place for someone who thought that way. It was a whaling port back in the first part of the nineteenth century, and whaling crews came from all over—then after the eighteen-forties, when ships got too big for the Innsmouth harbor, the Atlantic whaling fleet ran itself out of whales, and ships out of New Bedford and Nantucket pretty much monopolized the Pacific trade, it became a bit of a backwater. So you had a lot of poor New Englanders living here, but you also had black folks, Portuguese, Chinese, even some Polynesians who'd taken jobs with the whaling fleets, ended up in Massachusetts, and went looking for a place where rents were low and people weren't too uptight about brown skin. By the twentieth century, there'd been a fair amount of intermarriage, and Lovecraft would have seen a good many mixed-race people here."

"So that was what happened in 1846," Owen said. "The end of Atlantic whaling."

Mrs. Marsh smiled and nodded. "Exactly. No plague, no fish-men, just an ordinary economic downturn. The fish-men make a better story, I give the man that."

Owen laughed. "Oh, no doubt. What about 1928?"

Her expression turned serious. "That's something else again. Lovecraft wasn't the only one who got bent out of shape by the way things went here. Did you know the Klan had a foothold in Massachusetts for a while in the 1920s?"

"I've read about that."

"It was mostly in the west part of the state, but they had a Klavern in Ipswich, and in 1925 a whole bunch of them—more than a hundred—drove here to Innsmouth to make trouble. There were people beaten and shot at, a few killed, a lot of property destroyed.

"Then in 1928, the town got raided by Federal agents. That was during Prohibition, remember, and there was quite a bit of rumrunning all along the coast here, mostly managed by the Irish mob down in Boston. Innsmouth got a good share of the business because it had plenty of empty warehouses along the waterfront; they'd bring cargoes in from Canada or Europe via tramp steamer, anchor out past Devil Reef just after sunset, use small boats to bring it into Innsmouth harbor, and the steamer would be gone by sunrise.

"So one day in 1928 Federal revenue agents came busting into town, searched the waterfront, and found a whole lot of contraband that had just arrived. They weren't too happy because nobody in town would talk, so they smashed as many bottles and barrels as they could find and then just tossed some lit matches and walked away. The fire department did its best, but most of the wharves burned down, and a lot of other buildings too."

"And Lovecraft took those two things and put them together," Owen ventured.

"That's certainly what it looks like."

It sounded reasonable enough, Owen admitted to himself.

"If you have the time," said Mrs. Marsh, "you're welcome to do as much digging as you like in our historical collection—that's next door in the library, but you can get there that way." She motioned toward a door on one side of the office. "The library's officially open Sunday through Wednesday, but that's because I'm the librarian, and I'm on this side of the wall the rest of the week. If you'd like to take a look, by all means."

"Thank you," Owen said, "and please, if it's not any trouble."

"None at all." Mrs Marsh got up and went through the door she'd indicated, and light switches clicked on the far side of it. Owen put his chair where he'd found it, and followed.

A long corridor led to another door, and that opened onto the library itself: a single big room with wooden shelves around the outside, a few tables in the middle, and a desk for the librarian near the front door. Old-fashioned ceiling fans with narrow blades hung overhead like bats waiting for sunset. Windows that clearly hadn't been cleaned in many months let in a bleared gray light, to which the lamps made their own pallid contribution.

She led him over to a set of shelves under a sign that read LOCAL HISTORY COLLECTION. "There's a section of the card catalog just for the collection—yes, I know, we're frightfully behind the times, but we've never had the funds to get the catalog digitized." She pulled one book off the shelf. "This is probably the best place to start. It's a bit outdated, but for what you're after it should be fine."

"Thank you," said Owen. As he took the book, gold glinted on the third finger of Mrs. Marsh's right hand: a wedding band, he guessed, but it was of an unusually pale gold, and it looked like a tiny, twisted blade of kelp with a pale sea-green stone. "That's a lovely ring," he told her.

She dimpled. "Thank you. My husband Jeff brought it home from Indonesia for our wedding. He used to be in the merchant marine." With an unreadable look that reminded him oddly of the clerk at the hotel: "Well, I'll leave you to your work. If you need anything at all, you come right over and let me know."

* * *

The collection was about what he'd expected, the sort of thing you find in any small town with a history behind it: mostly popular books on the history of Massachusetts' north coast, along with a few scholarly titles, a complete set of the Essex

County Historical Bulletin, and a variety of staplebound pamphlets and other oddities. Still, Owen took the book Mrs. Marsh had given him and half a dozen others over to the nearest table, sat down, pulled his laptop out of the backpack, then looked around for an electrical outlet and couldn't find one. The laptop was old enough that the battery wouldn't last him more than a couple of hours, so he shoved it back into his backpack, pulled out a spiral notebook with a black and orange Miskatonic cover, fished around for a pen, and started taking notes.

The book he'd been handed by the librarian was a history of Innsmouth, somewhat unoriginally titled *A History of Innsmouth*. It was as bland and formulaic as the title suggested, the sort of standard account from settlement to whenever that practically every American town pupped at some point in the twentieth century. This one dated from 1948, when the wartime boom hadn't yet trickled away and taken the last of the regional economy with it, but the black and white photo of downtown Innsmouth facing the title page didn't look much more cheerful than the views Owen had seen walking through town.

He paged through the chapters on settlement and colonial times, the whaling boom of the early nineteenth century and the hard times that followed it, pages after pages of tidily marshaled facts that might have helped an economic historian but didn't do Owen any good at all. He leafed past maps of the town in its earlier days, a Currier and Ives print showing the barque *Sumatra Queen* coming out of Innsmouth harbor past the old lighthouse, and the long list that named every young man from the town who left to fight in the First World War, followed by a photo of the memorial for the ones who didn't come back.

After that, finally, he got to the section on Innsmouth in the 1920s, and the few pages discussing the Klan's visit in 1925, the Prohibition raid in 1928, and the ordinary happenings in an ordinary small town between and around those events. It all matched the story Mrs. Marsh had given him. He copied down the account, glanced through the last chapter on the Depression and the wartime boom, then closed the book, pushed it away, opened one of the others.

It was past one o'clock before he was done with the last of them. He glanced at the big clock over the librarian's desk, considered lunch, decided against it, put the books back in their places and went over to the card catalog. It took him a few tries to figure out which set of narrow drawers had the cards for the local history collection, and a few more tries to work out how the cards were arranged, but once that was settled he started looking up topics and scrawling references into his notebook. LOVECRAFT, H. P. (HOWARD PHILLIPS) got him a dozen articles in the Essex County Historical Bulletin, both of Annabelle Marsh's among them. Very little of it covered anything that he hadn't found already, but there were a few things worth footnoting here and there, and plenty of primary sources in the bibliography wouldn't hurt his thesis a bit.

It was almost four-thirty when he finished with the card catalog. Common sense told him to leave, thank Mrs. Marsh for her help, and wander back toward the hotel with an eye toward spotting somewhere to have dinner, but there was also the letter, the man in the long black coat, the questions and uncertainties that pressed around Innsmouth and whatever Lovecraft had or hadn't seen there. He glanced around the room, decided to see what else might be in the Innsmouth public library.

At first glance the collection could have been in any other small-town library with no funding to speak of: the fiction section heavy on romance novels and popular authors from thirty years back, the sparse nonfiction section mostly featuring old books in the heavy library bindings of an earlier time, two racks of paperbacks with garish covers that had seen many better days, and a children's book section that looked as though most of the books had seen heavy use. He turned around, and noticed something green on a chair at one of the nearby tables. Someone had left a book sitting there, a thin volume in a plain green library binding; Owen picked it up and, in a moment of idle curiosity, opened it.

The pages inside were photocopied rather than printed. The original had been hand-typed, and there were drawings in black ink: undersea scenes, with a little curly-haired girl in most of them. In one picture she seemed to be playing a game with fish and octopi, in another she was hiding from a shark in a sea-cave, and in a third she was looking with delight toward the spires of an undersea city. He flipped to the title page and nearly dropped the book. It read:

A PRINCESS OF Y'HA-NTHLEI
by Laura Marsh

He blinked, stared at the title for a long moment, and then turned the page to start reading the story. Just then, a muffled noise from the direction of the Historical Society building caught his attention. He glanced that way, then at the clock, and realized that the librarian would be closing up. He considered asking her about the book, decided against that. As quickly as he could without making a noise, he put the book back where he'd found it and went back to the table where his backpack sat. He was hoisting the pack onto one shoulder when the old woman came through the door.

"I hate to interrupt your work," she said, "but it's closing time, and I should head home."

"I was just packing up for the night," he told her. "Thank you for all your help—I've found some really useful data points."

"Delighted to hear it." He headed down the corridor to the Historical Society office while she turned out the lights in the library and followed after him. "Will you be coming tomorrow?"

"If it's not any kind of inconvenience."

"None at all," she assured him. "Any time after noon."

They shook hands and said the usual things, and Owen went out into the evening air. The sky had begun to clear, and a few pale stars were just visible over the rooftops to the east. Owen had thought about trying to see more of the town that evening, but there were few streetlights and most of the ones he could see showed no particular interest in lighting up. He compromised by turning left and going around New Church Green. He passed the old Masonic Hall with its faux-Greek columns; the Masonic square and compass had been taken down a long time before, but if the place was being used by the Esoteric Order of Dagon, as Lovecraft's story claimed, there wasn't a sign to announce the fact. Two churches and any number of big rundown houses made up the rest of the circuit and brought him back to Federal Street and the route back to the hotel.

He kept an eye out for restaurants, but didn't find one until he'd crossed the Manuxet gorge again and was back in Innsmouth's town square. The place he'd seen on his arrival was still open for business. The sign above the door said BARNEY'S SEAFOOD AND GRILL, and the sandwich board on the sidewalk said something about the best fish and chips on the north coast. Every restaurant from Marblehead to Newburyport made the same claim, granted, but Owen figured it was worth a try.

There weren't many people inside, just a group of locals sitting around a table at the far end of the place and one waitress who looked like a cousin of the hotel clerk, with the same brown hair and eyes and the same hard-to-place ethnic quality to her face. She led him to a table not far from the door, gave him a menu and ducked back into the kitchen, coming out again with an order pad and a pen a moment later. He ordered the fish and chips, asked about beers, settled for something decent from a Boston brewery. There was an odd saltwater scent in the restaurant, or so he thought when he first sat down at the table; it was only after the waitress went back to her seat and the scent went away that Owen realized it had come from her. Some kind of local perfume? He didn't try to guess.

The beer came promptly, and the fish and chips followed soon after. The beer and the fries were ordinary, but the fish was good enough to justify the claim on the sandwich board, perfectly cooked and seasoned, and so fresh he guessed it must had been caught that day. He finished the meal feeling highly charitable toward Innsmouth, and left as big a tip as he could afford when he paid up and headed back to the hotel.

Back in his room, he sat on the edge of the bed, got his laptop plugged in and charging up, and paged through the notes he'd taken in the library. He hadn't had time to make notes on his unsettling final discovery, and so took a moment to note down the title and author of the curious children's book he'd found, along with a brief description.

It was an odd thing to find in the Innsmouth library, no question. He guessed that the author was from Innsmouth—the Marshes were one of the old families there, he'd learned that from the town history, and he'd noted the librarian's last name as well—but why would a local writer take something out of a piece of fiction that everyone there loathed for good reason, and use it for a children's story? The little girl in the drawings—the princess of Y'ha-nthlei, he guessed—didn't look particularly fishlike, much less like the sort of half-fish, half-frog, less than half-human horror with which Lovecraft had populated the town. She looked like an ordinary little girl with bare feet and curly hair, and the only tentacles he'd seen anywhere in the story were being brandished by the playful octopi.

He shook his head, got up and went to the desk where his laptop sat, woke it up. As he'd suspected, the hotel didn't have internet service; he wondered whether anybody in town was online. Still, the lack of distractions would be useful. He clicked on his thesis, for want of anything better, and then stared at the screen for a long moment before finally starting to type.

* * *

He woke up early the next morning. The sky had cleared off during the night, and pale autumn sunlight splashed over as much of the Innsmouth streetscape as he could see from the hotel window. To all appearances, it was still just one more old New England fishing town sinking into quiet decay now that the fisheries were gone. He watched gulls and gannets wheel through the air, considered the drear brown expanse of the marshes behind town and the distant line of trees that marked the edge of higher ground off toward Ipswich, and tried to make sense of the uneasy feeling that had haunted him since nightfall.

Showering, shaving, and pulling on clothes, the little rituals of morning, distracted him briefly but left all the bigger questions unanswered. Nothing he'd seen in Innsmouth either confirmed or contradicted any of the hints in Lovecraft's letter or made sense of the things that had happened since he'd found it. The closest thing to a mystery he'd found since arriving was the children's book in the library, and what he'd seen of it neither proved nor disproved anything. Even if he wanted to follow up on that, a glance at the clock showed that the Innsmouth library wouldn't be open for another five hours. He decided to walk around the town for a while, find some breakfast, and then visit the library again before catching the bus back to Arkham.

As he went out into the hallway, he nearly ran into the housekeeper, a gray-haired woman with the same unfamiliar ethnic look he'd seen in the desk clerk and the waitress at the restaurant. "I'm sorry," he said, stepping back; as he did so, he noticed the same saltwater scent he'd smelled from the waitress at Barney's.

"Quite all right," she said. "Will you be checking out now, or later?"

"Later, thanks."

She nodded, pushed her cart of cleaning supplies down the hall. Owen waited until she was past, went to the elevator.

Outside the air was brisk, and smelled of salt and seaweed. He turned east along the edge of the town square, past the restaurant—it was closed and dark, and the sign gave the Sunday hours as eleven to eight—and past the Rexall drugstore on the corner of Marsh Street. He kept on going past boarded-up storefronts. The next corner was State Street, or so the rusty sign said; the street itself angled south and east toward the waterfront. Owen glanced down it and then, having no better goal in mind, started walking along it.

It took a block and a half to go from buildings that were rundown but still apparently occupied to bare brick shells with empty windows and roofs half fallen in. Two more blocks brought him to the edge of the harbor, and a desolation even more complete. Most of the buildings along Water Street were ruins, interspersed with bare vacant lots where summer's goldenrods stood brown and dead among a profusion of hardier weeds. On the other side of the waterline, the stumps of old pilings from long vanished wharves rose from the harbor like decayed teeth. Off across the water, a bare tongue of sand curved along the breakwater, and a heap of stones discolored by seaweed at the breakwater's far end showed where the lighthouse once stood. If there had been dories, lobster pots, and fishermen's shacks on the sand in Lovecraft's time, as his story claimed, every trace of them had long since vanished.

Further along Water Street was a cluster of warehouses that probably dated from the wartime boom and hadn't yet fallen in on themselves, and a single long wharf reaching well out into the harbor, roofed and sided in corrugated metal gone dark brown with rust. One of the big doors on the landward side was pulled slightly open; Owen glanced inside, saw dim heaped shapes he couldn't identify, then noticed the gaps here and there in the floorboards of the wharf and decided not to investigate further. Past the wharf was a flat area just above the water's edge where stones were heaped in great piles, and beyond that the last traces of the town went away and a shore that probably didn't look much different when the Pilgrims arrived curved south and east toward the mouth of the Ipswich River.

He climbed up onto one of the piles of rocks, found a place to sit, perched there and stared out at the water for a long time. The tide had just started to ebb, and the sea was quiet in the lee of the breakwater, with only the smallest waves rolling in toward the shore before him. A black line on the horizon's edge had to be Devil Reef, but if any Deep Ones were capering about they didn't show themselves. The spires of Y'ha-nthlei stayed unseen.

The other choice is to go deeper, the man in the long black coat had said. How can I do that, Owen asked himself bitterly, when every route I can find that goes that direction ends in a closed door?

After a while, he shook his head and started to clamber down from his place atop the pile of rocks. As he did so, something heavy splashed into the water not far away. Once he was down on solid ground, he turned to look, but nothing was visible but ripples and swirls where whatever it was had plunged into the water.

Puzzled, he walked over toward the water's edge, wondering if a harbor seal might have been sunning itself there. Nothing surfaced, but when he got close to the water he happened to look down, and saw the footprint in the wet sand.

It wasn't the mark of a seal's flipper, or anything else he recognized. One end looked like the print of a human heel, but the other splayed out like a duck's foot or an unusually short set of frogman's flippers. He stared at it for a moment, swallowed, and then nodded slowly to himself.

"If any of you are still here," he said aloud, "I'd like to talk."

Only the wind answered him, but then he expected nothing more. After a long moment, he turned and began to walk thoughtfully back the way he'd come.

It was a little after nine in the morning when he got back to the hotel, and he went up to his room and spent an hour and a half reading before he packed up and went back downstairs to check out. The same young woman was sitting behind the desk; she took his key and said, "I hope you enjoyed your stay in Innsmouth, Mr. Merrill." He said something more or less appropriate and went back out into the morning.

Breakfast was at Barney's Seafood and Grill again—the fried-oyster omelet was delicious—and then he walked up Federal Street to the library, circled New Church Green twice before Mrs. Marsh appeared at the library's front door and the sign went from CLOSED to OPEN. Once inside, after fielding the librarian's calm greeting, he went to the local history section of the card catalog again and tried to think of something that would keep him looking busy until she left the room. He ended up with a stack of Essex County Historical Bulletins, sitting at a table much closer to the children's books, and hoping that something got her out of the room before any other patrons arrived.

He was in luck. Fifteen minutes after he got settled at the table, while he was in the middle of an article about the long-exhausted gold mines on the upper Manuxet and the very modest gold refining industry at Innsmouth, the sound of a phone ringing came faintly down the corridor connecting the library with the Historical Society. Mrs. Marsh excused herself and went to answer it. As soon as she was out of the room, Owen slipped over to the children's books. The book he wanted wasn't on the chair where it had been, so as quickly as he could he checked every thin book in a green library binding he could find on the shelves. None of them was the book he wanted.

He muttered something rude under his breath, listened carefully, heard Mrs. Marsh's voice talking. She was still busy, then. He went back to the card catalog, found the section that covered the children's books, and started searching. It took him only a few minutes to discover that the library officially didn't have a book titled *A Princess of Y'ha-nthlei*, nor did the catalog list anything at all by an author named Laura Marsh.

He gave the brown wooden bulk of the card catalog a bleak look, walked back to the table where he'd been sitting, sat down heavily in the chair. The article on the local gold industry sat there waiting for him, as though in mockery. No doubt, he thought, Mrs. Marsh had seen the book while closing up the evening before, and taken it back into the librarian's room, and no doubt there was some perfectly ordinary reason why it wasn't in the card catalog. No doubt.

A minute or so later Mrs. Marsh came back from the phone call, gave him a smile and settled into her station behind the librarian's desk. Five minutes after that, the library door swung open to let in children's voices and then the children themselves, twenty or so of them, shushed at intervals by the two middle-aged women who shepherded them. They looked as though they'd come straight from the local Sunday school, Owen thought sourly. Did the Esoteric Order of Dagon have a Sunday school?

Still, there was nothing left to do but play the game. He worked his way through the whole stack of Essex County Historical Bulletins, collecting maybe a dozen footnotes for the thesis, before the clock told him it was time to leave. The children were long gone by then, replaced by a trio of elderly ladies who hovered around the romance novels, buzzing with quiet conversation like so many bees.

"I hope you found what you were looking for," Mrs. Marsh said to him with a bright smile. "If you need anything else, call or come by, you hear?"

He promised he would, said his goodbyes, headed out the door and down Federal Street. Twenty minutes after he got to the sidewalk in front of the hotel, the bus back to Arkham pulled up. He climbed aboard, handed over his round trip ticket, trudged back to the same seat he'd taken on the way out, slumped into it as the door moaned shut and the driver pulled away from the curb. The desolate gray and brown streetscapes of Innsmouth rolled by. Owen glanced out the window, then closed his eyes and tried to come up with some reason his trip there hadn't been an utter failure.

CHAPTER 4

THE PARTING OF THE WAYS

B y the time he got back to the Dyer Street bus station, the
stars were bright overhead, and his mood was less dour
than it had been when he'd left Innsmouth. Sitting in the
bus as it rattled south on the Federal Pike with a book open
in his lap, while the sun sank toward the hills and one abandoned farm after another rolled past, he'd reviewed the trip
to Innsmouth and everything that led up to it, and decided
that he'd done as much as he could. Whatever secret might be
behind the letter from Lovecraft, he told himself, pretty clearly
wasn't for him to discover, and it was time for him to follow
the advice he'd gotten from Professor Akeley and the man in
black, leave the whole baffling business behind him, and refo-
cus his efforts on getting his degree, finding a doctoral program, and trying to claw his way to a teaching job before those
dried up completely.

He walked the four blocks from the bus station to the house
on Halsey Street without incident. After the unsolved puzzles
of Innsmouth, the familiar shabbiness of the house comforted
him; he hung up his coat in the entry, went into the living
room. Jenny Parrish was curled up in her usual place on the
couch, and voices and the clatter of dishes came through the
dining room doorway.

"Hi, Owen," Jenny said, looking up from her book.

"Hi."

"How was your trip?"

"Not too bad. I'm feeling better now."

"Good." She gave him an odd look then, and seemed to be about to say something else, but just then Barry came through the doorway and said, "Hey, welcome back. Where'd you go?"

"Caught the county bus up the coast, stayed overnight in a cheap hotel in an old fishing town. I just needed a break."

"I bet," Barry said. "Me, I'd head for Boston and get some real night life for a change, but whatever floats your boat."

A few minutes later Tish wanted to know where he'd been, and he repeated the same half-truth to her, all the while getting dinner made—this time it was minute rice and microwaved canned tamales. Back out in the living room with dinner, he slumped into his favorite chair, asked the others about their weekend, got to hear more than he really wanted to know about the ongoing scandal in the English department. He didn't mind; it was a welcome relief from the uncertainties he'd been contending with over the previous week.

When he'd finished with his meal; he headed upstairs, pleading unread emails and work on his thesis. He'd barely gotten settled in the chair at his desk when a tentative knock sounded at the door. "Come in," he said.

It was Jenny. "Owen," she said, "I didn't want to mention this in front of the others, but something kind of strange happened when you were gone."

He gave her a startled look. "Strange how?"

"Somebody came here Saturday afternoon to talk to you. He said he was in your critical theory seminar, and that the two of you were working on a project together. I told him you were gone for the weekend, and he got upset and started talking about how you were starting to act really strange, things like that." Her frown deepened. "The thing is, there was something really creepy about him. I don't know what it was. Maybe I was just stressed out."

"I'm not doing a project with anyone in that class," Owen said, baffled.

"Well, that's what he said."

"Did you get his name?"

"Jim something. Or—no, what was it? That's funny; he told me his name and now I can't remember it at all."

Owen shrugged. "I suppose it doesn't matter. If he shows up again and I'm not here, get him to leave his name and email and I'll find out what's going on."

"I'll do that," she promised, and left the room. Owen shook his head and got to work on a weekend's worth of unread emails.

* * *

"Man is the measure of all things," said Professor Peaslee. "You've seen that line over and over again. You've read the Presocratics, Plato, Aristotle, right on down to *Zen and the Art of Motorcycle Maintenance*, right? Good. Discuss."

Owen sat back in his chair, waited for the inevitable fireworks.

"I'll bite," said Maria Sanchez. "Man is the measure of all things, for man. Each of us can only experience the universe through human senses and a human nervous system, right? So our universe is a human universe, the only kind of universe humans can know."

"I'd argue that it's the only kind of universe there is," Shelby said. "Without human reason, you have matter and energy and space in various combinations, but you don't have a universe in any sense that matters."

"Okay, let's say there are intelligent alien jellyfish in the oceans of Alpha Centauri III," said a guy from comparative literature whose name Owen had never been able to pronounce. "They're rational beings who perceive a universe. Is jellyfish the measure of all things?"

"For jellyfish," said Sanchez.

Jim Malkowski got Peaslee's nod. "Fair enough. When computers become sentient—"

"If," said three other students at once.

"When," Jim snapped back. "Then computer will be the measure of all things, for sentient computers. Assume they're smarter than we are and learn to access sensory data we don't have. Their 'all things' contains more than ours does, and they tell us about it. Is man still the measure of all things?"

That got a low whistle from someone near Owen. "Let's take that in another direction," said Luellen Blair, the ministry student. "Different people have different capacities for experience. When we say Man, whose capacities are we talking about?"

That spun into a long argument about the role of the senses in knowledge, which finally wound down in a flurry of quotes from Hobbes, Berkeley, and Thomas Aquinas. When that ended in a pause, Owen got Peaslee's nod and said, "Okay, let's take it another step. Is Arthur Jermyn the measure of all things?"

"Howard!" half a dozen of his classmates shouted.

"You can't draw conclusions from an imaginary human-ape hybrid," said Shelby. "Those can't exist for biological reasons."

"Statistically," said Owen, "everyone in this room who's of European descent is supposed to have something like four per cent Neanderthal genetics. If that's true of me, am I only ninety-six percent the measure of all things?"

"Good," said Professor Peaslee. "Take it from there."

Owen drew in a breath. "It seems to me that we're avoiding the big question here, which is the relationship between this thing we're calling Man and individual human beings. Arthur Jermyn isn't Man, agreed. Neither am I, and neither are you. What goes into this abstract concept Man, and who makes that call?"

"That's an issue," Luellen said. "If I suggested that Woman is the measure of all things, I think we all know what kind of reaction I'd get."

That got an uncomfortable silence; more than one Five-Ninety-Five session had turned into a screaming fight over gender politics.

"Can we say that each individual is the measure of all things, to that individual?" Maria asked, breaking the silence.

"Does the phrase 'all things' still mean anything at all at that point?" Jim shot back.

"What I think Owen's suggesting," said Luellen, "and correct me if I'm wrong, Owen, is that when you say 'Man is the measure of all things,' you've made a political statement. You're holding up one particular abstract concept of what individual human beings can be, and saying that all things ought to correspond to it."

"All things," Owen said, "but also all people. That's the one that matters. Start out by defining this abstraction called Man as this or that measure, and you end up demanding that everyone measure up to it, and punishing the ones who don't."

"The only way to avoid that is to not impose any common measure on human beings at all," Jim said.

"I'm good with that," said Owen.

"That's a copout," said Shelby. "Reason gives us a basis for measure. As human beings we can tell the difference between the rational and the irrational. We know that what's rational is based on reality, and what's not rational isn't. That's what distinguishes us from the rest of the universe. To say man is the measure of all things means that reason is the measure of all things, and that's a valid standard for measuring everything, including human beings."

"That would imply," said Maria, "that you can judge human beings based on whether they measure up to your notion of rationality."

"It's not a matter of my notion or yours," Shelby said at once. "Reason is what it is. Statements, ideas, and beliefs are rational, or they're not. We can recognize that and solve our problems as a species, or we can ignore that and just keep floundering in the mud, the way we've done for all these thousands of years."

The next person who got Professor Peaslee's nod wanted to explore how Man in any sense of the word could measure anything, and before long most of the class was cheerfully wrestling with the linguistic roots of the Greek word for "measure."

Owen tried to follow the discussion, but his thoughts kept circling back to the earlier exchange. The argument Shelby had made, with its facile claims about the infallibility of human reason, reminded him rather too much of what little he'd found out about the Noology Program. Was that what they were teaching over in Belbury Hall?

He wondered bleakly whether Lovecraft's fish-men from Innsmouth were the measure of all things, and then thought of the little girl in the children's book he'd seen, playing with fish and octopi. Which of those was the measure of all things? The girl, the fish, the octopi?

Great Cthulhu?

When the class finally ended, Owen pulled himself out of his chair and left the classroom for the walk to Morgan Hall. Shelby got out ahead of him and was waiting outside. "I've mentioned you to Dr. Noyes," she said. "He'd really like to see you this afternoon."

"I've already told you I'm not interested," Owen said.

She looked irritated. "You're really being difficult about this."

"That's right," he said. "You know what? I'm just going to get more difficult until you drop it." He pushed past her and headed for the stairs.

* * *

Dead leaves crackled under Owen's shoes as he climbed the slope behind the new parking garage, weaving around the black clawed shapes of bare trees. Up ahead was the broad green whaleback shape of Meadow Hill, and beyond it the ravine, and the white stone.

He wasn't running from anything, he told himself. He didn't need protection.

The words rang hollow in his mind. Two more of his friends had recounted stories exactly like Jenny Parrish's, of people they didn't know, whose names they couldn't recall, who talked about how strangely he'd been behaving. Whatever was going on, it was too far from coincidence for his peace of mind.

He got clear of the bare trees and climbed the slope. At the crest he turned, looked out over the roofs of Arkham sprawled away to the south and the buildings of Miskatonic huddled to the east: Wilmarth Hall's baroque spires side by side with the gray concrete of the East Campus Parking Garage, Morgan Hall's bland brown brick, Pickman Hall all yellow brick and broad windows, and Belbury Hall off beyond it, pale and stark against the long row of trees lining Federal Street. The sky curved gray and bleak above him. He turned again and began walking north, toward the ravine.

The moment he started down from the crest, it was as though he had walked through a door. Even though he was only a few minutes' walk from campus and not much further from the busy streets of Arkham's north side, the green slope of the hill felt weirdly isolated, as if he'd suddenly stepped miles out of town. He could barely hear the traffic noise of the city behind him, and trees hid the campus to his right. He shook his head, kept walking.

To the north, the landscape spread out before him: a long grassy slope scattered with gray boulders some ancient glacier must have left behind, and then the ravine, a stark cut across the hillside, edged with tangled brush and great crannied masses of native stone. He found a way down into it after some searching. The bottom of the ravine was covered with thick grass, and rising out of it on the far side, just before the land rose back up again, was the white stone.

Owen walked toward it. He knew about the stone, and not just from the references in one of Lovecraft's stories. The Arkham witch trials of 1692, though they'd never gotten the wider fame of the Salem trials, were still remembered among old Arkham families; teenagers in town dared each other to visit the stone at midnight, and the student Wiccan group at Miskatonic used it as an altar for their ceremonies when the weather was good enough, which wasn't often.

It was a vaguely cubical mass of hard pale stone jutting up from the grass. Owen looked around; it wasn't hard to imagine naked revelers dancing around the stone on May Eve, as the witnesses at the witch trials claimed they'd seen.

He got to the stone, glanced down at its surface. Someone had scratched words onto the stone: SHUB-NIGGURATH WAS HERE.

He laughed and turned back the way he'd come.

At that moment something stirred and crackled in the brush behind him. Startled, he turned around, but whatever it was had already ducked back out of sight. He stood there for a moment, and then caught the smell: a rank, animal scent, faint but definite. It was—there really was no other word for it—goaty.

He turned abruptly and hurried back the way he'd come, glancing back over his shoulder from time to time as he went. Nothing followed him but the smell, which lingered until the white stone was entirely out of sight.

* * *

Back on campus, he climbed the long winding stair that ran up the middle of Wilmarth Hall. He was distracted enough that he almost walked right past the seventh floor landing. Catching himself, he pushed open the door and started toward Professor Akeley's office.

There was someone standing at the far end of the hall, looking out the tall windows there toward the gambrel roofs of Arkham. At the sound of the door, he turned and came to meet Owen in front of the office door.

"You must be Owen Merrill," the man said, putting out his hand. "I'm Clark Noyes."

Owen shook his hand, tried to gauge the man. At first glance, he could have been any of a dozen other professors from Miskatonic's better-funded departments, wearing the whole successful Ivy League academic kit from rimless glasses and casually knotted silk tie to tastefully overpriced Italian shoes, with a bland and genial look on his face. A second glance drew back baffled, because Owen could sense nothing at all behind the costume and the vaguely friendly expression. It was as though the clothing and the face formed a shell around empty space. "Pleased to meet you," he managed to say. "Shelby's talked about you."

"I imagine so," said Professor Noyes. "Actually, that's part of why I came looking for you this afternoon. She's mentioned you to me more than once. I know you have some doubts about the project." He chuckled. It was a strange sound, as though he'd calculated exactly what a chuckle should sound like and decided to produce one just then. "No surprises there, of course. Like so many of our grad students, Shelby's got a somewhat single-minded view of the goals of our project. She really hasn't grasped just now much of the humanities are relevant to noology."

Owen made a noncommittal noise in his throat, and Noyes chuckled again. "I know, you're skeptical. Understandably so, in fact. Still, I've taken the time to check up on your work here at Miskatonic, and quite frankly, I'm impressed. You've got a good quick mind. You're doing your thesis on Lovecraft, right?"

Owen nodded and quoted the title of his thesis at Noyes, who said, "Good, good. And studying his sources as well, which might be very helpful indeed." Owen wondered what he meant by that. "Do I remember right that you're planning on a doctorate?"

"Yes," Owen said.

"Good. I'd like to encourage you to think about the possibility of doing that in our program. We've got plenty of funding for the next few years, and I think we could really use you in the lab."

Taken aback, Owen said, "I'll consider it."

"Please do. In fact, why don't you come up to my office sometime soon? When you have time, of course—I know your schedule's got to be pretty busy with the semester in full swing. Still, give me a call, when you've got an hour or two. I'd be delighted to show you around, introduce you to the team, give you a better idea of what we're up to and how we can use you. I think you'll be favorably impressed." He repeated the odd, almost mechanical chuckle. "Well, I won't keep you. Give my best to Miriam."

"I'll do that."

"Great. See you soon." He headed for the elevators, still smiling exactly the same vague bland smile he'd had on his face all along.

Owen turned to watch him go, then went into Professor Akeley's office, his thoughts in confusion. Having a doctorate program all but handed to him by one of the university's most influential professors was a grad student's wet dream—but the thought of getting involved in whatever was going on in Belbury Hall still woke the same cold sick feeling in the pit of his stomach. Worse, absurd as it was, he couldn't shake the thought that there hadn't actually been anyone there inside Noyes' fashionable clothes and smiling face.

The office was empty. A note scrawled on a bright orange pad on the desk read: *Owen—will be back 12ish. One more flustered cluck around the interdisciplinary studies program and I'm going to start tearing my hair out in clumps. —MA.*

Owen laughed, went over to the table, and looked over the old pulp magazines and letters from the Harriet Blake estate. The puzzling letter from Lovecraft was nowhere to be seen. He looked through the piles for the volume of Justin Geoffrey's poetry, in case Akeley had put the letter back where it had been, but had no more luck finding that than the letter.

He was just finishing his search when he remembered that the interdisciplinary studies program had its offices in Belbury Hall. Maybe it was just a coincidence that the head of the Noology Program had arranged to be waiting in Wilmarth Hall, while someone else from Belbury Hall made sure Professor Akeley was somewhere else when Owen got there. Maybe.

The words the man in black had said on the bridge over Hangman's Brook whispered in his memory: *Sooner or later, you'll have to take sides*, he'd said. *Nobody's neutral in this business.* Noyes pretty clearly wanted him on one side, the side of the Noology Program; so did Shelby, and one thing after another seemed to be lining up to push him in the same direction.

And the other side—was there another side at all? He'd gone to Innsmouth looking for it, and come back with nothing in his hands. Maybe the man in black was the other side, or part of it, but since the trip to Innsmouth there had been no sign of him. Owen sat down abruptly on one of the chairs, wondering yet again what he'd stumbled into, and whether he'd be able to get through it in one piece.

* * *

The next day he woke before dawn and couldn't get back to sleep. By eight he was finished with breakfast and feeling restless, and decided on the spur of the moment to spend the whole morning down in the Orne Library restricted stacks. He got to the library less than fifteen minutes later, clattered down the stair into the basement, pressed the door buzzer, waited until the door rattled open and Dr. Whipple's lean wrinkled face peered out. The old man looked even more distracted than usual, but his face brightened when he saw who was waiting. "Owen," he said. "Well. Come in, come in."

He stepped through the door, and realized as he was taking his pack off that he and Dr. Whipple weren't the only ones in the room. It took a moment longer for him to realize that the other person there was Shelby. She glanced up, saw him, and something tense and almost fearful showed in her face for a moment before she covered it with a bright smile. "Hi, Owen."

"Hi," he said, startled by her presence there.

She got up, took the book she'd been reading to Dr. Whipple, and handed it to him; Owen thought he recognized the cover of the book. "I think that's everything I needed, thanks."

He responded with a skeptical sound somewhere down in his throat, and she turned the bright smile on him before leaving the restricted stacks.

Owen watched the door close, turned to the old man, and thought he recognized the sour expression on his face. "Dr. Whipple," he said, "is she the one who keeps on asking for one book after another?"

"Why, yes, she's one of them. It's that program up at Belbury Hall, whatever it's called. They keep sending grad students down here to do that sort of thing—as though anything worth knowing about the old lore can be learned in any such manner." He shook his head dolefully. "Superficiality, Owen. It's the bane of education." He turned to take the book Shelby had been reading back into the stacks, then stopped. "What will it be this time? As I recall, you finished with the Eltdown Shards the last time you were down here."

"Yes, I did." A sudden thought came to him. "Do you have Justin Geoffrey's *The People of the Monolith and Other Poems*?"

The old man blinked. "Indeed I do. Curious that you should ask for that. Just a moment." He set down the book Shelby had been reading on one of the tables, went over to the far end of the stacks. When he was out of sight, Owen walked over to the table and opened the book. It had the crowded and ornate title page common in seventeenth-century books, but the top two lines read: *Necronomicon seu Liber de Legibus Mortuorum*. He closed the cover, stepped back to where he had been standing, and waited for Whipple to return.

"Here you are," the old man said. "That wasn't in the collection down here until a few days ago. They've got Lovecraft's own copy upstairs in special collections, full of scrawls." He shook his head. "But this is a good clean copy."

Owen thanked him and took the book to the nearest table while Whipple picked up the *Necronomicon* and took it back into the stacks. It was Robert Blake's copy of Geoffrey's book, no question of that. The letter from Lovecraft was gone, as he'd expected, but the paper it had been written on had yellowed the pages to either side of it. The left hand page was blank; the other had a sonnet printed on it:

```
HALI
The prophet's blood pools scarlet on the stone.
His eyes, that knew futurity and fate,
Stare blind and bleeding through a broken
gate
Into a burning fane, where he alone
Once heard the inmost whispers of the Earth.
Did they forewarn him of the cold command,
The pounding hooves, the weapon in the hand
That struck him down, the laugh of brutal
mirth?
Now muffled figures murmur in the night
His final words; now others gaze aghast
At fell shapes rising from the sleepless
past.
The age that dawned there, in the flame's red
light,
Shall end in flame when, as he prophesied,
Four join their hands where gray rock meets
gray tide.
```

He wondered what any of it meant. He remembered the prophet Hali from von Junzt and a few other books he'd studied, and something he'd read somewhere back a couple of months ago claimed that he'd been a historical figure, a priest of the city of Irem in Arabia in the second century BC. Nothing he'd read mentioned a violent death, and the prophecy of the last line rang no least bell of memory.

The faint yellowing there on the page reminded him of Lovecraft's warning. The question that mattered, he knew, was whether he'd tried to turn back in time.

* * *

He had his answer the next evening.

He went with Professor Akeley to her office after the afternoon class—she'd lectured on the impact of the cinema on popular culture between the wars, a fascinating topic though less relevant to his thesis than some of the others—and put something like four hours into helping her sort through the letters from the Harriet Blake estate. By tacit agreement, neither of them mentioned the fifth letter from Lovecraft. The weather had turned cold that day, and so the crotchety heating system in Wilmarth Hall went into overdrive as usual and kept the whole building stuffy enough that Akeley discarded her sweater and Owen felt overheated.

The letters included real treasures, no question. Some of them, the professor assured Owen, would keep scholarly dovecotes fluttering for years to come. Finally, though, they'd sorted through the entire collection and made a list of their authors and subjects. Through the window, stars shone bright and distant in a black sky, and the lamps around the empty quad glowed sodium yellow below. They wished each other a good night and Owen went down the long stair toward the ground floor and the walk home. The heating system was still running full blast; he slung his coat over his shoulder along with his backpack.

The main doors were working for a change. They hissed open, he stepped through, and a moment later realized that someone was standing out in front, waiting. It was Shelby.

Except that it wasn't.

She came toward him, her face fixed in a hollow smile. "Owen," she said, in a voice that was just as bland and empty as Professor Noyes' had been. "It's time for you to come with me. We've waited long enough."

The sense of vacancy he'd gotten from Professor Noyes had been uncomfortable enough, but Owen didn't know the man. With Shelby, things were different. He'd taken classes with her, argued with her, discussed career plans; he'd had a crush on her for a while, until he realized that there wasn't enough chemistry between them for anything to come of it. He knew her—but this wasn't her in any sense that mattered. Whatever was approaching him looked and sounded like Shelby, but there was no longer a person inside.

He tensed, backed away, and then suddenly out of the corner of his eye noticed someone else moving toward him.

Once in his Army days, out in Anbar Province, he'd been in a firefight and suddenly, with kick-in-the-stomach intensity, known that he had to get down. He dropped to the ground an instant before gunfire sprayed through the empty air where his face had been. This felt exactly the same way. He knew he had to run, and he ran. Shelby sprang after him and grabbed one end of his coat; he twisted, shed coat and backpack, and sprinted out into the quad.

His footfalls drummed on the hard half-frozen ground. Another pair followed, went to one side, heading him off in case he tried to run for the main entrance to Armitage Union. Owen gauged his options, veered in the only direction that offered any hope of safety: the green belt at the foot of Meadow Hill. The ravine, he reminded himself. The white stone.

He rounded the southwest corner of Wilmarth Hall, hazarded a glance back over his shoulder. Shelby was standing in the middle of the quad, talking to somebody on her cell phone; his coat and backpack were on the ground next to her. His pursuer had lost ground heading toward Armitage Union, but was still on his trail. Owen sped up, sprinted past the south end of Wilmarth Hall to Garrison Street, which ran between campus and the green belt, knowing that any traffic there might leave him at his pursuers' mercy. Fortunately the only cars were a block away, and he dashed across the street, plunged into the black leafless trees on the other side.

* * *

The darkness beneath the trees was thick enough that Owen could barely see to run, but he kept moving uphill as fast as he could. The night around him was bitterly cold; the air burned in his throat. The footfalls of his pursuer slowed and stopped—on the street, from the sound of it—and after a moment he heard the faint buzz of a one-sided conversation as the man called someone else on a cell phone. Under the trees, Owen felt he had a chance; reactions he hadn't had to call on since he got home from Iraq surged through him alongside the adrenaline, reminding his muscles of every nasty close-quarter combat trick he'd ever learned.

Who had Shelby called? *Sooner or later, you'll have to take sides,* the man in black had said. *Nobody's neutral in this business.* The words burned in his memory. Whatever the sides were, whatever the stakes might be, he knew whose side he could never be on, and that left only one alternative—if there was another side at all. He shoved the thought away, kept moving.

He'd raised a sweat sprinting across the quad, and now that he had to move more slowly, his damp clothes turned painfully cold. He clenched his teeth to keep them from chattering, kept going. He tripped over a fallen branch, landed hard on his hands and knees, pulled himself up. What had the man in black said? *On the far side of the ravine is an old white stone. Go there if you're in danger—you'll find protection there, and guidance.* The words barely made sense to him. Keep going, he told himself; that at least was simple enough to understand.

He pushed ahead in the blind black shadows, finally came out onto the whaleback slope of Meadow Hill. The pale glow from Arkham's streetlights lit up the sky behind him, beyond the dark mass of Chapman Hall. Little light reached the hill, but it was enough that searchers might be able to spot him. No help for that now. He ran, fast and low, up to the hill's crest and over it.

As before, the moment he passed the crest he seemed to be in another world. The traffic noises and city lights behind him might as well have been miles away. Ahead, barely visible in the night, the hill sloped down toward the ravine, and the white stone.

Afterwards, he could never remember just how he found his way down into the ravine in the darkness without falling from the rocks and breaking his neck. Still, a few minutes later, he clambered down a steep slope onto thick grass crisp with frost, and saw the stone, pale in the night, not far away. He tried to remember why he was supposed to go toward it, but the memory wouldn't surface and the cold pressed him hard from every direction. He was stumbling, barely able to walk, by the time he reached it.

Someone was sitting next to it, wrapped in what looked like blankets and rags. He could barely see the face in the dim light as it turned toward him: dark-skinned, wrinkled, surrounded by shadows.

"Come here, child." A woman's voice, rich with the harmonies of age.

He looked at her blankly, came over to the stone.

"You'll catch your death of cold if you keep running on a night like this," she said, and patted the ground next to her. "Sit yourself down."

He stumbled over to her, slumped to the ground. There was a rank, animal scent around her, perhaps the smell of unwashed skin and clothing, perhaps something else. She turned and reached, and something that felt like a warm soft blanket settled over him; it smelled of fallen leaves and dry grass, of earth and weathered stone. The warmth brought a moment's clarity; he wondered if he was hallucinating, and then a moment later if he was dying of the cold.

"No, no, child," she said, laughing, as though she'd heard his thoughts. "No, you'll be safe here with me. What's got you out on a night like this?"

"They're hunting me," he managed to say

"Are they, now. Why is that?"

All at once, without any choice on his part, the whole story came tumbling out of him: the letter, the warnings, the trip to Innsmouth, all the way to the empty husk that had been Shelby and his desperate escape from the campus. All the while, the old woman nodded.

After Owen finished, the old woman nodded once more and then smiled; he could just see the gleam of her teeth. "Well, then," she said. "It's good that he sent you here."

"The man in black," he said then, guessing at her meaning. "You know him?"

"Oh, yes." Another laugh rippled through the air like wind in the branches. "Oh, yes, indeed. We go back a long, long time."

Then she leaned toward him. "Time to sleep now, child." When he opened his mouth to protest: "When you wake up, head north. There'll be a moon path waiting for you, child, and you're to follow it. North, you hear?"

"Yes," he mumbled.

"Good. Now go to sleep."

She seemed to rise up, becoming larger and more strangely formed, with great curving shapes rising from her head. He glimpsed her briefly, a vast dark presence that seemed to loom up into the night sky, though maybe that was just because he was slipping over onto his side. A moment later his eyes drifted shut. Something soft pressed against his head. The warmth of the blanket and its scent was all around him, and the softness under him drew him down, silently and gently, into blackness.

CHAPTER 5

THE OLD STRAIGHT TRACK

Owen woke slowly, out of strange dreams. At first he thought he must be in his bed in the house on Halsey Street. Then he blinked and stared in confusion, trying to think how he'd ended up outdoors in the gray dawn. Warmth still wrapped around him. As the last shreds of sleep cleared his mind, he found that he was nestled in a hollow in the ground next to the white stone, with fallen leaves piled under him and a great mass of them heaped above. He turned, pulled himself out from the pile, tried to make sense of his surroundings and the events of the night.

There was no trace of the old woman, no sounds but the wind and the rustle of branches. It took him a moment to realize that the gray light was coming from the wrong end of the ravine. Owen rubbed his eyes, but the pale smudge in the clouds that marked the sun's place was still in the west; it took him a moment to realize that it was setting, not rising. He'd slept through the night and most of the day.

As he sat there blinking, wings fluttered: a raven landed on the white stone, regarded him with one beady black eye. "Hi," he said to it.

The raven turned its head, looked at him with its other eye, and then opened its beak and let out its croaking cry. Maybe it was chance, but there seemed to be a word in the cry: "North."

"Yeah, I know," he told it. "I remember."

The raven gave a little nod, and then sprang into the air and flew off.

Owen blinked, got to his feet, looked at his wrinkled sweatshirt and jeans, then at the sky. There were clouds coming in from the west, alternately hiding and revealing the setting sun; it promised to be another cold night. Suddenly an idea surfaced; he took handsful of the leaves that had covered him, and stuffed them between shirt and sweatshirt, wriggling and shaking until they settled into an even layer. He could feel the extra warmth at once.

He looked around, then, and noticed something he'd missed at first. The grass around the white stone looked trampled, as though people had walked around it. Up toward the edge of the ravine was a place where mud had been washed down from the slopes above during the autumn rains; Owen walked over to it and saw fresh shoeprints, plenty of them. That made no sense at all. If the tracks were from the people who'd been hunting him, the ones Shelby had called, how could they have missed seeing him lying there asleep in a pile of leaves?

He shook his head, stood by the white stone, looked for the route north the old woman had mentioned—the moon path, whatever that meant. From the white stone, something that might have been a trail led up the far side of the ravine. Nothing else offered itself, so he clambered up past rock and thicket scrub to the edge of the land above.

There he could hear traffic noise again, though Meadow Hill and a mass of low twisted pines hid the town and the university. To the north, the land stretched out in a patchwork of old farms with stone-fenced fields. Off in the middle distance rose a line of hills, dark against the evening sky. He tried to see where the trail went, saw nothing but featureless grass, and stood there, uncertain, as the sun finished setting in the mountains to the west.

Then, as he looked north, he noticed his eye returning over and over again to a distant shape on one of the hills to the north:

not the tallest of them, nor the closest, but there was something atop it, something that he couldn't quite see but that felt oddly important. Staring at it, he noticed other things that seemed to line up with whatever it was: a pool close by, a bit of old lane, a low mound, a ragged stone at the corner of a pasture. There was something else, too, or maybe it was a trick of the first pale radiance of the moon in the eastern sky: something that was neither light nor dark, but took up the moonlight and drew it like a current across the land. It seemed to flow in a straight line between each point and the next, insubstantial as a spider's web but unquestionably there.

He shivered, and not from the cold. There was something uncanny about the alignment and the faint current that swept along it, something that scraped and jarred at his nerves. A murmur like distant voices and a sense of unseen presences seemed to move along the path, if that was what it was, drawing him onward toward the distant hill and whatever threat or blessing it might hold. He felt himself leaning forward, as though the path was pulling him and a single step might commit him irrevocably to it.

The traffic noise of Arkham muttered behind him. He wondered what his housemates were thinking and doing, and the thought of going back hovered in his mind for a moment. Then he thought of what Shelby had become. He'd barely escaped a trap, he felt that in his bones, and stepping back into it wasn't an option he was willing to consider. After another moment, he started walking, following the faint line of light down the grassy slope to the north. If it wasn't the moon path the old woman had mentioned, he decided, it was close enough.

He learned quickly that he could only see the path when he was on it. If he strayed to either side more than a few feet, the alignment and the subtle current vanished, and he was standing on an ordinary bit of undeveloped real estate outside an ordinary college town. Once he found his way back to the path, though, the world went strange around him. The half-seen irregularity on the distant hill again became a compelling presence, the flowing moonlight pointed the way there, and the grass, the brush and the scattered stones around him seemed to gesture and murmur to one another.

After a little while, he came to the pool he'd seen from the crest of the ravine. Gray flagstones that might have been part of some long-abandoned farmyard stood beside it, carrying the path past the mud and reeds. As Owen got there, another raven—or perhaps the same one he'd seen earlier—swept down from a nearby tree to perch on a branch beside the pool. It dipped its beak in the water, then gave Owen another sidelong glance.

"You're telling me," he said aloud, "that I ought to drink."

The raven perched there, watching him, and after a moment Owen laughed nervously. "Probably a good idea," he told it, knelt on one of the flagstones and brought water up to his mouth in cupped hands. Only when he tasted it did he realize just how thirsty he was, and he scooped up water again and again until he felt filled. The water was cold and clean, and something like the moon-current shimmered and tingled in it; he washed his face and hands in it for good measure, then got up and gave the raven a questioning look. It croaked "North!" at him again, and flew away.

He kept going. The night deepened around him as he walked. The hills in the distance turned into black silhouettes against the cold and distant stars. He found that if he kept his gaze on the peak of the one hill that mattered, he didn't need to pay attention to his footing. The moon path guided him—it felt at times as though it carried him—and all he had to do was keep putting one foot in front of another.

Though nothing human came near him, he was not alone in the night. As he crossed a half-overgrown pasture, following the path from one gap in the stone fence to another half a mile away, bats fluttered above him; as he walked under bare trees, a great gray owl ghosted silently past. Deer looked up from their browsing to watch him go, and a fox darted onto the path ahead of him, trotted before him for a time, then turned aside and vanished into the underbrush.

There were still supposed to be working farms north of Arkham, but no dogs barked at him, and he passed no human handiwork except weathered stone walls that had been cleansed by the weather of many harsh seasons. The path he followed was not a route for tame things, and the longer he walked on it, the more he felt like a wild thing himself, alert to sounds and scents, one with the wind and the autumn night. He'd had the idea early on of keeping watch for signs of pursuit, but somehow that thought slipped away from him as he walked. While he was on the moon path, he seemed to be in some other world, where pursuing footfalls and whatever hid within Belbury Hall were dim legends from the far past or prophecies of some distant future.

He scarcely noticed when the land began to rise, when the one hill that mattered stopped being a silhouette against starlight and turned into a curving mass blotting out the lower arc of the northern sky. He began to breathe heavily, but the path led onward and he followed. A final climb led him up through resin-scented pines, and then the darkness fell away from the northern stars and the thread of moonlight wound to its end.

He was on a low bare hilltop with nothing above him but the heavens. The moon was high above; he guessed from its position that the time was around midnight. All around him, jagged black shapes jutted upwards to blot out patches of the sky. It took Owen some moments to realize that they were standing stones, a ragged circle of them crowning the hill.

A dark shape, man-high or taller, detached itself from one of the standing stones. Owen turned to face it, waited as it approached and stopped.

"Well done," said a voice he'd heard twice in Arkham, the voice of the man in the long coat and the broad-brimmed hat. "I thought you would find the way."

Owen blinked at him in the darkness, tried to think of something to say, and failed.

"Come with me," said the man, taking his arm in a strong grip. "We have only a little while, and shelter's near."

* * *

Light flared in blackness: a tiny flame on the end of a long sliver of wood. It moved, kindled the wick of an old-fashioned oil lamp. A pool of yellow light spread around it, revealed the lean dark face and hawk's nose of the man in the black coat; spread further to show a stained and cracked wooden table, stone walls off to the sides, rough oaken rafters overhead. The man set the lamp on the table, motioned Owen to a rusted but serviceable metal chair by it, bent to get something on the floor.

"What is this place?" Owen asked. His own voice sounded strange to him.

"This? An abandoned farmhouse. All the farms in these hills went bankrupt long ago, but some of the houses are still weathertight. This one serves me for shelter now and then when I need it." He set a bag on the table next to the lamp, sat down in another chair.

"Were you waiting for me up there the whole time?"

"That depends a great deal on what you mean by 'there' and 'time.'"

"Who are you? What—" Owen stopped in confusion, unable to find the words even to frame the questions he wanted to ask.

"All in good time," the man replied with a soft laugh. "As to my name, though, you should know that by now, or at least you should have guessed it."

Owen opened his mouth, closed it again, swallowed though his mouth felt suddenly dry. The man in black watched him with inscrutable eyes. "You're—" He made himself go on. "Nyarlathotep."

"That's correct," the man said.

"That's—that can't be true."

The man leaned forward, elbows on the table, propping his chin on his hands. "You already know that some of what Lovecraft wrote about was real. You've seen the letter—as far as we know, the only one he wrote on that subject that hasn't been hidden or destroyed. You've been to Innsmouth, and seen things there. You've come here along one of the old straight paths, and sensed some of its magic." In a voice that was little more than a murmur: "And you've seen something of what the other side can do."

"If that's true," Owen said then, "if you're Nyarlathotep, if—if the rest of it is true, then everything I've ever been taught about the world is a lie."

"Essentially, yes."

Owen gave him a bleak horrified look.

"I don't ask you to take that on faith," said Nyarlathotep. "All I ask is that you make room for the possibility, and don't pretend that you don't see and hear the things that happen around you. One thing more: when I tell you to do something, you'll need to do it at once, without question. Your life is only one of the things that could be at stake."

"Okay," said Owen. "I can do that much, I think. You've already saved me from—from—I don't know what they would have done to me, but I think I'd rather be dead."

"Tell me what happened."

Owen drew in a breath and told him.

"That's what I thought. You can't go back to Arkham now, or ever again, you know. Do you have family?"

"Not any more. My parents died in a car crash when I was seven."

"That's something. But your friends, your college plans, your career, all of that is over."

Owen stared at him for a long silent moment, and finally nodded. "You told me at Hangman's Creek that there wouldn't be any way back," he said slowly. "What's going to happen when I—" His voice faltered.

"When you disappear?" Nyarlathotep shrugged. "If the other side's doing what they usually do, they've already spread claims that you were acting strangely—always convenient if someone has to disappear. If they think they have a chance of catching you, they'll toss a few garments of yours in the nearest available river and try to make people believe that you drowned yourself. If not, the rumors will be enough. People will decide that you had a nervous breakdown and ran off one night, and isn't it sad that nobody's seen you since. After a while, the search will stop, and a few years down the road, you'll be presumed dead."

Owen stared at him again for a while in something close to shock.

"I'm sorry," said the man in black.

Owen started laughing. There was an edge of hysteria to the laughter; he felt it, and hated it, but couldn't make himself stop. "You're sorry? You're Nyarlathotep, the Crawling Chaos, the nightmare herald of the Great Old Ones, and you're *sorry*?"

Nyarlathotep leaned back in his chair, folded his hands behind his head, and smiled. After a moment Owen stopped laughing. "Of course. That's what the other side calls you."

"They're not entirely wrong," said Nyarlathotep. "I am the herald of the Great Old Ones, and to them, that makes me a nightmare indeed. As for crawling chaos, that's a more complex matter than you realize; we'll discuss it another time." He opened the package on the table. "First, a more basic issue. I hope you don't mind cold sandwiches. That's all that I could find on the way here."

It suddenly occurred to Owen that he hadn't eaten for most of two days. "Thank you," he said, and took a sub sandwich wrapped in paper. When Nyarlathotep didn't take the other sandwich in the bag: "You?"

"I don't eat," the Old One said.

Owen gave him a dubious look, then nodded and went to work on his sandwich. Nyarlathotep reached down to the floor again, brought up a clean metal cup and a metal bottle, filled the cup with what looked like water and pushed it across the table. Owen managed to thank him through a mouthful of sandwich.

When he finished the first one, Nyarlathotep gestured at the bag. Owen nodded, took the other and unwrapped it, but sat there looking at the Old One for a long moment.

"You told me that I'm going to have to take sides," he said. "I don't know what this whole business is about, or why I'm suddenly in the middle of it; I don't have any idea what the sides are, and I don't know what your side is for, but if you're against—" He tried to find words. "Against whatever it is they're doing in Belbury Hall, against the—deadness, if that's the right word—then I may be on your side. For whatever that's worth."

"It may be worth little, or much," said Nyarlathotep. "We'll have to see."

* * *

Owen finished the second sandwich and sat back in the chair. "And now?"

"We have more walking to do. They're hunting you along the roads, hoping to catch you before you reach me, or to stop us before we can get to safety, so the moon paths are the only route that's open to us just now."

"Hunting me," Owen repeated. "Why?"

"That's a question I can't answer yet," said Nyarlathotep. "Clearly the other side wants you, badly, and they're willing to mobilize quite a few of their resources to catch you."

"So this is more than just the people at Belbury Hall."

The Old One gave him a wry look. "Very much more than that."

"Oh." Owen thought about that for a moment. "Where are we going?"

"Innsmouth." He motioned toward the door, got up, and extinguished the lamp. Owen followed him out of the little stone house and across the slope. The Old One seemed to know exactly where he was going. He led Owen to a place below the hilltop and stopped, pointing off into the distance to the northeast. "Look. What do you see?"

Owen stared across the dim land, gray and formless beneath the moonlight. There were low mounds in the distance, a standing stone atop a hill, stone fences dividing long-abandoned fields. Off on the edge of the sky was a thin line of different hue that had to be the sea. After a time, though, he caught a first dim sense of flow across the landscape, stretched out like a spiderweb across the vista from one subtle landmark to another. His breath caught. "A path," he said. "Like the one I followed earlier."

"Good," said Nyarlathotep. "Come."

They started walking down the slope. Within moments Owen felt the same strange sense of murmuring presence around him that he recalled from the first part of the night's journey. He glanced at the tall figure beside him, who seemed to follow the strange path effortlessly. "The thing that flows down the moon path," he asked. "What is it?"

"Voor," Nyarlathotep said.

Owen considered that. "That's in von Junzt," he said after a moment, "and in some of the other books, but I never could figure out what they were talking about."

"No?" The Old One considered him sidelong. "Voor is the life force, the twofold current that flows along the old straight tracks, through the body of the living Earth and through every other body above and upon and beneath it. There's a bright voor that descends from the sky and a dark voor that rises from the Earth's heart, and the two dance together along the surface of land and sea and make manifest the kingdom of Voor. Do you know the riddle of the Alala?"

"No," said Owen, feeling more than a little overwhelmed.

"'Find me the place where the light goes when it's put out, and find me the place where the water goes when the sun dries it up.' There was a time, long ago, when human children all over the world knew that riddle by the time they could walk. The answer is the kingdom of Voor, the realm of the unseen, that holds the realm of the seen in existence moment by moment."

They walked on, following the thread of light down the hill-side. "Lovecraft never really understood that," the Old One said. "I tried to explain some of the deeper meanings of the lore to him, more than once, but he wouldn't have any of it." He held up a hand suddenly, before Owen could respond. "We'll need to leave the path. Follow me."

Immediately ahead, the slope turned steeply downhill, plunged into shadow. Nyarlathotep led the way off to the left, down a shallower slope, and then back across at an angle to return to the path. The faint shimmering presence of voor enclosed them again.

"You knew Lovecraft?" Owen asked then.

"Oh, yes. I met him several times, when he was living in New York City. I ran with plenty of authors in those days. Quite a few people in the New York literary scene liked to dabble in magic, sometimes in the latest fashionable nonsense, but sometimes in deeper and truer things, the sort of things I deal in. Lovecraft did some of both, though you won't learn that from your scholars; he burned all the papers and books that had to do with his occult studies before he went back to Providence, and cobbled together some story about a burglary. He learned quite a bit—enough, for example, to realize who and what I am."

Nyarlathotep laughed again softly, shook his head. "But of course that wasn't something he was willing to face, not for long. He made his choice, fled home to Providence, turned his back on his dream-quests and his studies, and made himself believe that the things he'd learned might just as well be turned into raw material for pulp-magazine stories and spread among his fellow authors. We tried to warn him, but—" A silence. "He refused to believe the other side could be the more ruthless of the two."

"The other side," Owen said then. "Who are they? What do they want?"

Nyarlathotep glanced at him, kept walking. "We'll discuss that another time, when you're well clear of their grasp."

* * *

The night wore on, and the faint shimmering of the moon path stretched out before them. Here and there, where the ground required it, Nyarlathotep led the way off the track and then back onto it, moving with a sureness that left Owen wondering: had the Old One traveled the same unearthly path many times before, or did he perceive it in some profounder way than human senses could?

That something of the sort was involved, he had no doubt. Somewhere in the silent dark hours, the part of him that wanted to insist on the impossibility of what he'd seen and heard had gone tumbling away with the cold night wind. It still startled him that he was walking alongside a figure out of Lovecraft's stories and the old lore behind them, but it was the same sort of surprise he might have felt if he'd been riding a county bus and had someone from Congress or the movies take the seat next to him: a sense of something improbable, but not unreal.

Partly, it was the animals. He'd learned on his solitary journey north from Arkham that wild things seemed to seek out what Nyarlathotep called the old straight tracks, but except for the raven, they had behaved like every other wild animal Owen had seen: wary, poised, busy with their own affairs and uninterested in his. With Nyarlathotep, it was different. Deer walked shyly up to him to nuzzle his hands, and a fox crossing the path ahead of them spotted him and came over at a trot, then sat there with its head cocked to one side as the Old One crouched on his heels and seemed to commune with it in some way Owen couldn't follow.

Once when they were crossing an open field, the Old One suddenly raised a hand with one long finger extended. When he lowered the hand, a bat was hanging from the finger, its wings furled around it, its eyes beady and bright. As Owen watched, fascinated, Nyarlathotep's lips moved, though no sound seemed to come out of his mouth, and the bat hung attentive on his finger. After the conversation, if that was what it had been, Nyarlathotep flung his hand upwards again, and the bat fluttered away into the night.

Still, there was more to it than the behavior of the animals, more even than the weird murmuring space that wrapped around them as they followed the shimmering voor of the moon path. After a day sound asleep and a night spent walking, Owen's mind felt clearer than it had in weeks. During the silences of the night, when he wasn't talking with Nyarlathotep or watching the wild beasts follow him and lick his hands, Owen thought over his last month in Arkham and the rising tide of strange events that had swept him out of the life he knew, returning again and again to his last encounters with Shelby, the things she'd said, and the empty shape with her face on it that had confronted him, there at the last. What had they done to her on the ninth floor of Belbury Hall? Or—the question forced itself on him—what had she done to herself?

The night brought him no answers. He kept walking.

Finally, as they came out of a thicket of shore pines along the edge of an ancient mound and crossed a long-abandoned field, a first faint edge of gray showed along the eastern horizon. "On the other side of this field," said Nyarlathotep, "we leave the track, and go east to Pickman's Corners. I have a friend there. That's as well; tomorrow will be the most dangerous part of the journey. We'll have to travel by day, and we won't have the protection of the old straight tracks."

Owen took that in. "What are they? The tracks, I mean."

"Part of an ancient enchantment on the land. The people who built them vanished from this land long before the ancestors of the ancestors of the Wabanaki crossed the mountains to settle here, and they built on foundations laid by the serpent-folk of Valusia before the Atlantic Ocean was born." He started walking again, stretching his long legs, and Owen hurried to catch up. "It's given your archeologists no end of trouble to keep insisting that colonial settlers were somehow responsible for all the mounds and standing stones in New England."

"They know otherwise?" Owen asked, startled.

"A few of them, yes. The rest—you know how that happens at least as well as I do. They think what they've been taught to think, and they find out very quickly that asking the wrong questions is an effective way to end a career."

Owen was silent for a while. "Like asking the wrong questions about Lovecraft," he said as they reached the end of the field, and Nyarlathotep turned and led the way down a disused lane. "I sure walked into that one face first."

"You saw the letter," said the Old One, "recognized it for what it was, and didn't dismiss the evidence of your eyes. There are still universities and fields of study where that's acceptable, but not at Miskatonic—not where Lovecraft is concerned."

"And here I am."

"Do you regret that?"

Owen glanced at him. "No," he said finally. "No. I probably should, but I don't. Whatever all this is about, it feels important, more important than anything else I could do. And—" He looked down. "If I'd stayed in Arkham, I think that whatever got its claws into Shelby would have gotten me too."

"The question," said Nyarlathotep, "is exactly what that is."

"You don't know?" Owen asked, startled.

"No. I have my suspicions, nothing more. It's just possible that you can help turn those into knowledge." The lane opened onto a road. In the still faint light from the east, Owen could just make out the cracks that ran across the pavement, the weeds that pressed close to the road's edges and sprouted in potholes here and there. "This way," the Old One said, gesturing. "The sun will be up soon. You'll need to get what rest you can before the last part of the journey."

CHAPTER 6

THE WITCH OF PICKMAN'S CORNERS

Pickman's Corners was a little cluster of buildings huddled at the intersection of two old county roads. Most of the structures had tumbled in on themselves years before, and those that were still occupied—two houses and a rundown convenience store with disused gas pumps out in front—looked as though they weren't far from the same condition.

Nyarlathotep seemed to know exactly where he was going, though. He went straight to the gap between the convenience store and one of the houses, pulled open a rusty gate in the low chain link fence that stood there, stepped through. A big mixed-breed dog came around the corner of the house at a dead run, teeth bared and growling, but the moment it saw Nyarlathotep, it stopped in its tracks. It came up to him then, ears flattened, head down and tail wagging, making little whimpering noises in apology. The Old One let it lick his hand, scratched the top of its head, and went by. The dog sniffed at Owen as well, then trotted along behind him as Nyarlathotep went around to the back door and knocked on it in a complex rhythm.

A few minutes later the door opened, and an old woman in a frilled nightgown and a worn velour bathrobe peered out. "Magister! I thought I knew that knock. Come in, come in. You too, young man. Tobias, no, not you."

The door clicked shut in the face of the disappointed dog, and a light went on. They were standing in a kitchen that had seen many better days. "Sit down, sit down," the old woman said, waving them to chairs around the table. "You'll want food, of course. Tea, coffee?"

"Tea, please," Owen said.

"Half a moment." A kettle went on the stove, and pans clattered. "You've spent a night out of doors, that's plain enough."

Owen looked down ruefully at his crumpled clothing. The old woman glanced back over her shoulder, considered him with bright eyes, and laughed. "No surprises there. It's been years and years since I traveled with the One in Black, but I remember well what sort of mess the mirror showed me when I got back home. I don't imagine you keep a gentler pace now than you did then, Magister."

Nyarlathotep smiled, and said nothing.

She bustled about the kitchen, and before long the tea put in an appearance, followed by eggs and sausages, fried potatoes, toast and jelly, and more tea. The old woman sat down and had her own breakfast along with Owen, and talked with Nyarlathotep, partly about the route ahead, mostly about people and places Owen didn't know, though Innsmouth featured in the talk now and then. The old woman was on friendly terms with the Innsmouth folk, he gathered, though there seemed to be some sort of rivalry with them as well.

By the time the meal was over, the morning light came pale and clear through the kitchen curtains. The old woman gathered up the dishes and took them to the sink, and then said, "Magister, I've a question I'd ask your young friend, if I may."

Nyarlathotep gestured for her to go on.

"Young man," she said, "you're wrapped in something that's been touched by power, and not by our friend here. Seeing as such things are my trade, I'd be glad to know what it is."

Owen blinked again, and then suddenly realized what she had to be talking about. "It's leaves," he told her. "When I left Arkham, I went to a place near it—"

"The white stone," the old woman said.

"Yes. There was an old woman there, sitting by the stone, wrapped in—old blankets, or that's what they looked like. I don't know who she was, but I don't think she was just a homeless person or anything like that. She talked to me and—put me to sleep, I think. When I woke up I was lying in a pile of dry leaves, and I put some under my sweatshirt to help me stay warm during the night as I walked."

The old woman was staring at him when he finished. "You were at the white stone of Arkham," she said in a wondering tone, "and you don't know who you met there."

"He has much to learn," Nyarlathotep said.

"I'll say." Then, to the Old One: "May I—"

He held up a hand, silencing her. "Owen, will you accept my advice?"

Owen nodded at once. "Of course."

"Take off your sweatshirt, so we can see how many of the leaves are still intact." Gesturing: "You'll want to stand up."

Owen got up, went to the middle of the kitchen, and pulled the crumpled Miskatonic sweatshirt off over his head, as gently as he could. Leaves fluttered to the floor around him. The old woman gasped, slid out of her chair and knelt on the floor. She picked up an oak leaf the color of hammered gold, and set it down again quickly, as though it had scorched her fingers.

"Take nine perfect leaves, three at a time," said Nyarlathotep, "and give them to your hostess as a gift." Owen knelt down on the floor and did so, handing them to the old woman, who pressed them to her heart and then reached up to set them on the table. "Now take nine more, three at a time, and place them in her hands so that she may make a charm with them, for your safety and help." The old woman beamed. Owen did as he was told, and handed her the leaves. "Now take four more, all at once, and give them to me to place in the four corners of this house, to keep it and all within it safe this day and always." Owen gave Nyarlathotep the four leaves, and glanced around him; there were no more intact leaves left. "The pieces should go onto your garden beds, Abigail, to bless the earth and everything that grows there. You can sweep them up if you like."

For all her years, the old woman got up off the floor without the least trouble, went to a closet, and brought back a dustpan and a whisk broom. Owen stood up also, turned his sweatshirt inside out and shook out broken scraps of leaf from it. The old woman scurried about, sweeping up the bits of leaf, and then ducked out the back door, fending off the dog's renewed attempts to get inside.

Owen stood there in the middle of the kitchen for a long moment. "Neither of you could take the leaves," he ventured, "until I gave them to you."

"Good," said Nyarlathotep. "I could have taken them unbidden, but it would have cost them all their virtue. As for our hostess, Abigail Price is a witch and a very skilled one, but even she could touch them only for a moment, until you gave them to her."

Owen blinked. "She's—"

The door opened again, and the old woman came in, shooing out the importunate dog. She turned to Nyarlathotep at once. "There's a helicopter maybe two miles to the south of us, flying low, back and forth." Her hand mimed the motion. "Unless I'm an old fool, it's hunting for something."

"For us," Nylarlathotep said. "Yes, I expected as much."

Owen gave him a startled look, then remembered what the Old One had told him in the deserted farmhouse during the night. If the other side could call on a helicopter to help them, there was much more than Belbury Hall involved. How much more was not a question he wanted to ask just at that moment.

* * *

At Nyarlathotep's suggestion, he bedded down on the couch in the living room, and got to sleep without too much difficulty. His dreams were troubled; he seemed to be wandering the streets of Arkham, looking for something he'd lost and could no longer quite recall. Then a hand was shaking him awake; it was Nyarlathotep's. The Old One leaned over him, a tall shadow against the homely decor of the witch's living room.

"Time for us to go," Nyarlathotep said. "The hunt's strayed well north of us, and I don't think they'll expect us to travel by daylight; we may reach Innsmouth without more trouble."

Owen rolled to a sitting position, then stood up. "Sounds like a plan," he said, trying to sound more confident than he felt.

The old woman was in the kitchen, singing something in a low voice; Owen couldn't make out the words. When he and the Old One came into the kitchen, she was straightening up from a crouched position, with something in her hands.

"Here you be," she said to Owen, and held out a little packet of red cloth with a loop of red cord tied to it. "If any witchery known to me can keep you safe from harm, this will do the trick. Place the cord around your neck and put the amulet down under your clothes, next to your heart; it'll have most power that way."

Owen opened his mouth to thank her, but before he could speak she raised a hand. "No, no thanks. The spell won't stand it. You do have plenty to learn, don't you?" She waited while he put on the amulet, then nodded once, as though something was settled. "That'll do. Go with the Great Old Ones' blessings." She curtseyed to Nyarlathotep. "Magister—"

"We'll talk," he said, "another time."

"Of course."

Outside the air was still, and the sun came down vaguely through a blue autumn haze. The dog came trotting up enthusiastically as Nyarlathotep came through the door, licked his hands and eagerly accepted a moment of scratching behind each ear, then followed along with them to the gate and stood wagging its tail while Owen and the Old One walked back out onto the cracked and weedy road. "This way," Nyarlathotep said, pointing north. "We're not far from the Ipswich River. There's an abandoned railroad bridge over it that's still safe to cross, and on the far side of that is the old branch line from Ipswich to Innsmouth."

"Lovecraft didn't mention that one in his story," Owen said.

"Understandably. It was built in 1942."

"Oh."

"Fortunately for us, it goes straight across the marshes to Innsmouth, and stays away from the road from Ipswich except for one point half a mile from Innsmouth itself, where the two come close together. So long as the other side doesn't figure out which route we're taking, we should be safe."

"What will they do if they catch you?"

Nyarlathotep allowed a smile. "That's not the issue. They can't catch me, and I doubt they'll be fools enough to try. No, it's you they're hunting."

Owen thought about that as they walked down the road. "I still wonder why."

"My guess at this point," said the Old One, "is that they think you know enough about what's being done at Belbury Hall to make a difference. They may be wrong, of course."

The road turned across an old railroad line, two rusted rails running over rotted ties, with weeds clinging to the gravel all around. Nyarlathotep motioned for Owen to follow, and they left the road and started along the track. Up ahead in the middle distance Owen could see an iron railroad bridge angling across a dip in the land that had to be the Ipswich River. It took him a little practice to match his steps to the gaps between the ties, but before long he was keeping pace with the Old One.

"You said," he ventured, "that Abigail Price is a witch."

"That's correct."

"I'm guessing you don't mean she does Wicca."

Nyarlathotep gave him an amused look. "If you ever want to see the sharp side of Abby Price's tongue, ask her what she thinks of Wicca." He shook his head, with a soft noise that might have been a chuckle. "No, she's a witch in the original sense of the word. All the local farmers who haven't been bullied into obedience by their ministers or the public schools go to her when they've got a sick child, lose something they need to find, need ill-wishing taken off their cattle, or the like. She's capable of much more than that, of course, and does a great deal more, but she has her living to earn, and it's an old and honorable profession."

They walked on for a time. "Are there many witches around here?" Owen asked finally.

"Not as many as there once were," said the Old One, "but if you know how and where to look, or who to ask, you can find one or two in most of the small towns locally."

Owen glanced at him. "I really do have a lot to learn, don't I?"

"The world is a much bigger place than you've been taught," said Nyarlathotep.

* * *

Not long thereafter they reached the old railroad bridge and picked their way across the rusted span. The roofs of Ipswich were a dim presence in the hazy air to the west. A few hundred yards on, the track split two ways and joined the abandoned branch line between Ipswich and Innsmouth. Nyarlathotep led the way along the right hand curve, onto a low causeway that ran straight out into the marshes, a broad line traced across a landscape of brown reeds and pools of still water. Ahead was a thicker haze, tinged with the scent of the sea.

They were a few hundred yards out into the marshes when a red-winged blackbird came flying low and fast from the south, making loud shrill cries as it flew. Nyarlathotep turned suddenly to face southwards, then said to Owen, pointing down to the northwest side: "Get down behind the embankment."

Owen, startled, scrambled down to the edge of the marsh just as the blackbird flew overhead. A moment later Nyarlathotep skidded down the slope to join him. "Trouble," the Old One said. "There's a surveillance drone coming straight toward us. The blackbird says there are men in cars south of Falcon Point, and the drone came from there." He glanced at Owen. "You'll need to be completely silent until I say otherwise."

Owen nodded, said nothing. After a moment, Nyarlathotep nodded as well, turned and broke off a double handful of dry reeds from a hummock next to the causeway. He knotted the reeds into a mass, and murmured something over it that Owen couldn't make out, then threw the reeds up into the air.

The moment it left his hands, the mass of reeds turned into a bird and flew up above the embankment.

Owen stared as the bird's heavy wings whipped the air. It looked like a hawk, but it was black to the smallest of its feathers. Once it had gained some height it began to circle, still beating the air with steady strokes of its wings, catching a thermal over the causeway and riding it high up into the hazy air.

As it rose, he heard a high mechanical whine off somewhere in the middle distance, and knew at once that it was the drone.

The bird rose higher and higher until it was barely a black speck against the sky, and then with terrible suddenness turned and stooped. Owen heard a sudden impact and then a splash, and the whine vanished.

"Quickly!" said Nyarlathotep. "We'll need to hurry." He climbed back up onto the causeway. Owen scrambled after him, did his best to match the Old One's pace. Off to the southeast, circular ripples were spreading in one of the larger ponds.

"They know which route we're using now," Nyarlathotep went on as they followed the causeway. "If we're fortunate, they won't have time to get anyone onto the Ipswich road before we pass the narrow place. If we're not—things may get interesting." Glancing at Owen: "Yes, you can talk now if you wish."

Owen nodded, but could find nothing to say. He was breathing heavily now, trying to keep up with Nyarlathotep's long stride, and simultaneously trying to process what he'd seen. The image of reeds blurring and flowing into black feathers and a hawk's strong form hovered before his mind's eye. He shook his head, tried to clear it. Now of all times, he told himself, he couldn't risk being distracted. Nyarlathotep's words whispered in his memory: his own life was only one of the things that could be at stake.

They hurried on. After a while, vague green shapes in the haze to the right turned into trees, a line of them marking the edge of higher ground. The line drew closer, and Owen could just make out the long gray shape of the road from Ipswich to Innsmouth beyond the trees. There was no one on it. He put on a burst of speed, caught up to Nyarlathotep, looked ahead to where the first dim shapes of Innsmouth's buildings could just be seen through the sea haze.

At that moment, the sound of car engines sounded somewhere off behind him.

Nyarlathotep glanced back over his shoulder. "They'll get to the narrow place before we will," he said to Owen. "Listen carefully. When I tell you to run, you're to run as fast as you can, straight on down the track to Innsmouth—no matter what happens, no matter what you see or hear, or who or what tries to stop you. Keep running until you get to Innsmouth. Do you understand?"

Owen nodded. "Yes."

"If anything stands in your way, press the amulet Abigail gave you against your chest. That should offer some help."

"Okay."

The sound of engines got louder and louder, and finally the cars themselves came roaring down the road from Ipswich, three big gray SUVs with tinted windows. They drove on past and stopped maybe a hundred yards further on, where the road came closest to the old railroad line. The doors flew open and men in gray urban-camo military outfits spilled out of them.

In response, Nyarlathotep slowed to an ordinary walking pace, bowed his head, and raised his hands in a great arc to either side, fingers spreading like talons.

An instant later, something low and black sprang past Owen, went at a dead run down the embankment into the marsh and across it toward the men and trucks. Another followed, and another, and then more: dogs, Owen realized, but dogs of a breed he had never seen before. They were long and lean, with pointed muzzles and pricked ears; they ran like greyhounds, low to the ground and fast as the wind; they had blank feature-less eyes, like the eyes of blind things, and the only sounds they made as they ran were the scrape and clatter of gravel beneath their paws and the splash of the water as they plunged through the pools and raced toward their prey.

Gunfire rang out from among the trees. Some of the dogs fell, but the rest raced onwards, and more of them streamed over the railroad embankment with every passing moment. Nyarlathotep kept walking, head still bowed and hands still raised, and the dogs swarmed past him and flung themselves toward the men. Owen walked alongside him, watching him, adrenaline coursing through his bloodstream, every instinct screaming at him to fling himself down on the far side of the embankment and get out of the line of fire.

A hoarse scream tore through the hazy air, and another. The dogs had reached the road and were hurling themselves on the men there.

"Run!" Nyarlathotep shouted.

Owen ran. The railroad line stretched out in front of him, straight toward the half-seen buildings of Innsmouth in the middle distance. He tried to shut everything else out of his mind, concentrate solely on covering that distance as fast as he possibly could.

All at once raw blind panic surged inside him, and something like a voice seemed to be shouting in his mind: Down! Get down! They'll shoot you dead as you run! He almost slackened his pace, then remembered Nyarlathotep's words and flung himself forward, clutching one hand to his chest and pushing the amulet against his heart. Gravel scrabbled and sprayed beneath his feet. The voice, if it was a voice, kept shouting at him, but the words dissolved into meaningless noise as he sprinted toward the looming buildings ahead.

Then all at once he was free of it, as though he'd torn through something and come out the other side. Brown water of a river curved near to his left, and the land to his right rose up out of the marshes; the buildings of Innsmouth were close. He kept running. His blood pounded in his ears, his breath came in gasps.

Another track swung in from the right to join the one he was following, and then all at once he was under the rusting canopy of the railway platform alongside the abandoned Innsmouth station. He slowed to a trot, then to a walk, panting hard, trying to catch his breath.

Footfalls sounded behind him. He turned, to find Nyarlathotep hurrying after him with great bounding strides. His long coat billowed out behind him like a cloak. Two of the terrifying dogs trotted alongside him, and half a dozen others stood on the track behind, looking back toward the road to Ipswich.

"That was well done," said the Old One, as he came close enough to talk. He gestured to the dogs, who trotted silently back the way they had come and vanished into the undergrowth beside the track.

"Thank you," Owen gasped.

"Can you walk a few more blocks?"

"I'll manage."

Nyarlathotep motioned toward a side street that led away from the river. "You've been to the Gilman House Hotel, as I recall," he said. "I think I can promise you a less guarded reception this time."

* * *

The gray streets of Innsmouth were a blur. It took Owen most of a block to catch his breath, and by then half his muscles were pulsing with pain; it had been too many years since he'd last run really hard, and now he'd done it twice in less than two days. He managed to follow where Nyarlathotep led, and scarcely noticed that the Old One was walking at maybe half his usual pace.

Finally they turned into an alley, and stopped at what looked like a service entrance on the back of some feature-less brick building. Nyarlathotep knocked in a complicated rhythmic pattern on the door. A moment later it opened. Owen blinked; through the haze of exhaustion, he recognized the Gilman House Hotel housekeeper he'd seen on his earlier visit to Innsmouth.

She curtseyed to the Old One. "We heard you were coming, Lord." Then: "The Grand Priestess asks to speak to you as soon as possible."

"Good. I need to speak to her as well." He took Owen by the arm, brought him forward. "This is Owen Merrill, a friend of our cause. He's had a bit of a rough time—he's walked here from Arkham, and we just had to get past a Radiance negation team." She gave him a horrified look, and he went on: "Not to worry. They've been taken care of."

"Father Dagon," the woman said, shaking her head. "Well." She stepped back from the door. "Mr. Merrill, if you'll come with me."

"He'll do well here in Innsmouth," Nyarlathotep said to her, and then to Owen. "I'll be back later. You're in good hands."

CHAPTER 7

THE CHILDREN
OF THE OLD ONES

The staff at the Gilman House Hotel, Owen gathered, were used to having people show up tired, hurt, and friendless, bringing nothing with them but the clothes on their backs. The housekeeper, as though it was the most natural thing in the world, asked if he'd taken a gunshot or any other injury, and then quickly ran through a list of his needs, all the while guiding him through the hotel to what he gathered would be his room for the time being. It turned out to be much like the one he'd stayed in while visiting Innsmouth the first time, a clean little space with furniture that looked most of a century old. He slumped in the chair while the housekeeper went for toiletries and linen, blinked awake from a doze when she came back, and when she left again, undressed and showered, leaving his rumpled clothing on the floor as she'd requested. The amulet he'd been given by the witch of Pickman's Corners stayed with him; he hung it over the hook on the bathroom door, put it on again as soon as he'd toweled off.

A shower and shave did a good deal to make him feel less feral, if no less tired, and he came out of the bathroom to find his clothes gone and another set piled neatly on the bed: the sort of thing he dimly remembered his grandfather wearing, wool slacks, a pressed cotton shirt, a knitted vest whose pattern somehow made him think of fishermen in old photos.

Still, they fit comfortably enough, and he had time to towel his head again and drag a comb through his sand-colored hair before a knock came at the door.

"Better?" the housekeeper asked. "Good. Supper's still an hour or so off, but Miss Marsh would like to speak to you if you're willing."

"Sure," Owen said.

The housekeeper nodded and led the way through the windings of the hotel, and then through a door with a peep-hole in it. On the other side was what looked very much like a living room, with a big old-fashioned couch and a low table on one side, a scattering of chairs on the other. A brown-haired woman in a white blouse and a long brown woolen skirt was sitting on the couch, reading a book, her feet tucked up under her where they couldn't be seen.

"Laura my dear," said the housekeeper, "Mr. Merrill. Mr. Merrill, Laura Marsh."

She turned. To Owen's surprise, it was the woman he'd seen behind the hotel's front desk on his earlier visit to Innsmouth. She was clearly just as startled to see him. After a moment, she motioned to the other end of the couch and said, "Won't you have a seat. Would you like tea, coffee?"

"Tea, please," Owen said.

"Good." She smiled unexpectedly. "Tea's been an Innsmouth thing since I don't know when: back to the days of the China trade, probably. We've got coffee, but—" Her nose wrinkled. "Not my favorite."

* * *

"Nyarlathotep said you'll get along well here," said Laura Marsh. "No offense meant, but I'm not so sure of that."

The two of them were sitting on opposite ends of the couch, teacups in hand. The housekeeper had vanished after introducing them, returned a moment later with the cups and a full teapot in a cozy, vanished again. The saltwater scent he'd noticed around the waitress at Barney's and the housekeeper surrounded her as well. Perfume? He suspected not.

"Why?"

"You're human. Most people in Innsmouth aren't—not entirely, or not at all. Humans don't always handle that well."

"I suppose I'll just have to see."

"We could put that to the test right now, if you like."

He finished his cup of tea. "Sure."

"More tea?"

"Please."

All at once something long and slender snaked out from beneath her skirt: a smooth tentacle the same color as the rest of her skin. It was neither squamous nor rugose; it looked like ordinary human skin and flesh, drawn out somehow into an unhuman shape and tapering to a flattened point. It wrapped its tip three times around the handle of the teapot, lifted the pot, and brought it over to the couch. Owen, who had somehow managed not to drop his cup in surprise, held it steady while the tentacle bent, deftly filling it with tea. It filled Laura's cup as well, set the pot back down, and then curled in a graceful spiral on the couch between them.

After a moment, he looked up from the tentacle to her face. She had been watching him the whole time. "Good," she said. "I've seen humans scream and toss themselves out the nearest window for less than that."

He sipped tea to cover his shock, set down the cup, drew in a ragged breath. "May I ask you a very personal question?"

"Go ahead."

"How many of those do you have?"

Her hand went to her mouth, stifling a laugh. "Just two. Are you disappointed?"

"Well—"

She shook her head, obviously amused. "Under—certain circumstances—people here are born with tentacles in place of the more usual sort of body parts. Usually it's the arms, the legs, or the lips that are affected."

"The lips—oh. Of course."

"Just like the Dreaming Lord. In Innsmouth we say that it's very good luck to have a child like that. I have a great-uncle with mouth tentacles; he used to make my sister and I laugh ourselves into hiccups sometimes. He'd take a spoon in every single tentacle when ice cream got served, and …" She mimed a flurry of movement ferrying dessert to mouth.

Owen laughed; the image made the concept of tentacles less unnerving to him. "That would be something to see."

"Oh, it was." Then, in a more serious tone: "Here in Innsmouth, though, that sort of thing is normal. When you're growing up, some of your friends have tentacles, the rest don't, and if you're lucky you have an aunt or an uncle in Y'ha-nthlei who comes to visit now and then, and takes you swimming in the deep water out past Devil's Reef when the weather's good. If you met my sister Belinda, I promise you you'd be out the window screaming the same minute, but to me, she's family, and that's just what she looks like."

Owen considered the tentacle curled up between them on the couch, tried to think of some way to ask what he wanted to ask. "You want to touch it," she said suddenly, as though she'd read his thoughts.

He looked up at her, embarrassed. Laura was watching him with something just a little too ambivalent to be called a smile. "Well, yes," he said. "But I didn't want to be rude."

"You're not. For a human who's just seen something of the real world, you're being astonishingly polite. You haven't even mentioned that we all smell like fish here."

"You don't," Owen said, startled. She put her hand to her mouth, stifling another laugh, and he went on. "I noticed the—salt smell, if that's what it is."

"Yes. If you've got ancestors from Y'ha-nthlei, you inherit that. It's—I forget the phrase; it's been too long since high school biology class."

"A dominant gene," Owen guessed.

"That's the one." The tentacle uncurled, flowed over his hand and wrapped itself gently around his wrist; the gesture felt oddly intimate. "The Deep Ones get rid of the salt in sea water through their skins, and so do we. If Innsmouth folk drink fresh water too often we get sick."

"That makes sense."

She considered him. "You're taking all this amazingly well. Still, you've traveled with Nyarlathotep. I don't know which of his powers he used when you were with him."

"I've seen his dogs," Owen said.

She shuddered. "Those terrify me."

"Me too," Owen admitted. "I saw him do a few other things. Mostly, though, it's—it's finding out that so much of what I thought I knew about the world is wrong."

The tentacle gave his hand a reassuring squeeze, then slipped back off it and coiled on the couch between them. "I can hardly imagine what that would be like," Laura said. "To be taught all your life that there are no elder races or elder gods, that humans are the only thinking beings that ever lived on Earth, that history started just five thousand years ago—it seems so bleak and barren to believe that." She shook her head. "And then to find out that it's all wrong, and that everyone you trusted to teach you how things are had either been deceived or was deliberately lying to you. That's got to be hard."

"Well, yes," said Owen. "But it's got its good side. I'd rather find out that the world is bigger and richer and stranger than I thought, instead of constantly being told that it's smaller and poorer and less wonderful than it seems."

"The sort of thing the other side says," she said.

"Yes." Then: "Who are they? What are they after?"

"You should probably ask Nyarlathotep about that," Laura told him. "He knows the whole story better than anyone— well, other than the King."

Before Owen could think of a response, the housekeeper came into the room. "Supper's ready," she said.

"Of course," said Laura. She stood up in a fluid motion that would have been impossible for someone with legs. "You like seafood, I hope?"

"Of course."

"Then Nyarlathotep may have been right after all. He usually is." Walking with an odd but graceful gliding motion, she led the way into the next room.

* * *

Dinner was a thick seafood chowder, homebaked bread, and slices of cold raw fish that they taught him to spear on the end of an oddly shaped two-tined fork and dip in any of half a dozen sauces before eating. There was water to drink, in two pitchers, one for fresh water and one for salt. He didn't recognize half the ingredients in the chowder, but it would have been tasty under any circumstances; after the harrowing journey he'd had, it was beyond delicious. When he sat back, sated, the warmth in his belly and the weariness of the road very quickly had him struggling to stay awake.

"I think," said the housekeeper, "that our guest needs to turn in."

"No, I—" he started to say, and then had to stifle a yawn.

Laura laughed, not unkindly. "I'm curious. Where did you sleep last night?"

"I didn't," Owen said, fighting back sleepiness. "We walked all night. I got a couple of hours this morning on a witch's couch. Before that, I spent most of the day sleeping in a pile of leaves in a ravine." Suddenly he started laughing at the absurdity of it. "I know how silly that sounds," he said, still laughing, "but that's what happened."

"Doesn't sound silly at all," said the housekeeper. "You travel with Nyarlathotep, by all accounts, that's the sort of thing you can expect."

Laura made a shooing motion with one hand. "For Dagon's sake, go get some sleep. You don't have to settle for dry leaves or spare couches tonight, at least."

"You'll want to be shown the way, I'd guess," the house-keeper said to him, and without waiting for an answer led him back through the living room to the stairs, the hall, and the door of his room. "Sleep well," she told him.

He thanked her and went inside. The little room seemed indescribably peaceful just then. He got ready for bed as quickly as he could, tucked the witch's amulet under his pil-low in the hope that that would protect him through the night, and settled into bed. He was asleep moments after his head touched the pillow.

He woke to find clear autumn sunlight splashing in through the room's one small window, stretched, and wished he hadn't. The muscles in his legs were still far from happy about his run out of the Miskatonic campus, the long walk that followed, and the last sprint into Innsmouth. Still, he felt comfortable and warm in the bed, and let himself lie there for some minutes before finally tossing back the covers and getting up.

As he got to his feet, though, the warmth trickled out of the sunlight, and the little room stopped feeling quiet and com-fortable. The furniture and wallpaper took on a decrepit air, as though rot had spread through them during uncounted years of decay. The ceiling pressed down; Owen found himself wondering if the hotel was structurally sound, and whether the whole structure might suddenly fall on him. He shook his head, trying to clear it, but the thoughts clung to him the way a dog's jaws cling to a rat.

He made himself shower, shave, and go through the rest of his normal morning routine, but the sense of something profoundly wrong would not let him go. Everything seemed twisted and menacing; the water in the shower was always either too hot to too cold, the towel felt clammy and slippery on his skin, the little bathroom crowded in on him from all sides. When he finally stumbled out of the bathroom, he was pale and shaking, his thoughts in tatters.

Something could protect him, he recalled vaguely. What was it?

The cord of the witch's amulet looping out from beneath his pillow reminded him. As he reached for it, though, voices seemed to shout in his mind, warning of unspeakable consequences if he let himself so much as come near it. Something in the voices seemed oddly familiar to him, though it was a moment before he placed the memory: they reminded him somehow of the not-quite-voice that had tried to stop him on the last run into Innsmouth.

Remembering that broke whatever grip the voices had on his mind, and he reached for the amulet. The moment his hand touched the cord, the sense of nightmare menace vanished.

He blinked in surprise, looked around. The little room was as comfortable as he remembered it from the night before, the elderly furnishings and wallpaper were pleasant rather than foreboding, and the sunlight slanting down through the little window was as clear and warm as it had ever been.

He pulled the amulet out from under his pillow, then deliberately set it on the desk and let go of it. As soon as he did so, the sunlight turned pale and cold, and the dreadful pressure and the sense of menace began to build around him again.

"No, you don't," he said aloud, and reached for the amulet. Once again, as soon as he touched it, the sense of nightmare stopped. He put the cord around his neck, settled the amulet in place above his heart, then got dressed and left the room.

He was able to find his way back down to the living room with only a moment or two of perplexity in the corridors. When he got there Laura Marsh was sitting on the couch, reading a book, just as she'd been the day before. She glanced up as the door opened, wished him a good morning, then gave him a second look and said, "Something's wrong?"

"Yes," Owen said. "I think someone's trying to mess with my mind."

"Do you need—" she began, and stopped, gave him another close look. "You've got a protective amulet, a strong one. Good." She motioned him to a seat on the couch. "Tell me exactly what happened. Please."

He settled onto the couch, described his experience in the room. Laura was nodding well before he was finished. "That's one of their usual gambits," she said then.

"So this is from—the other side?"

"Of course," she said, as though startled by the question. "They'll have something of yours—do you know about voor yet?" At his nod: "Okay, good. Anything that's been in contact with you, especially if it's something you care about, is linked to your voor, and they can use the link to focus one of their machines on you."

Owen nodded, thinking about the coat and backpack that had ended up in Shelby's hands, and everything he'd left behind in his room in Arkham.

"This may be difficult for you," she said then, "but would you be willing to take off the amulet for a few minutes? It'll be much easier for me to figure out exactly what sort of machine they're using, and how best to work a counterspell."

"I hope you won't mind my asking," said Owen, "but—are you a witch?"

"Me? No, I'm an initiate of the Esoteric Order of Dagon. We know some of the same things as the witches do, but if you want to have somebody's ill-wishing taken off your cows, I'm afraid I can't help you."

"I'll keep that in mind," Owen said, laughing. "Yes, I think I can stand another dose." He took the amulet from around his neck, set it on the couch between them.

The moment it left his hand, everything in the room pressed inwards toward him. The light from the lamps turned pale and cold, the couch radiated corruption and decay, and

Laura's face became a pretty mask over infinite malignity. His imagination served up images of her mouth opening to reveal jagged yellow fangs, a dozen tentacles surging out from underneath her skirt to hold him helpless the couch while she drained his blood and battened on his flesh. He tried to force the images out of his mind, with no success.

"Don't do that." Laura's voice seemed to come from measureless distance. "Bring the images to the center of your attention. Turn them into objects of awareness, so you don't confuse them with yourself as the subject of awareness. Does that make sense?"

"Y-yes," he managed to say, and tried to do what she'd asked. The images were elusive once he tried to pay attention to them, but after a time—how long a time, he could not tell—he managed to fix them in his attention, and as he did so the sense of dread and the images that clustered around it lost a little of their grip on his mind.

"Good," she said then. "With your permission, I'm going to do something now to take most of the pressure off you."

"Please."

She began to sing in a low voice. The words were in a language he didn't know—it sounded like bits of the elder speech he remembered out of Lovecraft's stories—and the tune rose and fell hypnotically. Within moments the song was the only thing in Owen's mind. Every trace of dread and every scrap of imagery had dissolved; he barely noticed Laura moving her hands in curious gestures, her eyes focused intently on him.

The song ended and she lowered her hands. A moment later he blinked, as though waking up. He could still feel the pressure of whatever the other side was trying to do to him, but it was far off. He found he could set it aside and ignore it, like a quiet but annoying noise. "Thank you," he said. "That's a lot easier to deal with."

"I'm glad," she said, blushing a little at the praise. "You should use the amulet only when you really need it—it's strong, but its power can be used up, and you may need it for something much worse someday. And get some breakfast, too—even with magical help, you'll need to keep your strength up to deal with an attack like that."

"And you?"

"Oh, Becky and I ate something like three hours ago—it's after ten. Nyarlathotep must really have run you ragged." Then, with a look he couldn't read: "When you've eaten, if you don't mind, I'd like to ask you some questions about that amulet."

* * *

Breakfast was as good as supper, though equally strange, and there was more raw fish; Owen guessed that it was an important part of Innsmouth home cooking, and wondered whether they'd gotten the habit from the Deep Ones in Y'ha-nthlei. Still, the meal left him feeling fortified, and when he went back into the living room he found that Laura had gotten a pot of tea made. She was sitting with the tips of her tentacles peeking out from under her skirt. He felt somehow comforted by that, as though it was a gesture of confidence in him.

When he'd settled on the couch and she'd poured him a cup of tea, he said, "You wanted to ask me about the amulet I have."

"Yes. If you don't mind, I'd like to know how you came to have an amulet that's been blessed by Shub-Ne'hurrath."

It took him a moment to parse the name. "So that's how it's pronounced."

"Yes. If Lovecraft wasn't long since dead, I'd go find him and slap him silly for turning her name into a cheap racial slur."

"You make it sound personal."

"Well, actually, it is." She considered him for a long moment, then said, "I'm one of her children. Of course we all are, but in my case it's a little more direct."

Owen took that in. "Thus your—" He stopped in mid-sentence.

She put a hand to her mouth, stifling a laugh. "You really can mention my tentacles. It's not considered rude or anything." Then: "But you have something that's been blessed by my mother, and I'm wondering how you came by it."

He nodded. "It's simple. Nyarlathotep told me, before I came here to Innsmouth that first time, that if I had to run to get away from—the other side—I should go to the white stone in the ravine north of Arkham."

"I've heard of it," she said. "It's one of her holy places."

He told her about his flight from the Miskatonic campus, his arrival at the stone and the old woman who greeted him there. "I'm—I'm not really sure what happened after that. She put a blanket over me to keep me warm—I'm not sure if it was actually a blanket, but that's what it felt like. She told me that I was safe, and that I should follow the moon path north when I woke, and then she told me to sleep. I remember—" He stared into his teacup, trying to recover the last fragmentary memories of a shattered night. "She bent over me, and she was—huge. Bigger than anything human. And—" In a whisper: "I think she had horns."

Laura nodded. "She often appears that way. Then you woke up?"

"In a pile of leaves."

"You mentioned that last night."

"But I wasn't the one who piled up the leaves. When I woke up it was dusk, and I knew it was going to be another cold night. I didn't have a coat, so I stuffed some of the leaves into my sweatshirt for insulation, to keep me warm. And they did; I was comfortable all night."

"I bet," said Laura. "You just had the feeling that you should have the leaves with you."

"Pretty much." He described his journey by night, and the distribution of the leaves in the house of the witch at Pickman's Corners. "And that's how I ended up with this amulet."

"Fair enough," she said. "Thank you."

He considered her for a while, sipping his tea, and then asked, "May I ask a question?"

"Of course."

"Are there many—children of the Old Ones?"

"Oh, yes. A dozen of us in Innsmouth these days, many more in Y'ha-nthlei—I don't know if anyone but Nyarlathotep knows how many there are all over the world, but you'll find us wherever the elder races mingle with humans, or where humans still remember and reverence the Great Old Ones. That's to say nothing of crosses between humans and the elder races, which happen all the time. The only people in Innsmouth who don't have plenty of relatives in Y'ha-nthlei are people who were born somewhere else and moved here."

"Do all the children of the Old Ones have tentacles, then?"

"No, not by a long way. One in two or three, maybe, comes out with tentacles in place of something or other, and then every so often you get an epigenetic cascade and the child doesn't look human at all. My sister's like that. With me, though, it was just the legs."

He considered the tentacle-tips before him. They looked familiar and alien at the same time, human skin and flesh molded into an unhuman shape. "Your sister Belinda."

"Yes."

"Is she here in Innsmouth?"

"No, she mostly lives down in Y'ha-nthlei. Most of the really unhuman-looking crossbreeds go there once they grow up, if they can breathe water. It's safer that way, and the Deep Ones are glad to have them." She gestured with the tip of one tentacle. "These are more useful in water than on land, and Belinda has lots of them."

"Y'ha-nthlei," Owen said then. "When I was here in Innsmouth earlier, I saw a book about a little girl who went there. I think you might have written it."

Unexpectedly, she blushed and looked away. "My stepmother thought you might have seen it."

"Your—oh. Of course. Mrs. Marsh, the librarian."

"Yes."

"I didn't have time to read it," Owen said, "just to look at a few of the pictures—which were really pretty good, you know."

She mumbled something inaudible that might have been thanks.

"I'm sorry," Owen said then. "Shouldn't I have mentioned it?"

"No," she said, composing herself with an evident effort. "No, it's nothing like that. It's just—I wrote that the year I finished high school. One of those things you do, and then get teased about for years."

There was more to it than that, Owen guessed, but he let it pass. "I'm sorry if I stepped on a sore—" He stopped in confusion.

Laura laughed. "Tentacle," she said. "As I said, you really can mention them."

CHAPTER 8

THE CRAWLING CHAOS

That evening at supper the housekeeper—her name was Rebecca Eliot, Laura Marsh mentioned in passing—announced over dinner that Nyarlathotep had left Innsmouth that morning. "He was in lodge with the elders and the grand priestess all night, and on his way with the sunrise," she said, passing a bowl of dipping sauce for raw fish down to Laura's end of the kitchen table. "Sally Waite tells me she's rarely felt such a voorish dome around the lodge hall."

"Well, of course not," said Laura. She took the bowl, dipped three slices of raw fish in it with deft motions of the little fork, set the slices on her plate and handed the bowl back. "We've got some very good initiates here, but Nyarlathotep is—well, Nyarlathotep."

"True enough." Mrs. Eliot motioned with the bowl toward Owen, offering it.

"Please," he said, took it, and managed to dip a few slices of fish in it without feeling too clumsy. "Did anyone say where he was going?"

"Out the old rail line toward Rowley," the housekeeper said. "Other than that, who knows? He roams the world, they say. Certainly we don't often see him here for more than a day or two at a time."

Owen nodded, said nothing. Though he knew that Nyarlathotep doubtless had plenty of things to deal with that were far more important than a stray grad student from Miskatonic, the Old One's absence left him feeling adrift, uncertain of his place.

Laura seemed to guess at his thoughts. "Don't think there'll be any problem with you staying here, Mr. Merrill," she said. "We have guests stay with us for years, sometimes, when that's necessary. That's one of the reasons the Gilman House Hotel is here."

"Did they have to get away from—the other side—the way I did?"

"Sometimes," said Laura. "Sometimes it's other reasons. Last spring we said goodbye to a woman who'd been with us for most of two years, who was here to have her baby. She'd mated with one of the Old Ones, and there might have been trouble for her if the child didn't happen to look human enough to pass—and he didn't, not a bit."

"I still miss her," said Mrs. Eliot. "And her little Willie—as sweet a thing as you'd ever want to meet."

"He was a little dear, no question," Laura agreed. More dipping sauce traded places. "Once Nyarlathotep comes back, doubtless he'll sort things out. Until then—" She gestured with the little fish-fork. "You're welcome to our hospitality."

"Thank you," said Owen, meaning it.

The days that followed went past in much the same fashion: meals in the kitchen, conversations with Laura and Mrs. Eliot, silent times spent staring out his room's one window at a narrow slice of Innsmouth's sky and wondering what it all meant, or trying to come to terms with the sudden end of everything he'd planned to make of his life. The pressure from the other side remained, but Laura's counterspell kept it from being more than a very slight annoyance. He took to leaving the witch's amulet in the dresser in his room, though he tried not to think too much about Laura's warning that it might be needed to protect him from something worse; the thought made his skin crawl. Exactly who the other side was, what it wanted, and why it had pursued him so relentlessly weighed on him, a question he had no idea how to answer.

At breakfast on his third day in Innsmouth, feeling the push of habits he'd spent years cultivating, he asked about visiting the library and checking out some reading material. "Of course you can," Laura said, setting more than one of his worries to rest—he'd wondered more than once whether he might be confined to the hotel for the duration, a prisoner in all but name. A few hours later on he walked up Federal Street to the library under a sky full of billowing clouds. Annabelle Marsh was sitting at the librarian's desk, and greeted him cheerfully when he came in. "I hear you're staying with us now, Mr. Merrill."

"Not something I expected, but—" He smiled, shrugged. "I'm glad to be here."

"I can well imagine. Nyarlathotep told our grand priestess about the trouble the two of you had getting here. He had some good things to say about you."

That startled him. "I'm glad to hear it."

She smiled. "Well, there you are. The upshot, though, is that if you're minded to read something from the private stacks in back, you certainly may."

"Please."

She got up from her chair, led him to an inconspicuous door, unlocked it with a heavy key she took from a pocket of her sweater. Beyond the door was a small room lit by a single skylight overhead, and with one large bookshelf against the far wall. She gestured at the books with one hand, said, "Help yourself," and went back to her desk.

Most of the books were reprints from the middle years of the twentieth century; Owen guessed that they kept the really valuable books somewhere else. Still, he had no difficulty finding interesting reading. He chose the 1951 Librairie Azédarac edition of *Les Sept Livres Cryptiques de Hsan*; a 1974 paperback reprint of *The Greek Pnakotica* from a small occult press in London; and a plump hardback with a garish dust jacket shouting *The Book of Nameless Cults* on the spine, which he thought at first was the expurgated Golden Goblin Press edition of 1908 but turned out to be a real find, a 1932 Boston reprint of the Bridewell translation, with corrections and an able commentary by the famous occult scholar Etienne-Laurent de Marigny. Not even Miskatonic University had a copy of that edition, though he'd heard of it.

He brought the three books to the desk. The librarian deftly pulled cards out of little paper pockets inside the front covers, stamped them with a rubber stamp and handed the books back to Owen. "You can bring these back or give them to Laura when you're done with them," she said. "You've read these before?"

Owen nodded. "Like everyone in Lovecraft studies." Then, with a rueful laugh: "I didn't expect to be taking them anything like this seriously."

She laughed as well. "Oh, yes. It's been a few years, but I remember what it's like getting used to things here."

"You're not from Innsmouth, then?"

"No, I grew up in Newburyport, and moved here after Jeff and I met." She glanced down at her wedding ring, and then back up to his face. "For what it's worth, I'm sorry about telling you so many lies when you were here last. I'm sure you understand why, but—" She shrugged. "I wish it wasn't necessary."

Owen thought about that all the way back to the hotel. In the days that followed, between meals and conversations and long comfortable hours curled up in a corner of the living room couch, exercising his slightly rusty French on the enigmatic prose of the *Books of Hsan*, Mrs. Marsh's words kept returning to him. Finally, one night a week after his arrival in Innsmouth, as he was settling under the covers to sleep, the thing that had been trying to surface in his mind finally managed the feat, and he rolled onto his back and lay there laughing quietly for a good ten minutes. It had never before occurred to him to think of the Innsmouth folk, as Laura called them, as just one more American religious subculture preserving an old tradition into the modern world. Like Mennonites, he thought, but Mennonites with tentacles.

He stopped laughing, then, and wondered just how many groups there were, scattered across the country and the world, who secretly worshipped the Great Old Ones. *Were* there Mennonites with tentacles? The night offered him no answers.

* * *

The next day, Nyarlathotep returned.

Owen was in his usual place on the couch, still wrestling with the layered obscurities of the *Books of Hsan*. Laura was out behind the front desk, doing whatever a hotel manager does, and Mrs. Eliot was at her housekeeping, when a faint rhythmic pattern sounded somewhere off beyond the living room door. Owen glanced up; he heard footsteps in the hall outside, clatter of a lock being opened, murmur of Mrs. Eliot's voice, and then the tones of a deep voice that he recognized instantly.

He was on his feet as the door opened and the tall figure in black came through it. "Good," said the Old One. "I hoped you'd put the time to use." He indicated the book in Owen's hand. "That might be valuable when things start happening."

Owen opened his mouth to ask a question, and stopped, suddenly uncertain what he could or should say.

"You want to know," said Nyarlathotep with a slight smile, "when things might start happening, and where I've been for the last week, and why, all of which is quite reasonable."

"Thank you," said Owen. "Yes."

"I don't yet know the answer to the first question. The second and third—that's a long and complex matter. The short and simple form is that I've been trying to figure out what the other side is doing, and why your escape from Arkham concerned them so much. I still don't have the answer to that, though my suspicions are a good deal more precise than they were." Then, with another smile: "Does that answer your questions?"

"Yes," said Owen, "except for one." He considered the tall figure before him, who figured so strangely in the ancient tome he'd been reading, and made himself go on. "When we were walking—the old straight tracks, as you called them—I asked you about the other side, and you said we should talk about them later, when we were out of their grasp. I don't know if this is a good time to ask again, but—" He gestured with the book in his hand. "These talk about your side—our side, I suppose I should say now—not about them. I want to know." Then, raising his eyes to meet those of the Old One: "No. I need to know what I'm up against."

Nyarlathotep regarded him for a moment, then nodded. "Understood. Yes, we can talk about that, but it's lore best learnt under open skies. Are you up for a walk?"

"Sure."

They left the hotel by the front door, after the Old One murmured a few words to Laura in a language Owen didn't know. The afternoon was bright and cold, with great heaps of high white cloud scudding by on the wind, veiling and revealing the sunlight by turns. Wind danced down the silent streets of Innsmouth, bringing with it the tang of salt spray and the mutter of the waves.

"This way." Nyarlathotep motioned across the town square. Owen nodded and followed. The two of them walked in silence across the Federal Street bridge, with the Manuxet splashing over its three falls below them and the gulls wheeling overhead. Owen thought of his walk to the waterfront on his first visit to Innsmouth, and shook his head slowly, measuring the gap between the narrow world he'd inhabited then and the vaster space he'd fallen into since that time.

They reached the other side, turned onto River Street and went past the lengthening shadows of the old Marsh Refinery to Water Street and the seashore. North of the breakwater, there were no pilings from old wharves to break the restless surface of the sea, just a steep gray beach, surf rolling in from the Atlantic, and the black bulk of Devil Reef drawing a line under the eastern horizon. The buildings along the waterfront had been abandoned long ago; the best preserved were windowless and roofless shells scarred by winter storms, while many of the others were low crumbled walls or bare foundations just visible here and there amid the beach grass.

A well-worn trail led from Water Street, angling down onto the beach. Owen followed the Old One along the trail, walked beside him as the sea hissed and surged toward them over the gray shingle.

Finally they came to a big driftwood log lying a few yards above the waves' highest reach. A mass of kelp and bladderwrack was caught under the near end of it. Nyarlathotep walked over to the mass of seaweed, knelt beside it, and glanced up at Owen.

"Look closely," he said, and flipped the seaweed aside. The rocks beneath the weed and the bottom edge of the driftwood were aswarm with living things: barnacles, sea lice, a pale worm squirming out of sight, three little beach crabs who scurried for cover. "What do you see?"

Owen opened his mouth to reply, but before he could say anything, Nyarlathotep went on. "The crawling chaos."

Owen looked up from the beach and stared at him. "But it's not really chaos, is it?" he said after a few moments. "Every biology teacher I've ever had talked about the order of nature."

"Good," said the Old One. He stood up, walked halfway down the driftwood log, and sat on it, stretching his long legs out in front of him and looking out to sea. After a moment, Owen followed, sat next to him.

"Tell me this," said Nyarlathotep. "Is this order of nature, the order you find under stray seaweed or anywhere else where nature does what it wants, the kind of order that humans usually mean when they use that word? Is it neat, simple, clean, logical?"

"No." Owen admitted.

"Good," said Nyarlathotep again. "So, chaos. But also, crawling. Wet. Slimy. Squirming. There's a long list of adjectives your human languages use for actual, biological life, and in most languages every single one of them carries a burden of loathing and disgust.

"Look at your horror fiction—Lovecraft's as good an example as anybody. Cthulhu has tentacles, wings, scales, claws, all the shapes of the animal creation: therefore he must be supremely horrible. Men go mad at the mere sight of him, though I've never yet seen humans lose their minds at the sight of an octopus or a bat. Worse, he refuses to keep to one side of the hard line that human thinkers like to draw between life and death. He's *fhtagn*, as we say—abiding in himself, until the stars are right—but he dreams, and those dreams don't stay neatly locked up in drowned R'lyeh. They rise up to form a world unto themselves, and become the nightmares of those who want to place the world under the iron rule of abstract reason."

"The other side," Owen said.

"Exactly."

"Who are they?"

"You've met one of them," said Nyarlathotep. "One of their adepts, who calls himself Clark Noyes just now. Behind him, behind the powers he commands and serves, there's quite a lot of history. You need to know something about that if you're going to make sense of the challenges ahead of you—and a great deal of what you've been taught about history has been distorted to hide exactly those things you need to know most."

Owen nodded. "Go ahead."

"It all started about three thousand years ago. In those days humans lived alongside the elder races, one of seven intelligent species on the planet."

Owen blinked and, after a moment, nodded. "What happened to the others?"

"They're in hiding now, for obvious reasons." The Old One gestured toward the sea in front of them. "The Deep Ones under the oceans, others in their own havens. But three thousand years ago, that wasn't the case. You've read legends of human interactions with elves, goblins, merfolk, and so on? Those are folk memories of earlier times, or of places more recently where the elder races hadn't yet been driven into hiding.

"Humanity has only been around for a little more than half a million years, so it's the youngest species of the seven—thus the term 'elder races' for the others. Each species has its gifts. Among yours is a capacity for certain kinds of cleverness, and in particular for abstract thinking. It's easier for you to distance yourself from the the natural flow of things, from the rhythms of nature and the dance of the bright and dark voors, than it is for members of the elder races: a remarkable gift but also a dangerous one.

"It was about three thousand years ago, as I said, that certain ideas began to circulate for the first time among certain groups of human priests and scholars in the lands between the Euphrates river and the shores of the Mediterranean. They became obsessed with the difference between the kind of order that humans like to imagine, and the kind that actually exists in the universe: the crawling chaos, if you will, the natural order of life and magic and the great cycles of time. They came to see nature, magic, and the Great Old Ones as the three principal enemies of your species, standing in the way of humanity's manifest destiny as rightful masters of the cosmos—but it was more than that, more than just the craving for dominion that's one of your species' persistent bad habits. To their way of thinking, the natural order had to be false and evil and wrong, because human reason said that the real order of the cosmos must be neat, simple, and logical. If human thinking didn't correspond to the world as it actually exists, it wasn't human thinking that was wrong—it was the world that had to be a lie.

"If you know the intellectual history of the ancient world, you can trace the way those ideas spread over the centuries after that. Eventually, the movement became large enough to attract certain allies from elsewhere, and lay plans that came to fruition a little more than two thousand years ago. You've heard of Alexander the Great, but you don't know the real motive behind his wars of conquest, or why he took a cadre of philosophers with him all the way across south Asia—that's all been suppressed. The point of the whole exercise was to seize control of certain very ancient holy places, far older than humanity, centers of the voorish currents within the Earth, so certain things—terrible things—could be done there at the right moments."

"When the stars were right?" Owen guessed.

Nyarlathotep shook his head sharply. "When the stars were very, very wrong. The desecration of the holy places changed the voor of the Earth in certain ways, weakened the powers of magic and the Great Old Ones, and gave to the initiates who did the deed—to them, and to their heirs—powers that the sages and sorcerers of the elder races couldn't match, and the Great Old Ones themselves couldn't overturn, not until the cycles of the stars ran their course. All so they could pursue their dream of a perfectly rational world, freed from the natural order, without any interference they couldn't brush aside for the window of time they'd bought by their acts of desecration.

"And that's what they did, with results anyone else could have predicted. Civilizations crashed into ruin, wars over pointless abstractions swept the face of the world, whole countries were reduced to lifeless deserts, and yet they never learned the lesson of those disasters. The only possibility they were willing to consider was that they hadn't gone far enough, hadn't done enough to force the world to obey them and their idea of reason.

"Of course one of the things that wouldn't obey them was the rest of humanity. They tried any number of gambits to people to follow their kind of order instead of the crawling chaos, the living order of nature. They decided that they needed to stop human beings from perceiving voor and experiencing the natural order directly, and so they tried to breed that sense out of humanity—that's why, for so many years, people who showed any talent for sensing voor got walled up in monasteries or nunneries, where they couldn't have children and pass on their genes. When that didn't do the trick, they tried to exterminate the genes in question by way of the witch burnings, and more recently by insisting that perceiving voor is evidence of mental illness, so they could drug into oblivion anyone who admits to experiencing it."

"You make it sound as though the ability to sense voor is—" Owen fumbled for a word. "Biological."

"It is, in part. How much do you know about the pineal gland?"

"Almost nothing."

"It has much the same structure as one of your eyes, but it's not adapted to light." Owen gave him a questioning look, and he went on. "It sees voor. In the elder races, and in humans in past ages, it was well developed. In most humans now, much less so. There are exercises that can restore it to its proper function, and we teach those. Simply being in the presence of one of the Great Old Ones will do the trick over time, too, but we've got another strategy as well."

"Interbreeding?" Owen guessed, thinking of Laura.

"Exactly. Two of the six elder races are related to humans closely enough to be interfertile, and the crossbreeds have much more pineal function than most humans do these days. Then there are the children of the Great Old Ones—we can take on the necessary biochemistry when that's useful, and mate with humans, and the children have the voor-sense to a degree that even the other elder races don't. Laura Marsh is a good example; she'll almost certainly become the next Grand Priestess of the Esoteric Order of Dagon here in Innsmouth. She's got a great deal of work ahead of her, but she's got the potential."

"But the other side," said Owen. "What are they? An order, or—"

"Yes, though, they work through a constantly shifting network of front groups—these days, most of them in universities, big corporations, and government bureaucracies. The group at Miskatonic University, the one you brushed against, is a typical front. Its members call it the Inner Circle; they've got one adept, initiates of various levels, and a negation team—those are their paramilitary units, like the one that tried to stop us on the road here. Then there are a great many others who think they're part of the Inner Circle and are simply its dupes."

"The Inner Circle," Owen said. "But the order itself has a different name?"

"The Radiance," said Nyarlathotep.

Owen took that in.

"That's the most recent name," the Old One went on. "They've had many others. The original name was *Dumu-ne Zalaga*—that's Sumerian; it would be 'Children of Light' in English. All their names are along those lines, because that's the cold heart of their ideology: they're the enlightened ones, the guardians of the radiance of reason, and everyone else—the Old Ones, the elder races, other humans, anyone who disagrees with them or their plans for whatever reason—wallows in darkness."

"So—" Owen began, and stopped. "The Illuminati," he ventured.

"That was one of their names, yes."

He considered the Old One for a long moment. "And they're still chasing this failed dream of theirs, after three thousand years."

"But they don't think it's failed," Nyarlathotep said at once. "That's exactly it. The vision of a world made perfectly ordered, perfectly rational, perfectly obedient to the human will—to their will—it hovers in front of them like a mirage, always just one more step further than they've gone yet. They think of the grandeur of the conception, all the hopes that have gathered around it, all the sacrifices that have been made for it: how could they turn back?

"But all the while, without their ever quite noticing it, they've changed—or their goals have, which amounts to the same thing. At first they wanted to understand nature—provided, of course, that nature let them understand it in the terms they wanted. When that didn't work out, the dream of understanding nature shifted slowly into the craving to dominate nature, to bully her and turn her into humanity's obedient slave. And when that failed, as of course it had to, the craving to dominate turned into a rage to punish, to poison, to ruin. So first they insisted that Man was the measure of all things, until they found out that all things weren't sized to fit a human measure; then they proclaimed Man the lord of creation, until they couldn't ignore the fact that creation wasn't interested in the least in acknowledging humanity's supposed lordship; and then—about five centuries ago, now—the rhetoric shifted to Man the conqueror of nature. You don't conquer something unless it's your enemy, and if you can't conquer it, sooner or later you decide to destroy it instead. That's where they are now."

Owen gave him a long dismayed look, and then turned away. Something on the beach in front of him, right at the upper reach of the waves, caught a glint of the sun. After a moment, he recognized it. He got up, walked down to the water, picked it up: a piece of plastic made to hold a six-pack.

He turned back to Nyarlathotep, holding the thing up. "What you're telling me," he said in an unsteady voice, "is that this sort of thing is—intentional. All the pollution, the destruction, the species dying out, the rest of it, was planned." With a short harsh laugh: "It's not a bug, it's a feature."

"Essentially, yes."

Owen stared at him for a moment, then shook sea water off the tangled plastic, crumpled it savagely and stuffed it into a pocket. "Can they actually do it? Kill the Earth?"

"They think they can."

"And all the talk about colonizing space—"

Nyarlathotep shook his head, dismissing the idea. "They know better than that. Human beings can't live in space any more than fish can dance on mountaintops. The radiation, the long-term effects of weightlessness, a whole flurry of other things—a few years, maybe a decade at most, and a human body in space simply shuts down. There are intelligent beings who live in space, but their biochemistry isn't anything like yours."

He leaned forward, abruptly serious. "No, the point of the talk about space colonies is to encourage people to look forward to the thought of living in a lifeless, artificial environment, supported by machines rather than the cycles of nature. It's the same reason they've been pushing all those government regulations to keep parents from letting their children play outside. As the Earth's surface becomes uninhabitable, they plan to retreat to shelters deep underground, where they think they can finally achieve their utopia of perfect reason."

"There's no way they could get seven billion people underground."

"Of course not."

Owen turned away abruptly. He could too easily imagine, could not stop himself from imagining, a dead sea streaked with oil forever throwing scraps of plastic onto a dead shore, a dead land covered with ruins and bones reaching into the barren distance under a dead and poisoned sky.

"Fortunately," Nyarlathotep said behind him, "they aren't unopposed."

The Old One's voice had changed somehow. Owen turned back to face him. The lean figure in black was still sitting on the driftwood log, but something seemed to hover in the air above him, towering up past the old ruined buildings of the Innsmouth waterfront, past the billowing clouds, past the sky itself. Owen sensed, or seemed to sense, a presence that enfolded the solar system, a mind and will that spanned space, memories that swept back without a break to the sun's first kindling. An instant later, all of it had vanished, and he was looking at a tall lean man in a black coat who considered him with a wry smile.

Owen, shaken, tried to find words for the questions he wanted to ask. "The Great Old Ones," he said finally. "How many are there?"

"In the cosmos as a whole, unimaginably many. Here on Earth? A few hundred. There was—a choice, of sorts, when things went the way they did, when the holy places were desecrated and the Radiance began to clutch this world in its fist. To stand apart from the Earth or stand with it, to remain free from its burdens or to accept a certain mode of embodiment here, along with the limits embodiment brings with it. Some few of us, mostly those who'd been here for a long time already, chose the latter—until the stars are right."

"But if you've been here more than three thousand years," said Owen slowly, "people must have known—oh. Of course."

Nyarlathotep leaned back, smiled, said nothing.

"Of course," Owen repeated. "You're—you're Anubis, aren't you? You're Hermes the soul-shepherd, the Black Man of the witches, the crossroads devil the old bluesmen used to sing about. You're the dark messenger who shows up all through the world's mythologies. And—" He was staring now. "And Shub-Ne'hurrath is Astarte, Danu, the Magna Mater. The King in Yellow, Cthulhu—you're the old gods and goddesses of nature."

"That's correct," said Nyarlathotep.

Owen stood there staring for another long moment, and then went over to the driftwood log and sat down next to the Old One, shaking his head.

The waves hissed and foamed on the beach before them. "Laura was right," Nyarlathotep said after a time.

Owen glanced at him, startled.

"She told me you were taking all this remarkably well."

After a moment, Owen started to laugh. "I think I've just used up my lifetime supply of oh my God," he said. "I've slept in a heap of leaves by the white stone of Arkham while men who were looking for me went right on by. I've walked on a path made of moonlight. I've watched you have conversations with ravens and bats, make a live bird out of marsh plants, and call dogs out of nowhere—not just any dogs, either, the spooki-est animals I've ever seen. I've stayed for a week now with a delightful young woman who has tentacles in place of legs. I've had someone use a machine to put nasty thoughts into my mind, and the only things that keep those at bay are a spell cast by that young woman and an amulet I got from a witch. And now it turns out that I'm hanging out with the Devil or with Hermanubis, take your pick, and most of what I thought I knew about human history is a lie cooked up by psychopaths."

"Do you doubt that?" asked Nyarlathotep.

"No. That's just it. Those things actually happened to me— and the fact that they happened at all means that I've been fed a lifetime of lies." He drew in a long deep breath of the sea air. "I'm surprised you haven't tried to go public with all of this."

"It's been tried," said the Old One. "You've heard of the poet Justin Geoffrey, I imagine."

"Of course."

"He wrote quite a bit about all this in *The People of the Monolith* and some of his other poems, and was drafting a prose book on the subject. The Radiance did what it usually does in cases like that—they got a doctor to certify him insane, threw him into an out-of-the-way asylum they controlled, and had one of the staff give him a fatal overdose before we could find him and rescue him. When you read that this or that student of ancient lore died in a madhouse, that's usually what happened."

THE CRAWLING CHAOS   139

Owen took that in. "So what—" He stopped, then went on slowly: "What should I do?"

"That's a question I can't answer," said Nyarlathotep. "I told you early on that sooner or later you'd have to choose sides, and you've made that choice. There's another choice ahead of you, though. Of the people who know what's actually going on, there are those who help in various ways but stay out of the fighting, and then there are those who take part in the struggle. You could do either—and you'll have to decide before much more time passes."

* * *

Behind Owen, the door clicked shut, leaving him to the solitude of the little hotel room. He walked over to the chair, slumped into it, sat there looking at nothing for a long moment. In the dimly lit stillness around him, images of things Nyarlathotep had mentioned in their talk on the beach—the Great Old Ones, the elder races, the Radiance—seemed to hover, watching him.

The Old One had dropped him off at the hotel and left at once on some errand he hadn't explained. Laura was gone as well—up at the Esoteric Order of Dagon lodge hall, or so Mrs. Eliot had explained—and so he ate dinner with the housekeeper, asked her questions about Innsmouth that he hoped were harmless, tried to make sense of the answers. Once dinner was over, the housekeeper returned to her chores and Owen found his way to his room. Questions that were far from harmless tumbled over each other in his thoughts.

Too many of them revolved around what would become of him now that that door back to Arkham and the life he'd been leading was closed for good, but there was more to his discomfort than that, more than he could name just then. Above all, though, was the question Nyarlathotep had raised there at the end. Was it his job, would it become his job, to join the struggle against the Radiance—and what might that demand of him?

The gap between his past and whatever future might be waiting for him was difficult enough to deal with all by itself. Day after day, he'd caught himself over and over again, thinking that this thing would make a good addition to his thesis or that thing ought to be discussed with Miriam Akeley, and then stopped short and had to remind himself that his thesis, his assistantship and everything that went with it had gone tumbling off into the past once and for all. The pursuer who'd chased him across campus, the shoeprints circling the white stone in the ravine, the men with guns who'd come piling out of the SUVs on the Ipswich road: even if all the rest was nightmare and illusion, those remained, cold warnings of just how real the threat was that blocked the way back to his former life. What life might be available to him now that he'd passed through that barrier wasn't a question he knew how to answer just then.

He rubbed his eyes and raised his head from his hands, and only then noticed the book on the desk in front of him: a thin volume in a blank green library binding.

He opened it to the title page, and found:

A PRINCESS OF Y'HA-NTHLEI
by Laura Marsh

Owen considered the book for a long moment before turning the page. Laura must have left it there for him to read, he guessed, but how to make sense of that action was as much a mystery to him as any of Innsmouth's other riddles. Finally, he turned on the desk lamp, sat back in the chair, and turned to the first page of the tale.

Most of the page was an ink drawing of a barefoot, curly-haired child in summer clothes standing on a beach, looking out toward the broad sweep of the sea and the billowing clouds above it. Below the drawing was typed:

```
Once upon a time there was a little girl
named Melanie who lived in a town by the
seashore. Her mother was one of the under-
sea people, and her father was one of the
shore people. She lived with her father,
but she knew that someday she would visit
Y'ha-nthlei, the city of the undersea peo-
ple far away beneath the waves.
```

He turned the page and let himself be drawn into Melanie's adventures, as she learned the ways of the sea on her journey underwater to Y'ha-nthlei. It wasn't a work of great literature by any measure, just an engaging story for children past the beginning-reader stage, pleasantly told and illustrated with lively drawings. The prose had a storyteller's rhythm, and he found he could easily imagine a younger Laura Marsh recounting Melanie's adventures to a rapt circle of schoolchildren like the ones he'd seen at the Innsmouth library. Did some of the children have tentacles? It seemed likely enough; certainly most of them had parents or relatives among the Deep Ones, or so Laura had said.

When the story was finished and Melanie was reunited with her mother Pth'thya-l'yi beneath the sea, he sat there looking at nothing in particular for some minutes, thinking of the spires of Y'ha-nthlei and wondering if he would ever see them. Oddly, that thought comforted him, and so did the story, for no reason he could name. The sense of comfort remained with him as he got ready for bed, settled underneath the covers, and went to sleep.

CHAPTER 9

THE SILENCE BETWEEN
THE STARS

The next morning he woke early, feeling restless and troubled. Whatever comfort had come from reading Laura's story had trickled away in the silent hours of the night. He considered taking the book with him when he left his room, decided against it—for all he knew, Laura might not want anyone else to know that he'd seen it—and headed downstairs, hoping to find a chance to talk to her about the story that day.

The housekeeper told him, though, that neither Laura nor Nyarlathotep were there; nor, she said, would they be back for some hours yet. He stifled his disappointment, had an Innsmouth breakfast with Mrs. Eliot—he noted, almost with surprise, that he'd become quite fond of the raw fish—and then perched uneasily on the couch in the living room. The restless feeling wouldn't let him go, and finally he asked the housekeeper if it would be any problem if he took a walk around Innsmouth.

She gave him an odd look but said, "No, I can't see that there would be any harm in it, so long as you don't go past the town limits—Innsmouth's well guarded but outside, it's another matter. You'll want to be back well before dark, mind you. They'll be finished at the lodge by then; they'll likely want to speak to you again, and I don't know what all else."

He promised to be back in a few hours, and let her shepherd him out the back door into the alley behind the Gilman House Hotel.

It was another bright cold morning, though the clouds had begun to thicken off to the west. Owen wandered aimlessly through the gray streets of Innsmouth, past the few tenanted buildings south of the Manuxet and into the ruined area beyond them. He came to the abandoned railroad station where he'd tried to catch his breath after that last frantic dash into Innsmouth, and glimpsed the drear brown level of the marshes beyond it. The sight put a chill down his back, and he turned and walked the other way, toward the waterfront.

The town square looked as empty as ever, though Barney's Seafood Grill and the drugstore were both open for business. He thought briefly about stopping at Barney's for lunch later, then remembered that he had no money—his wallet had been in his backpack, one of the many things he'd left behind when he sprinted across campus toward the ravine and the white stone. He walked on. A few blocks further he was crossing Main Street, passing the husk of a long-abandoned church, and two more blocks brought him to Water Street and the harbor. To his left, the Water Street Bridge leapt across the Manuxet in an arc of gray steel, leading into the populated part of Innsmouth, but he turned right and walked south along the old harbor front instead. He wanted solitude, not the wary kindness of the Innsmouth folk or the uncanny presence of the Great Old Ones.

The vague unease he'd felt the night before and the equally undefined comfort he'd gotten from the book had both found a name while he slept, and the name was Laura Marsh. It didn't matter how sharply he berated himself, or how much he brooded about his ignorance of whatever customs the Innsmouth folk had about relationships; it didn't matter how often he told himself that he was probably just reacting to the loss of his friends and his college career by seeking comfort from the first kind face to turn his way. He wanted—what? To get to know her better, certainly; maybe more than that, maybe much more. He couldn't tell. All he knew for certain was that her absence left him feeling troubled and lost, and the book she'd left for him to read—whatever she might have meant by that— made him feel as though, at least for a little while, the world had come round right again.

He walked down Water Street all the way to the last cluster of warehouses, thinking about Laura, about Innsmouth, about the things Nyarlathotep had told him about the Radiance and the hidden history of the world. He barely noticed his surroundings as he walked. It was only when he reached the last wharf with its rusted siding and roof, just north of the piles of rocks, that something broke into his thoughts.

It was the sound of a car engine, moving slowly, not far away.

He blinked and looked around. The car wasn't visible, but from the sound it was a block or two in from the waterfront, moving parallel to him. Something about the sound bothered him—or maybe it wasn't the sound; he couldn't tell. Whatever it was, it roused instincts he'd learned to trust in Iraq, drove a sudden overwhelming urge to hide from the car and its occupants.

The big rusted doors of the wharf still gapped open on one side, wide enough to admit him. Without thinking, he slipped through into the broken darkness inside. Light filtered in here and there through cracks and holes in the roof, and by that uncertain illumination he could just make out the broken places in the flooring that opened straight down into harbor water. He found a hiding place behind a stack of long-abandoned 55-gallon drums, where he couldn't be seen from the door, and listened.

The car came closer, still moving slowly, almost stealthily. He heard the broken pavement crackle under the tires as it slowed and stopped near the wharf. The car doors opened and closed with a whisper of sound; a voice murmured something he couldn't make out, and a weight came to rest on the gravel just outside the door. The sounds were too close for Owen's comfort, and he picked his way back across the fragile flooring to another hiding place further away.

Then, without warning, the world went mad.

The most terrifying thing about it was that nothing actually changed. The wharf still looked and smelled exactly as it had, the water still splashed against the pilings below, the lonely cry of gulls came muffled through the rusted metal walls and roof. Between one heartbeat and the next, though, all these things lost any connection to each other or to Owen. They became empty and alien, a world of blank surfaces with nothing behind them. It was as though the part of him that perceived meaning and value had been amputated; it was as though the silence between the stars had opened up between him and anything that mattered.

The transformation came suddenly enough that it nearly made Owen scream. He bit down on his lip, forced himself into silence. As his heart slowed its pounding, he realized that there was something familiar about whatever was happening. It wasn't anything like the attack he'd suffered that first morning in the hotel, but it reminded him of something. What?

Sounds by the door, and a voice:

"Owen."

Shelby's voice.

"Owen, I know you're in here. You wouldn't listen to me before. You have to listen to me now; it's more important than you can imagine."

That was when he recognized whatever was being done to the world, or to him. It reminded him powerfully of the emptiness that he'd seen in Professor Noyes' bland smiling face, the void that had swallowed Shelby and left a husk in her place, but the emptying hadn't happened to him. It had happened to the whole world.

* * *

"Listen to me," Shelby said again, her voice bland and calm. "I don't know what lies you've been told by the things that live here in Innsmouth, or the entities that control them. It doesn't really matter. You've been sighted in the company of one of their overlords, so no doubt you've been getting plenty of their propaganda. That's all it is, Owen. They're lying to you, trying to talk you into serving them and betraying the human race.

"Owen, these creatures are not your friends. They're not humanity's friends. They hate us and despise us. They enslaved humanity for half a million years, using our own superstitions and weaknesses against us, because they knew that we're more evolved than they are. We're capable of reason; we know the truth about the world. They aren't and they can't. All they can do is lie."

The sheer blandness of her voice gave it an oddly hypnotic effect. Owen shook his head, tried to force his mind clear. It didn't do much good.

"You don't have to be one of their slaves, Owen. We can get you out of here, take you back to Arkham, break the grip they have on you. There's a field protecting us now. I know it's uncomfortable right now, everyone finds it uncomfortable at first, but you'll get used to it. We can keep them from manipulating your mind, and then close your mind to them permanently. I've already had that done. I saw how you reacted to that, but that's because you were already coming under their control. We can free you. We can give you your reason back. All you have to do is come out of there."

An instant too late, Owen heard a floorboard creak behind him. An arm swung across his neck, seizing him from behind. Reflex took over; without thinking, he grabbed the arm in both his hands, dropped to one knee and threw his weight forward. The man who had seized him toppled forward over him and slammed hard into a stack of 55-gallon drums. As the drums came crashing down, Owen twisted away, ran deeper into the dark interior of the wharf.

"Get him," Shelby called out, her voice just as calm and bland as before. "Kill him if you have to—you have my authorization."

Just in time, Owen saw another dim shape moving through the near-darkness, lunging toward him. He flung himself out of the way behind another dark mass, slamming into something that felt like wooden crates and sending them toppling. He heard a cry of pain not far away as the crates toppled down onto something that wasn't the floor, and then Shelby's voice, saying something else he couldn't make out.

The end of the wharf was right ahead of him, and there was only one way out. He found the nearest large hole in the floor, drew in a deep breath, and plunged feet first straight down into the black water below.

The moment his head was beneath the surface, the world suddenly went sane again. The effect, whatever it had been, vanished as though it had been cut off by a knife.

Down he plunged. The water beneath the old wharf was nearly lightless, but glimmers came filtering down from the surface here and there. The air in his lungs was already turning stale, and he knew he'd need to go back up to take another breath in another two minutes at most. The question was simply whether he could do that without taking a bullet in the brain.

He guessed which direction led into the deepest darkness, started swimming that way.

Something brushed against his leg, and then suddenly wrapped around it. An instant later other long shapes lunged out of the darkness, closing tight around him like ropes. A pulsing, buzzing sound rang in his head, confusing him, as whatever had him pulled him deeper into the black water.

* * *

Panic surged through him for a moment, and then he caught himself, remembered that he was in Innsmouth, stopped straining against the tentacles. As he did so, the buzzing sound in his head turned into recognizable words: "Nod if you can understand me."

He nodded.

"Good," said the buzzing sound. "I'm going to press a mouthpiece to your mouth. Get it between your lips and breathe normally."

Something hard pressed against his lips. He took it into his mouth, let out a long shuddering breath, then breathed in. He'd expected something like the harsh metal-tinged air of a scuba tank, but this was fresh sea air, tasting of salt and seaweed. He drew in a deep breath, let it flow out again, felt the pounding of his heart slow. Something pressed along the sides of his face, fastened behind his neck.

"I'm supposed to get you out of the way of trouble and keep you there for a little while," said the buzzing voice. "That means down to the bottom and then over to the breakwater. Let me do the swimming. No offense meant, but unless you're a lot better in the water than most humans, I'll get us there faster without your help than with it."

He nodded, felt most of the tentacles unwrap themselves from him. One stayed coiled around his right arm and shoulder, and drew him downwards into the depths of the harbor. Water surged and flowed around him as the other tentacles sculled through the deep. The patches of glimmering light from above gave way to a dim fading glow spread evenly above them— they were out from under the wharves, he guessed—but of the being that had rescued him he could see nothing at all.

Finally he felt himself slowing, and the tentacle turned him around and drew him down. Something hard pressed against him; he felt it with his free hand, touched slippery seaweed over firm angular rock, let the tentacle bring him down onto it.

"I'm sure you're bursting with questions," said the voice, "but don't try to talk. Unless you know the trick of speaking underwater, I won't be able to hear you. I'll just have to guess what you want to know." A bubbling laugh sounded in his head.

He nodded.

"As far as I know, everyone in Innsmouth is fine. I don't happen to know what the Radiance used on you, but the moment they turned it on, every sensitive in town felt it. We'd already gotten word in Y'ha-nthlei—the moment the Radiance crossed into Innsmouth the sentries alerted us—and a scouting party went up first while the main force of Guardians got ready. I came up with the scouting party; they wanted someone who could speak English and handle a half-drowned human if somebody had the good sense to go into the water."

Owen nodded.

"I was surprised, though. You're not from Innsmouth, are you? But you didn't carry on anything like as much as most humans do, when I caught you. You must have met children of the Old Ones before."

He nodded again.

"That'll explain it. Of course we didn't know."

Owen's eyes had gradually adjusted to the darkness in the water, or maybe it was that the sun had risen further. He found that he could see, very faintly, the pale shape of the tentacle holding his arm and shoulder, and part of another tentacle wrapped around one of the rocks that formed the breakwater, anchoring him and his rescuer safely down at the bottom of the harbor. Further off he could make out next to nothing: a vaguely cylindrical mass, maybe, with the slightest suggestion of another shape atop it.

He could also see, a little more clearly, the device that let him breathe. It seemed to be made of metal, a complex serpentine shape with many perforations that curved up the sides of his face from his mouth to below his ears, and fastened with a strap in back. He raised his free hand to touch it.

"It's an artificial gill," said the voice. "The Deep Ones have been making those since I don't know when." A pause, then: "Look up and you'll see something that not many humans ever get to watch."

He looked up. Dark shapes were swimming across the faint glimmering light from above. They didn't look anything like frogs or fish, as Lovecraft claimed in his story about Innsmouth. They looked much like humans, as far as he could tell at a distance, except that their hands and feet were webbed and they swam as fast as porpoises. They were naked, but yellow metal glinted on their heads, and each one carried a long menacing object of the same metal that ended in a sharp and baroquely curved head.

"The Guardians," the voice told him. "The things they're carrying are *g'thonwe*—you'd call them spear throwers. If one of those ever gets pointed at you, put your hands up and do as you're told. They work just as well in air as in water, and I've watched a spear from one of them go straight through a great white shark and out the other side."

There were hundreds of the Deep Ones, Owen realized, swimming straight and fast toward the Innsmouth wharves. He watched them go, wondering what was happening on the other side of the water. After a while the last of them went past, and then the dim flickering of light through the water was the only thing moving above him.

Another quarter hour or so slid by before something that sounded like a different voice, fainter and deeper, buzzed in his head, forming words he didn't recognize at all. The familiar voice buzzed a moment later, calling out something in the same language. Then, in English: "That was the signal. They've driven the outsiders off, and it's safe for you ashore. Here we go!"

Water billowed and roiled as tentacles sculled and he rose up from the base of the breakwater. A few minutes later they had crossed the narrow bay, and the surface glimmered not far above. "You'll need to take off the artificial gill," the voice told him. "It can't go out of the water without damaging the membranes. Take a breath." He did so, and the tip of a tentacle deftly unhooked the thing from behind his neck and pulled it away. "Up you go."

He swam upwards, broke through the surface of the water. The first thing he saw was the Water Street Bridge looming gray and skeletal above the mouth of the Manuxet; the second was a little sand beach not ten yards away, where the breakwater ended at a weathered concrete bulkhead and a steel stair with peeling paint rose up toward street level.

His sodden clothes weighed on him, but he managed to swim over, find his footing and stumble up onto the beach. He turned around, wondering if his rescuer might still be within sight.

Water roiled, and the head of a young woman emerged from it, brown-haired and brown-eyed, for all the world as though some human swimmer had been in the water with him. Her face seemed familiar, though it was a moment before Owen realized why. Around her, the sculling tentacles moved.

"Are you okay?" she asked.

"Yes," said Owen. "Thank you." Then: "You're Belinda Marsh, aren't you? I've met your sister Laura."

That earned him a sudden smile. "Glad to hear it. Can you bend down?"

He knelt in the wet sand, and she came up partway out of the water and planted a kiss on his cheek. He got a brief glimpse of a complex, half-human body shape surrounded by tentacles before she slid back into the water. "Give that to Lolo," she said. "Tell her it's from Bee."

"I'll do that," he promised.

She smiled again, winked at him, and vanished under the water.

* * *

Owen pulled himself to his feet. Sea water dripped from his hair across his face, and his clothes were soaked; he shook himself, made for the stair up to Water Street.

"Owen?" an unfamiliar voice called out.

He looked up. There were two men on the street above, looking down. "Yeah," he called out, and started up.

They met him at the top of the stair: a stocky man in his fifties with graying hair and a younger man who had the heavy muscular build of a longshoreman. Both of them had the skin color and the cast of facial features Owen had come to think of as "the Innsmouth look." The younger man also had tentacles in place of arms, though Owen barely noticed that at first glance.

"I'm Jeff Marsh," the older man said, shaking his hand. "This is Tom Gilman." Owen wasn't quite sure of the protocol for shaking a tentacle, but Tom held his out. It was as heavily muscled as the rest of him. Owen grasped it, the tip wrapped firmly around his wrist, and they shook in something like the ordinary fashion.

"You're not hurt, are you?" Jeff asked. "Good. Let's get you indoors; it's too cold to be out in the wind when you're that wet." They hurried him across the Water Street bridge and started toward the town square close by.

"Did anyone get hurt?" Owen managed to ask.

"Couple of ours had gunshot wounds," Tom said. "They'll be fine. One of the outsiders took a spear through the middle, and he won't be fine. The others got away, more's the pity."

"This whole business was quite a surprise," said Jeff. "They haven't tried to come all the way into Innsmouth since before my time. It's good that you had the sense to go into the water."

There were others standing here and there in the town square, more people than Owen had seen in any one place in Innsmouth before. Most of them were tough-looking young men, and quite a few of them had lumps in coat pockets or the like that Owen guessed were guns, though the shapes didn't quite look right. Some of them nodded to Jeff as he passed; others looked at Owen with a curiosity they didn't bother to conceal.

Owen was shaking from cold by the time they got him into the hotel. Laura was behind the front desk, the way he'd seen her on his first trip to Innsmouth. "Hi, Dad, Tom," she said, and then, with a degree of worry in her voice that startled him: "Are you all right, Owen?"

"Soaked and a little shaken," he said, "but other than that, not too bad."

"Oh, good," she said. Then, in a different tone: "Owen, there are some friends who want to see you as soon as you're ready."

"Sure," he said. "Give me ten minutes to get dried off."

"We'll be in the living room," she told him.

Not much more than ten minutes later, after a fast hot shower and a change of clothes, he went down to the living room. Laura was there, so was her father, and so were three others who he knew at once had to be Deep Ones. There were two men and a woman, naked except for jewelry and head-gear; the men wore smooth metal helmets and the woman an elaborate tiara, all of the same pale golden metal. All three had skin of a color Owen had never seen before, something halfway between olive and very pale blue-green. Their fingers were webbed and their feet splayed out exactly like the foot-print he'd seen in the wet sand on his first visit to Innsmouth; other than that, they looked quite human. One look at them told him exactly where the Innsmouth look came from.

"Owen, this is Mha'alh'yi," Laura said, indicating the woman. "She's a—sorceress, I think you'd say, from Y'ha-nthlei. If you're willing, she'd like to look in your mind, to see if we can figure out what the other side was doing."

"Sure," said Owen. Laura motioned him toward the couch. As he sat, she turned to Mha'alh'yi, and the two of them conversed in a language that sounded like bubbling water. "All you need to do," Laura told him then, "is look into her eyes. She'll do the rest."

He nodded. Mha'alh'yi sat down facing him; her lissome nakedness was a distraction, but he tried to ignore it, and raised his eyes to hers. They were remarkable eyes, sea-green with flecks of pale gold in them, and they held depths that drew him inwards until the rest of the world went away.

Then he was blinking out of something that felt very much like sleep.

Mha'alh'yi was still sitting on the couch facing him. She laughed, and said in heavily accented English, "You should get training. You went in trance easy, you learn fast."

He blinked again. There were many more people in the room, elderly Innsmouth folk by the look of them; one old woman in a plain blue dress and gray handknitted sweater had tentacles curling gracefully down from the bottom half of her face. "How long have I been out?" he asked.

"Almost an hour," Laura said.

"Wow," he said. Mha'alh'yi laughed again, and so did the others.

The old woman with the face tentacles spoke then. "We're still not sure what happened to you, Mr. Merrill," she said. "I would have said I knew all the tricks the Radiance can play by now, but this was new to me."

"Owen," said Laura, "this is Joyce Gilman. She's our grand priestess."

"Pleased to meet you, ma'am," he said.

The old woman smiled; the motion rippled down her tentacles to their tips. "Likewise." She nodded to him, and then turned to Mha'alh'yi, saying something in what Owen guessed was the Deep Ones' language.

All at once Owen heard footfalls in the hall outside, and recognized the long swinging stride at once. He got unsteadily to his feet. Everyone looked at him, and then suddenly all of them were standing, as the door opened and Nyarlathotep came through.

"I'm glad you've returned, Lord," the grand priestess said to him. "I need your counsel. We've had some very troubling news."

"You'll have it," the Old One said. He greeted the Deep Ones in their own language, and they bowed to him. He nodded to the others, and then said, "Owen, that must have been a ghastly experience, but it's paid off very handily for our side. We captured the machine the Radiants were using."

Joyce Gilman made as though to speak, and Nyarlathotep raised one hand. "No, it's not one of their usual technologies. This puts a very different face on things, and we'll have to move quickly." To the grand priestess: "How much time will you need?"

"Half an hour should be enough."

"Easily done. Owen, can you be ready to leave in thirty minutes? The machine needs to go north in a hurry, and you need to come with it. You'll want to have your amulet with you."

Owen blinked, but nodded after a moment. "I'll be ready."

"Good." The Old One turned to the others. "Now for counsel."

"Laura," said the grand priestess, "you and Mr. Merrill will need to leave us. This is a matter for the lodge elders and our guests from Y'ha-nthlei."

"Of course," Laura said, and led Owen out of the room, closing the door behind them.

In the hall outside, she turned to face him. "I know you'll need to get ready."

"It won't take me long. Before I go—I wanted to say two things." She nodded, and he went on. "First, I wanted to say thank you for lending me *A Princess of Y'ha-nthlei*. I really enjoyed reading it."

"Thank you," she said, looking away.

"Seriously, it's pretty good."

She bit her lip, then, and after a moment said: "A long time ago—well, when I was in high school—I used to daydream about having a career writing children's books, getting them published. Of course there was no way we could risk drawing that kind of attention to Innsmouth, so my stepmother made a dozen copies of that one book, gave them to a few people—I'm not sure where they all got to. But that was the end of it."

"Ouch," Owen said.

"It was necessary," she replied at once.

"I know, but still—ouch."

She looked up at him. In that moment something raw and vulnerable showed in her eyes, hid itself again when she lowered her gaze. "You said there were two things," she said then.

"Yes. This is the second." Owen leaned forward suddenly, kissed her on the cheek. "That's for Lolo, from Bee."

She stared. "You've met Belinda?"

"She's the one who rescued me when I jumped into the harbor."

"And—"

"She seems like a very nice person." He guessed a moment later what she was trying not to ask, and went on. "I must be getting used to tentacles. There wasn't a window for me to jump out of, but even if there had been, I don't think I would have."

Despite herself, she laughed. "Well, that's something." A moment later she surprised him by leaning forward suddenly and kissing his cheek. "That's for luck," she said. "You should get ready now." Then, blushing, she turned and hurried off. He stood there for a moment, then went up to his room to get ready for the journey.

CHAPTER 10

THE SIX THOUSAND STEPS

O wen came down the front steps of the Gilman House Hotel. A car was parked out in front; it was long and black, and at first glance Owen thought he recognized the make and model, though he somehow couldn't think of the name of either. A second glance left him even more puzzled, for the car didn't quite look like any other car he'd ever seen, though he wasn't able to put a finger on the difference.

The shrill cry of the hotel door opening behind him made him turn around. Nyarlathotep came out, took the stairs down to the sidewalk two at a time, and came toward him with a smile on his lean face. "I see you've been admiring my car. Tell me, does it have two doors or four?"

Owen blinked, realizing he had no idea. Nyarlathotep laughed, and waved him toward the passenger side. "It's less confusing from inside. Don't look at the license plates, though. If you do that, it'll take ten minutes for you to remember what letters and numbers look like."

There was at least one door on the other side, and Owen opened it and climbed in. The interior, as the Old One had promised, was less disorienting, and even more comfortable than he'd expected, with leather seats and plenty of leg room. He closed the door.

Nyarlathotep settled into the driver's seat. "You'll want to fasten your seatbelt," he said, shutting the door on his side. "You won't actually need it, but most people find that it makes riding with me less stressful."

Owen wondered what that meant, but fastened the belt. The engine rumbled to life, and the Old One turned the wheel and nosed the car out across the town square and onto Federal Street, across the bridge over the Manuxet and north through the middle of town. Innsmouth rolled past in a blur of decrepit buildings.

"You might like this," Nyarlathotep said, and punched a button on the radio. The speakers hissed and then started belting out the sort of old-fashioned roadhouse swing Isaac Jax and His Cottonmouths played in their Arkham gig.

Owen smiled, leaned back in the seat, and let the beat wash over him. After a few moments, he said, "I keep on thinking that I ought to know who this is."

"The Carolina Cotton Pickers."

Owen gave him a startled look. "I didn't think they ever cut a record."

"They didn't."

The car passed the Historical Society, the library, and the old Masonic hall.

"That's quite a trick," Owen said then.

Nyarlathotep gave him an amused glance, kept driving. "I saw them half a dozen times in the Thirties and Forties. This is from a Philadelphia gig they played in 1943. I spent a lot of time with bluesmen in those days."

"Let me guess," Owen said. "At the crossroads by midnight."

The Old One laughed. "Now and again."

"Did you actually give them their talent?"

"I didn't need to." The car slowed to take a patch of broken pavement. "They had as much of that as they needed, and more. You should know by now what I actually did."

"The pineal gland thing?"

"Exactly." The last of the inhabited part of Innsmouth slid behind them, and Nyarlathotep sped up. "Gatemouth Moore used to say that learning your instrument made you a good bluesman, but learning how to groove with the rest of the band and the audience made you a great one. You can't think your way to that; you have to sense it—and that's a function of voor."

"I won't argue," Owen said. The Carolina Cotton Pickers finished one number, started into another. "Is it okay to ask where we're going?"

"Just south of Chesuncook in Maine. There are—friends there, who know much more than anyone else about the sort of machine the Radiance is using. They'll need to see it, and they'll need to see you."

"Fair enough."

"Besides, it will confuse the Radiance if their adepts can't figure out where you are for a while. They can track you to some extent—they knew you were in Innsmouth, of course, but I'm pretty sure they can get more precise than that, using some object that's charged with your voor—and of course they can also project thoughts at you with their machines. The team with the machine was probably waiting somewhere outside of town, trying to influence you to leave the hotel long enough that they could close in on you."

"So I basically walked into their hands," Owen said bitterly.

"That's hard to avoid, until you learn how to close your mind to their influences."

"I'll want to learn that soon." He stopped, then, and glanced at the Old One. "I'm a little puzzled, though. I thought the Radiance was a bunch of rationalists."

"They are."

"Every rationalist I've ever met insisted that that sort of thing—influencing other people's thoughts—can't happen."

Nyarlathotep allowed a wry smile. "Of course. Influencing people's thoughts is so much easier when they don't believe that their thoughts can be influenced. So the ones who know keep their mouths shut, and encourage the ones who don't know to keep on repeating what they've been taught."

Owen thought about that while the Carolina Cotton Pickers played and the car passed the last abandoned houses on the north of Innsmouth. As those fell behind, Nyarlathotep turned off Federal Street onto a road that curved westwards along the flank of the long low hill north of town. He glanced at Owen and said, "You'll want to hang on at this point."

Owen gave him a startled look, but took hold of the grab bar on the door.

A moment later Nyarlathotep floored it. The engine roared, and the car shot up the road at something like a hundred miles an hour. Owen blanched, and clutched the grab bar hard enough to leave dents, but managed to keep his mouth shut. After a moment, as the initial shock wore off, he noticed the mathematical exactness with which Nyarlathotep took every curve.

"I'm glad you're not human," he said then.

The Old One chuckled. "Oh, granted. If I were human, we'd already be wrapped around a telephone pole." The car crested the hill, took to the air briefly, landed and shot down a long straight stretch of road on the far side. "It's always fascinated me that your species is so good at inventing things that are better suited to the Great Old Ones than they are to you."

"Like cars?"

"Exactly."

A curve loomed ahead; Nyarlathotep slowed just enough to take it without skidding out of control, sped up again as the road straightened.

"The one thing I don't get," Owen said then, "is why the Radiance seems to want so badly to catch me."

"You're not the only one wondering that," the Old One replied. "It's puzzling enough that they put so much effort into hunting you on the way to Innsmouth, but this latest attempt is well beyond that. As we drive, perhaps you can tell me everything you remember about the Inner Circle's presence at Miskatonic. There might be a clue somewhere in there."

"Sure," said Owen, and started telling him about the little he'd learned about the Noology Program: what he'd heard from Shelby, Professor Akeley, and Dr. Noyes, what he'd read in the flyer and the paper he'd found online, and what he'd sensed when he met Noyes and then, later, Shelby after her terrible transformation.

When he finished, Nyarlathotep nodded slowly. "All that fits what we already know. The one thing that's a surprise is how fast the change happened in the younger woman."

"Shelby."

"Yes. You didn't sense anything of the same change before that night?"

"Not really. I saw her the day before, and as far as I could tell she was still—human. If that's the right word for it."

"Very curious. Normally, with them, it takes years of training and intensive disciplines to reach that state: to get rid of feelings, passions, intuition, imagination, everything but the five physical senses and the rational intellect. Maybe it's just that they're hoping to prevent us from figuring out that they've found a way to accelerate it."

Owen nodded. Outside the window, the deserted landscape hurtled past.

* * *

Later—they were somewhere in southern Maine by then, and the sun was sliding west across the sky—they came to a little town in a fold of the hills. Nyarlathotep slowed, then startled Owen by turning off the road and pulling up to the drive-through window of a dilapidated hamburger place. The teenage girl who came to the window let out a gasp, turned, and called someone else over: a middle-aged man with an old-fashioned paper food-service hat on his head. He leaned out the window, smiled broadly, and said, "Welcome, Lord."

"Thank you, Harry," the Old One said, then turned to Owen. "What'll you have?"

Owen settled on a cheeseburger, fries, and a root beer. The man repeated the order to the girl inside, and he and Nyarlathotep talked as old friends do, referring to people, places and events Owen couldn't follow. Finally the man handed a white paper bag to Nyarlathotep, who passed it on to Owen; the man and the Old One said their good-byes, and Nyarlathotep rolled up his window and pulled away. The last thing Owen saw through the drive-up window was the face of the girl, who was staring after the car with an awed expression.

Owen sat back and ate his lunch. Nyarlathotep drove, the New Orleans Nehi Boys pounded out one blues classic after another on the radio, and the Maine woods hurtled past. Signs of human habitation became fewer and further between; the woods grew dark and tangled around them, and the mountains rose up higher to either side.

Later, some time after Owen finished his meal, Nyarlathotep spoke suddenly. "You've met members of one of the elder races now," he said. "What did you think?"

"They seem like—people," Owen said, remembering, with a flicker of embarrassment, Mha'alh'yi's naked body. "Where did Lovecraft get all that froggy-fishy business in 'The Shadow over Innsmouth'?"

"I have no idea," the Old One admitted. "Maybe it's just that he loathed seafood. The Deep Ones are close relatives of yours—it's only been two million years or so since your last common ancestors, which is why you interbreed so readily." He glanced at Owen. "The reason I ask is that in a little while, you'll be meeting members of another elder race who are less like you than the Deep Ones, and some other things that aren't related to you at all."

Owen took that in. "The friends you mentioned aren't human, then."

"Exactly."

"Okay," said Owen. "I'll deal."

Nyarlathotep gave him another glance, and a wry smile. "Good."

Not much further on, the paved road ended, and gravel crunched and sprayed under the wheels of the car as Nyarlathotep drove them further up into the hills. Owen watched the pine forest slide past, and thought about the elder races. The books he'd read at college, von Junzt especially, had plenty to say about intelligent species who inhabited the earth before human beings evolved: the ones who were closely related to humanity, like the Deep Ones, and the ones who were far older and more alien, like the serpent-folk of long-lost Valusia. The scholars who discussed von Junzt, and there weren't many of them, treated all those accounts of ancient species as legends spun by nineteenth- and twentieth-century occultists, but then they'd dismissed Nyarlathotep as a mythical being, too.

If I assume all of them are real, Owen thought, where will I end up?

The dark figure in the driver's seat, the Deep Ones in Innsmouth, the unknown beings ahead, all answered him: right here.

An hour later, as the sun approached the tops of the mountains to the west, the road twisted to the right and climbed a steep slope. The car roared up it, slowed at the top, pulled over to the side. The road stopped not far ahead, guttering out in a tangle of twisted pines.

Nyarlathotep turned off the engine. "Here we are."

* * *

They both got out of the car. Wind hissed in the pines and high clouds drifted past above them as Nyarlathotep went around the back, opened the trunk, took out a gray object the size of a small suitcase. He came to where Owen stood, handed him the thing. "You'll have to carry this. I may need both hands free."

"Sure." The thing had dials and a narrow blank screen on one side, and a shoulder strap fastened to heavy military-style swivels on its top. He took it gingerly, half wondering if he would feel any trace of the ghastly effect he'd experienced on the Innsmouth waterfront, but it remained inert, no more life-less and meaningless than any other manufactured object of plastic and metal. He hefted the strap up and across his body, got the machine settled as Nyarlathotep turned to go.

The Old One led the way up through the pines. He was fol-lowing a trail, Owen realized after a short time, though it was all but invisible most of the time. Long stretches of bare gray rock offered no guidance, and only here and there where soil huddled in folds of the ground and fed low tangled shrubs was it clear that other feet had passed that same way many times before. The route wound from side to side following the folds of the land, and Owen felt no trace of the voor that made the moon paths murmur and shimmer, but Nyarlathotep moved with the same certainty as before. Owen found him-self wondering how many senses the Great Old Ones had that humans lacked.

The trail ended at a ragged face of stone where part of a mountain must have slid into the valley below tens of thou-sands of years in the past. Without a moment's hesitation, Nyarlathotep led Owen to one side, around an outflung mass of gray rock, and then close in to the cliff. Not until they were right up against the stone could the gap between masses of rock be seen: a black jagged opening leading into shadow.

A moment later they were inside, picking their way across a rock-strewn floor by the dim light that came filtering in from the opening behind them. As they walked, Owen tried to get some sense of the space around him. At first it looked exactly like a natural cave; further in, as the darkness became thicker, he thought he glimpsed places where the stone seemed to have been shaped by something other than the forces of wind and water. Another few steps and he could see nothing at all.

Then Nyarlathotep took hold of his shoulder, stopping him. "One moment," the Old One said. "There's a door in front of us, and it won't open without the proper spell."

Owen felt rather than saw Nyarlathotep turn, raise his hands, place them flat against some dark presence ahead of them. A long silence passed, and then something almost too low-pitched to be a sound rumbled through the still air of the cave. Thin as thread, a line of green light split the darkness ahead of them, silhouetting Nyarlathotep's black form, and widened. A moment passed before Owen realized that the door was opening.

"Quickly," said Nyarlathotep. "It will only stay open for a few moments."

Owen stepped past him and went through the narrow opening. The Old One followed him, and then the door rumbled shut behind them.

They were standing in a roughly circular space hollowed out from the stone of the mountain. The floor was flat and smooth, and glowed green, sending a dim light upwards into the echoing space. The walls were of some more ordinary rock, but was carved in intricate fluted patterns that flowed together into the domed ceiling. The twin stone masses that sealed the door rose stark on one side. On the other, an archway opened; beyond it was a steeply sloping tunnel, and a stair of the same glowing green stone, plunging out of sight.

"This is green-litten Dhu-shai," said Nyarlathotep, "and these—" He gestured at the stair. "—are the Six Thousand Steps, which you might have heard of. We'll be met before we reach the bottom; the question is by what. You'll need to do exactly as I tell you."

"Of course."

They started down the glowing stair, Nyarlathotep in the lead. Their footfalls sent echoes chasing each other up and down the descending tunnel. An unpleasant acrid scent tinged the air, and the further they went, the stronger it became. It smelled, Owen thought, almost biological, and yet something told him it wasn't a biology he knew.

He followed the Old One around another turn in the descent, and stopped in his tracks.

Ahead of them, filling the tunnel, was what looked like a mass of dark iridescent bubbles. The acrid smell poured off it in waves. Indefinite and viscous, it seemed to flow slowly toward them, but what made the shape really unnerving were the eyes that opened and closed randomly across the bulk of it, as though they were being formed and dissolved as Owen watched.

"I'm guessing," he said in an unsteady voice, "that that's a shoggoth."

"That's correct," said Nyarlathotep. He walked up to it and calmly spoke to it in a language Owen didn't recognize at all: not the elder speech or the language of the Deep Ones, but something formed of musical notes across several octaves. The shoggoth produced a mouth on the part of itself closest to the Old One, and replied in what sounded like the same language. The two of them held a brief conversation as Owen looked on, at once fascinated and repelled by the shapeless being.

"Come forward," Nyarlathotep said then. "It wants to smell you."

It took an effort, but Owen did as he was told, and put out one hand as the Old One gestured for him to do. The shoggoth considered him with a seemingly random assortment of eyes, and then extruded a snout, which sniffed his hand thoughtfully before returning to the protoplasmic mass. A different orifice formed, and whistled something to Nyarlathotep; the Old One answered; and then all at once the shoggoth flowed away down the stair with surprising speed.

"There," said Nyarlathotep, and continued down the stair. "Now it and all its broodmates will recognize you and know that you're a friend. It'll let the others know, and we'll be met at the bottom."

"By shoggoths?"

The Old One seemed to find that amusing. "No. These caves were made by the voormis, one of the elder races. You should find them interesting."

"Voormis," Owen said, trying to remember what von Junzt had to say about them. "Any connection to—voor?"

"Good," Nyarlathotep said. "Yes. They're the children of the dark voor, the voor that comes from the Earth's heart. They have eyes, and see as well as you do, but it's the voor that guides them when there's no light at all, and that's when they're most dangerous, too. Be glad you don't have to face their hooked war-knives in some unlit place."

* * *

They walked on down the stair. Whether or not there were exactly six thousand steps, Owen didn't care to guess, but it certainly didn't seem like an overestimate. Finally, though, they came to the bottom of the stair and stepped into another round cavern with fluted patterns carved on the walls. There they found twenty or so of the voormis waiting for them.

They were short, not much taller than Owen's chest, and they stood half bent over, which made them look shorter still. They had short sturdy legs and long powerful arms that ended in yellow hooked nails; their skin was the color of yellow umber, and their fur—thin on most of their bodies, thick on their heads and spines—was much the same hue. They had huge pale eyes and protruding jaws; they wore loincloths, and some of them had short sleeveless tunics woven in brightly colored patterns; their limbs and heads were bare except for fur.

One of them—an elder, Owen guessed from the gray around his muzzle—bowed in a curious crouching way, and addressed Nyarlathotep in a language that sounded like the howling and yelping of dogs. The Old One answered him in the same language. They conversed for a time, and then the elder motioned for the two of them to accompany him and the other voormis deeper into Dhu-shai.

The realm of the voormis was a warren of caverns, some of them carved with fluted sides and domed ceilings, others seemingly natural with ragged walls, ceilings of various heights and shapes, and stalactites jabbing downwards from above. Some of the caverns were small, some were vast and echoing; some were empty, some had objects Owen didn't recognize piled or stacked or arranged in them; some had great stone basins catching dripping water from above, and still others had what looked like big shelf fungi, white and pale yellow and golden-brown, growing out of the walls. All were floored with the same smooth, featureless, glowing green stone. More voormis joined them as they went, and some of those who had been at the bottom of the stair went their own ways. For his part, Owen quickly lost all sense of direction in the intricacies of the route, and simply followed Nyarlathotep's lead.

After a while—how long, he could not guess—they crossed one of the big caverns with fungi on the walls, and went into a smaller cavern on the far side, where several more voormis were waiting. There the elder motioned for them to sit. The other voormis sat on the floor. Nyarlathotep folded his long legs and sat as easily as though he'd been in the habit of sitting on bare stone since the beginning of time, which Owen guessed was probably the case. Owen put the machine down and then sat beside it, and found to his surprise that the glowing green floor was soft to the touch, and faintly warm. Was it alive? It felt that way.

As he settled on the floor, one of the voormis spoke in their language. Nyarlathotep answered, and a conversation began, as opaque to Owen as the brief exchanges between the Deep Ones and the Innsmouth folk he'd heard earlier that day. He didn't mind. He was tired, and more shaken by the events of the day than he wanted to admit.

"Owen," said Nyarlathotep, startling him out of something close to a doze. "Please tell our guests who you are and a little bit about yourself. They don't speak English, but they'll learn what they need to know from the sounds of your voice."

"Sure," said Owen. "My name is Owen Merrill. I was born in Indianapolis, got orphaned in a car crash when I was seven, lived with foster families until I graduated from high school and joined the Army. Up until a few days ago I was working on a master's degree at Miskatonic in Arkham, and now—I'm not really sure what I'm doing."

The Old One's nod told him that he'd said enough. The voormis had been watching him carefully the whole time, and only after he stopped did they start talking again. After another long interval full of voormi-speech, Nyarlathotep spoke again. "They want to look at the machine now."

Owen hefted the device and gave it to one of the voormis, who passed it to another, who set it on the floor. A dozen more clustered around it. Weirdly shaped tools seemed to come out of nowhere as the voormis popped the case open, took out parts and passed them around, all the while yapping and whining and baying to one another like hounds on a scent. Before long it looked as though the whole thing had been broken down to a heap of spare parts. Then, just as quickly, they put the machine back together.

"They want to turn it on," Nyarlathotep said then, "if you can bear it."

"I'll manage," Owen said.

Clawed voormi fingers flipped a switch.

Owen braced himself for the same cold sense of total isolation and meaninglessness he'd felt under the machine's influence on the Innsmouth waterfront, but that didn't happen. Instead, the machine let out a low whine, which gradually faded into a faint droning sound. A purple glow surrounded the upper end of the machine, and then the whole cavern was filled with a faint glow of another hue, which didn't quite seem to be any color Owen recognized. He felt a curious sense of opening, as though the stone walls surrounding the chamber had become less solid than before, and faint presences seemed to move through the stone—but that was all.

"It's not the same," he said, baffled.

"I know." The Old One was watching him. So, he realized a moment later, were all the voormis. One of the creatures gestured, and another turned off the machine. The conversation resumed, and Owen, shaken, stared at the machine and wondered what was going on.

"Owen," said Nyarlathotep then, "the elders want to know if you need food and a place to sleep. I'd recommend it, for whatever that's worth."

"Please," said Owen. "And please thank them for me."

More voormi-talk, and then one of the voormis left the chamber. He—Owen guessed that it was a he—came back a moment later with two smaller voormis in tow, and motioned to Owen that he should go with them. Owen got up, bowed to Nyarlathotep the way he'd seen the voormis do, and went with them.

* * *

There were more of the smaller voormis outside in the big chamber—how many more of them, Owen wasn't able to tell, as they never stood still long enough to count. One of them took his hand and led him across the chamber to an opening in the far wall; the others scampered around them, baying and whining to each other like a pack of enthusiastic dogs.

The opening in the wall led through a passage and two smaller caverns into a huge open space, bigger than any of the others Owen had seen. In the middle of the space was an open pit at least a hundred feet across. Out of the pit, as he watched, a shoggoth emerged.

The voormis, talking cheerfully to one another, led him toward the pit. Owen blanched, but followed their lead. They stopped just back from the edge, not far from where the shoggoth was busy flowing over the lip and sliding across the glowing green floor. The pit plunged down into unguessable distance; here and there in the upper part of the pit, where enough light filtered down from above to allow him to see anything at all, Owen could make out more shoggoths sliding up or down the smooth stone walls. After a few minutes, he backed away, and the voormis, apparently content that he'd had a good look at one of the local sights, led him off in another direction.

On the far side of a maze of chambers and tunnels Owen was quite sure he could never retrace, they stopped in front of something that made him blink in astonishment: a plain wooden door with a doorknob, set into a rectangular opening in a flat stone wall. The voormis motioned for him to open it, which he did. Inside was a room that, except for the glowing green floor and the lack of windows, could have been above ground. A perfectly ordinary bed with a quilt on it stood on one side of the room, with a chest of drawers next to it, and a table and two chairs on the other. Past the table was a door with, of all things, a crescent moon on it.

The voormis, by way of gestures, managed to communicate to him that he could go in and sleep if he wished, or eat first. He considered that, wondering what voormis ate and what it might do to him, but the burger and fries were hours in the past and he decided to risk it. He and the voormis managed between them to make sense of his gestures, and five of them scampered off while the others sat down on the floor of the chamber outside the room.

He sat down with them. His guides seemed fascinated by his appearance and actions, and chattered excitedly to one another.

Were they voormi children? He added it to the lengthening list of questions he hoped to ask Nyarlathotep later.

He'd learned a little about the voormis from his reading in the restricted stacks at Orne Library, mostly from von Junzt. They were supposed to be a prehuman race, descended from a branch of the hominid family tree some distance away from the one that gave rise to humans. They'd lived in Greenland before the glaciers covered it, he thought he recalled, though they'd been pushed aside by humans in the last centuries before the ice came, and took to living underground in mountain caverns while humans spread across the surface. Sheer mythology, the scholarly literature on von Junzt claimed—but here they were, poking long clawed fingers at his shoes in evident amazement and talking to one another in their doglike voices.

A few minutes later, the five who'd left came back into the cavern, two of them hauling an enormous stoneware bowl with a bronze rim, the third with something large wrapped in cloth, and the others with a large pitcher and an assortment of small round cups. The bowl turned out to be full of something that looked and smelled very much like mushrooms and some kind of meat; the cloth wrappings opened up to reveal some sort of soft flatbread, grayish-brown in color and smelling of mushrooms as well, and the pitcher held water.

The voormis stood as soon as the food was set down, and all faced the same direction: toward Mount Voormithadreth beneath the ice, Owen guessed, remembering another scrap of lore from von Junzt. He stood with them, bowed his head as one of them recited something like an incantation. A few parts of it almost made sense to Owen; he was sure, or nearly sure, that some of the baying sounds included the name of the Great Old One Tsathoggua.

Once that was done, they all sat. The voormis showed him how to scoop the meat and mushrooms from the bowl with a folded piece of flatbread, and fell to eating. Owen decided he needed to ask about the meat, indicated a piece and gestured in what he hoped was a gesture of uncertainty. The voormis caught on at once, and one of them mimed with his hands the scuttling movements of a cave lizard. That was enough to settle Owen's worries, and he tried some. Inevitably, it tasted like chicken.

By the time the meal was finished, he and the voormis had worked out enough in the way of gestures to be able to communicate after a fashion. They mimed going to sleep; voormis, he gathered, or at least these voormis, liked to bed down in a pile like so many puppies, and they let him know that he could join them or sleep alone in the room, his choice. The thought of trying to doze off under a heap of young voormis amused him but didn't greatly appeal, and though they seemed disappointed they didn't try to argue. The dishes and cloth were hauled away, Owen gestured goodnight to all, and the voormis nestled down to sleep right in front of the door.

The door with the crescent moon on it turned out to be exactly what he'd guessed, which was one kind of relief, and the sheer ordinariness of the bedding and furniture was another. He slept hard but dreamed unquiet dreams. When he woke, the quiet sounds of voormi-talk filtered through the door; after he'd dressed, he opened it, and found his guides already awake and breakfast waiting. This time the stoneware bowl was full of mushrooms and cave fish, served as before with flatbread and water. After they'd prayed to Tsathoggua and eaten, the voormis gestured for him to come with them, and retraced the same route through the depths of Dhu-shai, past the pit of shoggoths, and back to the chamber where he'd left Nyarlathotep.

The Old One was waiting there, along with one of what Owen guessed were the voormi elders. "Not much the worse for wear, I see," Nyarlathotep said.

"Not at all," said Owen. "Please thank them for me."

A flurry of voormi-talk passed between the Old One, the voormi elder, and the small voormis; the latter scampered off, and Nylarlathotep and the elder turned and led the way through Dhu-shai's caverns and passages to the foot of the Six Thousand Steps. It was only when the voormi had bowed to Nyarlathotep and made off that Owen realized what wasn't with them.

"What about the machine?"

"The voormis will keep it for now. They've become very clever with machines these last thousand years or so." He gestured toward the stair. "We need to go. Up on the surface, the sun's about to rise, and there's much to do."

Owen gave the stair an unfriendly look, but started up it alongside the Old One. "Is it okay to ask about what the voormis figured out?"

"You're wondering why the machine didn't have the same effect on you as before." When Owen nodded, he went on. "That question's on a good many minds right now. The machine's an ordinary Tillinghast effect generator—do you know about those?"

"No."

"It's an elegant little bit of technology, come up with by an Arkham inventor back in the 1920s; we have them, and so does the Radiance. It emits waves that stimulate the pineal gland and awaken various senses that have atrophied in most humans, the voor-sense among them. What we don't know is why this one, this time, blanketed a good half of Innsmouth with the effect you felt. That's troubling—not least because we don't know what else they might be able to do with it." He shook his head.

The stair stretched on, rising up out of sight before them. "Can I ask another question?" Owen said finally. When Nyarlathotep nodded, he went on. "You've said a couple of times now that there are things you don't know. You're a god—don't you know everything?"

Nyarlathotep chuckled. "Oh, that. No, that's a story the Radiance circulates. They like to try to discredit the Great Old Ones, by making humans load expectations on us that nothing and no one can fulfill. We're neither omniscient nor omnipotent, and nobody in ancient times ever dreamed that we could or should be."

Owen thought about that as they climbed the six thousand steps. By the time they reached the top, his legs ached and breath burst harshly from his lips. He stood panting in the cavern at the head of the stair; Nyarlathotep went to the door, placed his hands against the two great stone slabs that sealed it, and stepped back as they pivoted open.

Owen went through. In the cave outside the door, the air tasted raw and wet, and pale morning light filtered in from the cave mouth. As Nyarlathotep followed, something small and dark came scurrying past Owen across the cave floor. The Old One dropped to one knee and seemed to commune with the creature, then gestured at it and rose to his feet as the animal scampered away.

"Trouble," Nyarlathotep said. "There are armed humans on the slope below, heading this way—more than a dozen of them; that's as high as wood-rats can count. If they're a Radiant negation team, this could be difficult."

"Let me know what I should do," Owen said.

The Old One indicated a jagged mass of stone that thrust out into the cave from one side. "Get behind that. If they start shooting, that should keep you safe until I can act."

Owen moved over and crouched behind the rock, making sure he was out of sight of the cave mouth. Nyarlathotep raised his hands, and out of nowhere in particular, two of his silent black dogs trotted over to stand beside him.

Something dimmed the light from the cave mouth. A moment later, footsteps sounded on the broken stone: just one person, Owen guessed. He tensed, watched the Old One.

"Lord Nyarlathotep." The voice was a woman's. "The King sends his greetings."

"I'm glad to hear it." The Old One lowered his hands, and the dogs trotted off and vanished into the shadows.

CHAPTER 11

THE YELLOW SIGN

"You can come out, Owen," Nyarlathotep said. "This is a friend." Then, to the newcomer: "You must be April Castaigne. I knew your father, of course."

The woman nodded. Owen, rising from behind the projecting stone, could see her only as a shadow framed by the light from the cave mouth.

"Am I right," said the Old One, "that the King had more than his greetings to send?"

"Of course, Lord." The voice sounded amused. "He's deeply troubled by the patterns the bones have shown him; he sees a juncture approaching where many destinies are knotted together. You're part of that juncture, Lord—and so is the Radiance."

Nylarhathotep nodded once, acknowledging. "I thought as much."

"He also asks me to remind you of the Weird of Hali."

A silence came and went. The Old One's expression did not change, but Owen, watching him in the dim light, sensed that something of immense importance had been said.

"Finally, he sends five heptads of the Fellowship." She motioned with her head, indicating the slopes outside the cave. "They're waiting below for your instructions. If you need more, that can also be arranged."

"It's that serious," Nyarlathotep said.

"So I was told."

The Old One nodded again. "We'll act accordingly. Do you have vehicles?"

"Of course."

"Good. We need to return to Innsmouth—the next step will have to be taken from there. We got here without trouble, but I don't expect to return so easily."

"Give us fifteen minutes lead time," said Castaigne, "and I can promise you a trip without interruptions."

"That would be welcome," the Old One said. "Let's proceed, then."

Owen picked his way through the cave, following Nyarlathotep. Outside, morning spread gray over the Maine mountains. In the clear light, Castaigne turned out to be a woman of maybe forty, tanned, blonde and wiry, dressed in the sort of nondescript clothing he'd expect to see on a casual hiker. The clothes looked out of place on her, and it took Owen a moment to realize why: she looked as though she belonged in uniform. The way she moved reminded him of Special Forces guys he'd known in Iraq.

She walked a short distance down from the cave mouth, put her hand to her mouth, and produced a perfect imitation of a whippoorwill's cry. A cry just like it came from further down the slope, and then all at once a dozen men and women rose out of hiding places Owen hadn't noticed. They were all wearing the same sort of unmemorable outdoors clothes as their leader, and none of them seemed to be carrying a weapon, but they moved like soldiers.

Castaigne turned to Nyarlathotep. "Innsmouth?"

"The Esoteric Order of Dagon lodge hall."

"We'll be there." She turned and set off down the trail. An instant later, the others down the slope had vanished.

Nyarlathotep stood there watching for a moment, then turned to Owen. "You asked a little earlier whether I know everything. There's your answer—this was a complete surprise to me. Welcome, in a sense, and very troubling in another." He started walking down the trail, rather more slowly than Castaigne had, and Owen quickly caught up to him.

"Who are they?"

"The Fellowship of the Yellow Sign—you might have heard of them. Servants of the King in Yellow, and among the very worst enemies the Radiance has."

"They're human?"

"Yes, or mostly. The Castaigne family is descended from the King, and so are some of the others in the Fellowship." They picked their way down a steep stony slope. "The others—they're humans who have some personal reason to want to see the Radiance darkened forever." A bleak smile creased one side of the Old One's face. "Pure abstract reason doesn't leave much room for compassion, and it's an endless surprise to the adepts of the Radiance how many people resent having their lives, families, careers, and reputations destroyed for some perfectly logical reason."

Owen thought of Professor Noyes and said nothing.

* * *

They got back to Nyarlathotep's car without seeing anyone or anything but a few squirrels and a distant soaring hawk. Owen managed not to look at the license plate, didn't even try to count the doors, and climbed in the passenger side. Nyarlathotep got in behind the wheel, leaned back and folded his hands behind his head. In response to Owen's unspoken question, he said, "I plan on giving them half an hour. Tom Castaigne rode with me more than once, but I'm by no means sure his daughter really understands just how fast I like to drive."

Owen laughed, settled back in his chair. After a moment: "Can I ask a question?"

"Go ahead."

"April Castaigne mentioned something about—the Weird of Hali," Owen said. "I don't know what that's about, but it felt important."

Nyarlathotep glanced at him. "Your pineal function is coming along nicely, I see. Do you know much about the prophet Hali?"

"Just what von Junzt says about him." Then, a moment later: "I read a poem about him, too. I think it was about the same person."

"Justin Geoffrey's sonnet?"

Owen nodded.

"Good. Yes, it's the same person—the last high priest of the Moon Temple of Irem. Do you recall what I told you about the desecration of the holy places? The Moon Temple was the last of those to fall to the Radiance. The soldiers they sent to Irem put out Hali's eyes and then hacked him to death before the sanctuary, and used his blood to pollute the great crystal mirror of the Moon before they turned their axes on it and shattered it forever. Everyone who took the smallest part in that deed died shrieking before the year was out, but—" The Old One shrugged. "The thing was done.

"Before they cut him down, though, Hali spoke his Weird— his death-prophecy, you might say, calling down doom upon the Radiance and all those who serve it. Nobody on our side knows exactly what he said. There were maybe two hundred priests and priestesses at the Moon Temple of Irem when the soldiers came, but only a few survived, and only one young priestess hiding in a storeroom was close enough to hear some of Hali's words. A few of the soldiers talked about what they'd witnessed before the curse took them, and a few others howled words from the Weird as they died. What we know is little more than what Justin put into his poem."

"'Four join their hands where gray rock meets gray tide,'" Owen quoted.

"Exactly. When the stars are right, where the gray sea meets the gray shore, four will join their hands together and open the way for the fifth. Then that which was bound shall be loosed, that which was broken shall be made whole, and an age that began in flame will end in flame. That's what we know."

Owen thought about that for a long moment, then shook his head. "I wish I understood what that means."

"So do I," said Nyarlathotep.

Owen gave him an uneasy look.

"I have my suspicions," said the Old One, "but that's all they are. And now the King in Yellow sees the Weird stirring as he watches the bones tumbling in the cold wind from Yhtill." He shook his head. "And I still have no idea what exactly the Radiance did to you in Innsmouth, or how to fight it." He reached for the ignition, started the car. "We'll just have to see."

Owen fastened his seatbelt, sat back as the car pulled out into the road. Gravel crunched under the tires as it moved through a tight turn and started back down the road the way they'd come the evening before. Fragmentary thoughts tumbled through his mind like the bones Nyarlathotep had mentioned: fragments of von Junzt, things he'd seen in Dhu-shai, and over and over again, the ghastly image from Justin Geoffrey's poem—the dead prophet with his eyes gouged out, lying in a pool of his own blood on the floor of the desecrated temple. He tried to recall the rest of the poem, and that brought back to his last visit to the restricted stacks of Orne Library, Dr. Whipple shuffling into the stacks, the slim volume of Geoffrey's poetry, the other book in its cracked leather bindings sitting on the table—

His breath caught suddenly. Nyarlathotep glanced at him. "What is it?"

"I've remembered something. I don't know that it means anything, but—" He swallowed, feeling the sudden gut-punch of intuition: it mattered.

"Go on."

"Some of the people in the Inner Circle were looking up things in the *Necronomicon*."

The Old One slowed and then stopped the car, turned in his seat to face him. "Tell me everything you know about that."

Owen nodded. "The day before I left Arkham, I was down in the restricted stacks in the library at Miskatonic. I didn't usually go there that early in the day, but—" He shrugged. "When I got there, Shelby Adams—the woman I told you about, the one they changed—was reading the Olaus Wormius translation."

"You're certain of that."

"I looked at the book after she left, when Dr. Whipple was getting me Justin Geoffrey's book of poetry. The title page read *Necronomicon seu Liber de Legibus Mortuorum*. I don't think it could have been anything else. And Dr. Whipple—he's an odd duck—"

"I know Abelard Whipple well, and yes, he is. Go on."

"He grumbled to me a couple of times on other days before then that people were coming to the restricted stacks and looking up things in one book after another. When I asked him about Shelby, he said that she was one of them, and the others—they were from Belbury Hall. From the Noology Program."

Nyarlathotep considered him for a long moment, and then nodded once, turned back to the wheel, and without another word started driving again. Owen watched the Old One for a long while. Once again, as on the beach at Innsmouth, something immense seemed to hover around the long lean figure in the driver's seat, something so vast and ancient it made the rounded gray mountains around the car feel tiny and temporary. Something stirred within the immensity, though, that Owen didn't remember sensing earlier: something that whispered of grief and pain and bitter memories, of terrible struggles fought through years beyond counting against a cold relentless enemy: and something else besides.

Something that felt, however improbably, like the first faint stirrings of hope.

* * *

They got back to Innsmouth early that afternoon. April Castaigne had been as good as her word; if the Radiance had sent negation teams to stop Nyarlathotep's car, they and their efforts had been brushed aside, and nothing interfered with the journey.

The Old One parked just off New Church Green, climbed out of the car and motioned for Owen to follow. "They'll be waiting for us," he said; those were nearly the first words he'd spoken since he'd questioned Owen in the car.

Owen followed. When he realized that they were heading toward the old Masonic lodge building, he asked, "Am I allowed in there?"

"Today, yes." Nyarlathotep glanced back at him. "It's one of the two large meeting spaces in town, and the school auditorium doesn't have the necessary protections."

Owen followed the Old One up the stair to the front doors, and through them. Inside were two old women he thought he remembered from the meeting of lodge elders in the Gilman House Hotel the day before. They curtseyed to Nylarlathotep and greeted Owen pleasantly. Then he was following Nyarlathotep up a spiral stair to the upper floor, and through an anteroom and a big double door into the Innsmouth lodge of the Esoteric Order of Dagon.

The lodge room was a great bare drafty space with lamps in white glass globes hanging from the ceiling. Below, an altar stood in the middle of the floor, with a closed book on it. Three massive wooden chairs carved with strange symbols stood at the room's far end, and a triple row of benches ran down each side, facing inwards. Close to a hundred people were already gathered there: Innsmouth folk in what looked to Owen like their Sunday best, Deep Ones naked except for pale gold jewelry, members of the Fellowship of the Yellow Sign sitting all together toward one end of the room. Even Abigail Price, the witch from Pickman's Corners, was there, in a green checked dress and a cardigan that had seen better days.

Nyarlathotep glanced back at Owen and motioned for him to take a seat, then proceeded to the far end of the hall and sat in the middlemost of the three ornate chairs. Joyce Gilman, the grand priestess, went to talk to him as soon as she saw him; she looked worried. Owen glanced around, saw no familiar faces, walked over to a cluster of vacant seats toward the back of the hall, and sat down. More people came into the hall, and then four he recognized came through the door, spotted him, and crossed the floor to where he was sitting.

"Mind if we join you?" Jeff Marsh asked.

"Please," said Owen, standing up and shaking his hand. He greeted Annabelle, who beamed, and Laura, who for some reason blushed and wouldn't meet his eyes.

"You've met my younger daughter Belinda, haven't you?" said Jeff, with a smile.

"Not formally," Owen replied, laughing.

Belinda looked a great deal like her sister from the neck up. From the neck down it was hard to tell, since she wore a gaudy flower-print muu-muu that concealed much more than it showed; two tentacles came out of each armhole, and more of them—Owen didn't try to guess how many more—peeked out from beneath the hem. She took his hand in one of her tentacles, gave it a squeeze, and laughed. "Oh, I don't know," she said. "Does a one-sided conversation on the bottom of Innsmouth harbor count?"

They got that settled, and Owen and the four Marshs sat down. More people came into the hall. "I hope your trip north went well," Laura said to him.

"I think so," Owen replied. "We didn't run into any trouble, and as far as I know Nyarlathotep got everything done that he wanted to. Oh, and I met my first shoggoth."

She gave him a look he couldn't read. "What did you think of it?"

"I was kind of nervous there at first, but—" He shrugged. "It seemed friendly enough."

Annabelle laughed. "You've got stronger nerves than I do. I didn't scream the first time I met one, but it was a close thing. The funny thing is, it wasn't much more than a broodling, and it was just as frightened as I was."

"I bet we look pretty strange to them," Owen said.

"Oh, we do," said Laura. "Strange and spooky. To them, something that doesn't change and flow the way they do, that always stares out of the same eyes and has stiff bones and hard sharp teeth—that's *really* scary."

Owen began to say something in response, stopped as the doors boomed shut. The benches along the sides of the hall were full, and so were the three chairs at the hall's far end: Nyarlathotep was in the central chair, the grand priestess Joyce Gilman sat to his right side, and an elderly female Deep One wearing an ornate gold tiara to his left. The hall went silent as Nyarlathotep got to his feet.

"I think you all know what happened here yesterday," he said. "I don't imagine any of you realize what it means. I wasn't aware of that last detail until a few hours ago. What it means is that the conditions that we've had to contend with for all these centuries, and you've faced all your lives, are changing at last.

"Those of you who were here when the Radiance used its machine yesterday know that the effect wasn't something we've encountered in the past. What's remarkable about that is that the machine itself is perfectly ordinary—the sort of Tillinghast effect generator they've been using since the 1920s. The question is how they got that result out of it.

"The answer is that they were using it to amplify the effect of a spell."

That sent a sudden murmur going through the crowd. Owen glanced at Laura; she was staring at Nyarlathotep with her mouth open.

"I'm all but certain they used the sixth Aklo formula, the one that projects thoughts from one mind to another. Use that spell when the Tillinghast effect has someone's inner senses wide open, and you can push one person's state of consciousness into someone else's mind with a great deal of force. If you were here yesterday and felt it, you now know more than you probably want to know about the state of consciousness of a Radiant adept."

Those last words started another murmur moving through the crowd. Owen closed his eyes and felt sick, thinking of Shelby's transformation.

"That's exactly the sort of clever trick we've learned to expect from the Radiance—except for one thing. The Aklo formulae are everything the Radiance despises, everything they've spent three thousand years trying to annihilate. The question is why they broke with their entire heritage by using one of them.

"The answer—that came from Carcosa this morning, courtesy of the Yellow Sign." The Old One nodded to April Castaigne, who stood, bowed a precise and shallow bow, and sat again. "The King asked me to remember the Weird of Hali."

What followed those words was not a murmur but perfect frozen silence.

"And of course that's the only thing that makes sense of any of it. Exactly when the stars will come round right again, no one outside the inner circles of the Radiance knows, if even they have that knowledge—but the window of time they claimed for themselves when they desecrated the holy places and bound the voor may finally be drawing to an end."

"If that's true, Lord," said Joyce Gilman, "no better news has ever been heard in this hall." Her voice shook as she said it.

"Granted," said Nyarlathotep. "But it's also a warning. We've wondered ever since this whole business began how the Radiance would react when they finally realized that their project was doomed to fail. Now we know. If they're prepared to use the Aklo formulae, there's nothing they won't do—and the shorter the time they have left, the more desperate they'll become and the more extreme the things they'll attempt. If we try to wait them out, we could lose far too much. It's not impossible that they could manage to destroy the living Earth itself before the Weird drags them down."

"Whether they get to that or not," the priestess said, "they're certainly going to try to destroy us here in Innsmouth, and soon. The Radiant initiates we spotted yesterday in the surrounding towns have been joined by negation teams. They're getting ready for something, and I don't think there's any question what it will be. I've already ordered an evacuation."

"Wise," said Nyarlathotep. "And if this were 1928, that would be the end of it—but this isn't 1928. We don't have to limit our response to retreat, evasion, concealment, the tactics we've used for two millennia. If the Weird is waking, new possibilities are opening up, and we can act accordingly. I've conferred with the voormis of Dhu-Shai, and they're more than willing to help. What I'm proposing is that we forestall their attack and seize the initiative—that we strike hard, now, with all our force, before the Radiance can finish mobilizing against Innsmouth."

"What exactly are you suggesting?" Joyce Gilman asked him.

"A direct assault on the Inner Circle's base at Miskatonic University," Nyarlathotep said.

* * *

Owen had wondered, ever since his conversation with Nyarlathotep on the beach, what he'd do when it came to deciding what part he was going to take in the struggle against the Radiance. The moment the Old One finished speaking, though, he knew. He waited out the brief discussion as the lodge elders and the leaders of the Deep Ones considered the options and agreed to Nyarlathotep's plan, the last few words the Old One said to them all, and the formal end of the meeting.

Then, as Joyce Gilman called for volunteers and April Castaigne went up to the far end of the hall, Owen got to his feet, said "I'll be right back" to Laura, and went to join the crowd of tough-looking young men who were assembling below the three thrones. Tom Gilman, the burly young man with tentacles for arms he'd met on the way up from Innsmouth harbor, was in the crowd as well; he spotted Owen, gave him a broad smile, and slapped him on the shoulder with a muscular tentacle.

April Castaigne moved through the crowd, nodding her approval, saying a few words here and there. She stopped in front of Owen. "You've got a military background."

"Army infantry," he said. "I was in Iraq."

"See combat there?"

"Yeah. We were out in Anbar Province a lot." As she took that in: "I know the Miskatonic University campus pretty well, too."

She considered that, and nodded, one soldier acknowledging another. A moment later she'd gone past him to talk to someone else.

"You'll be leaving tonight," said one of the lodge elders to the whole group. "Be in front of the hotel by ten o'clock, armed. We'll be sending you out in small groups through the night."

"You probably don't have weapons with you, do you?" Tom Gilman said to Owen. "Don't worry about it. I'll get you something."

"Thanks," Owen said.

"Hey, no problem."

The crowd of young men scattered. Owen turned and crossed the floor to the Marsh family, who were standing by the benches. "Okay, that's taken care of," he said.

"You're going?" Jeff asked.

"Least I can do."

Jeff nodded. "Have you got any plans before you leave? We're planning on an early dinner, and you'd be welcome to join us if you'd like."

Owen thanked him and agreed readily, and the five of them went out the door. At the top of the stair, Laura paused and bit her lip. Owen noticed and said, "Those don't look too easy for tentacles."

"She just doesn't have enough of them," said Belinda, and proved the point by moving past them both and descending with impossible grace.

"I've always hated stairs," Laura admitted.

"May I?" Owen said, and reached for her. She blushed, but put her arms around his neck, and he scooped her up and carried her down to the first floor, then right out the front doors and down to the sidewalk. They were both laughing by the time he put her down.

"Very convenient," Belinda said, laughing with them. "I say we keep him." Laura blushed again and said nothing.

They walked three blocks to a pleasant clapboard-sided house on Broad Street, talking about nothing in particular. Inside, Jeff and Laura sat with Owen in the living room while Annabelle and Belinda headed into the kitchen. Cups of tea made a prompt appearance, and the conversation, without anyone having to make an effort, managed to stay in that pleasant space between too general to be interesting and too personal to be comfortable.

After half an hour or so, Annabelle called Jeff into the kitchen to help with something. As soon as he was gone, Laura gave

Owen a somber look. "I'm going tomorrow," she said. "Joyce has asked for initiates to handle the magical side of things."

"Keep yourself safe," Owen said.

"I'll be well away from the fighting," she told him. She looked as though she was about to say something else, but Jeff came back into the room and she didn't go any further.

When dinner was ready everyone trooped into the dining room; Laura said what Owen guessed was grace in the elder speech, while Owen and the others bowed their heads. After that was done, the meal occupied everyone's attention for a little while, and then the talk picked up again; Belinda started telling stories about Laura's childhood, while Laura alternately laughed and blushed, and everyone else laughed.

"*And* she wrote a book," Belinda said.

"I know," said Owen. "I've read it. It's really pretty good."

That got another blush. "That was quite a year," Annabelle said reflectively. "There was the book, of course, and Laura was the class valedictorian—and she also played Cassilda in the school production of *The King In Yellow*."

"Oh, she's always been the smart one," Belinda said.

"Now, don't sell yourself short, dear," Annabelle chided her.

"I'm not. I'm better with my tentacles than she is with her hands; that's why she's an initiate and I'm an apprentice goldsmith."

"And part-time lifeguard in Innsmouth Harbor," said Owen, grinning. That got a general laugh, and a grin from Belinda.

Later, after pie and ice cream, they sat in the living room and sipped tea. Owen kept an unobtrusive eye on the clock above the mantelpiece while the conversation wound pleasantly down. Finally, as eight o'clock came close, he sat forward on the couch. "I hate to say this—I've really enjoyed this evening—but it's time for me to get ready."

"Of course," Jeff said. They all got up and said their goodbyes. Annabelle gave him a firm hug; Belinda, laughing, wrapped four tentacles around him and squeezed; Laura met his eyes, then hugged him awkwardly and gave him a kiss on the cheek. The women went off to the kitchen as Owen and Jeff headed toward the door.

"Before you go," Jeff said, "one other thing. I'm an initiate, and—well, let's just say that I can sense things. I think you're going to need a little extra help before this business is over."

Owen nodded, not sure of what the older man was getting at.

"I'd like to give you a Word of Summoning. I can place it in your mind. You'll only be able to use it once, understand, so don't speak it unless you don't have any other choice. If you speak it, it'll call on—certain powers—that might save you when nothing else will. Or they might not; you never know with the Great Old Ones. But I'd be happier if you had the Word."

"Thanks," Owen said, "and I'll be glad to have it."

"Good. Look into my eyes."

Owen did. All at once he felt something settle into place somewhere in the dark corners of his mind, and felt also the gesture of awareness that would awaken it.

"There you are," Jeff said. "Now stay safe, you hear?"

"I'll do that," Owen promised.

* * *

At quarter to ten, he came down the hotel steps onto the sidewalk and joined the crowd of young men milling around there. He could feel tension in the air; it reminded him of the morning at Camp Anaconda just before his unit first got deployed into Anbar Province. Instead of BDUs, a helmet and a flak jacket, though, he had on the same things he'd been wearing when he'd sprinted for the white stone: jeans and a black and orange Miskatonic University sweatshirt, the best kind of camouflage he could think of for an assault on Belbury Hall.

Tom Gilman pushed through the crowd to meet him. "You look good to go," he said. "Here. I didn't forget." He pulled an object out of his jacket pocket, handed it to Owen: a fist-sized shape of pale gold metal set with a single large greenish crystal on one side, and a strap that looked like scaled leather on the other.

In response to Owen's baffled expression, he laughed. "That's right, you haven't seen one of these before, have you? It's a *k'renth*—the Deep Ones make 'em."

"How does it work?"

"Put the strap around your hand, so the *k'renth* is on the outside—yeah, like that. Now look at the crystal. Point it at me, and think fear—not the word, the feeling. Just a little bit of it."

Owen did as he was told, recalled a few of the hours he'd spent huddling behind sandbags waiting for his number to come up, and thought some of that at the crystal. Tom blanched and gasped, and held up a hand. "That'll do." Owen lowered the *k'renth*, and Tom went on. "That was pretty good. Put everything you've got into it, and if you're close enough, the other guy's gonna be out cold for hours."

"Nice," Owen said. "What kind of range does it have?"

"About a hundred feet. It's best close up, though."

"Okay, good to know. Thanks."

"Hey, least I can do."

A car's tires crunched broken pavement. Owen turned to look, wondering if it was Nyarlathotep's, but saw a nondescript station wagon pull up to the sidewalk. "I've got room for eight," the driver called out through the open window; the eight closest of the young men piled in, and the station wagon drove off. Five minutes later, a thirty-year-old sedan did the same drill; ten minutes after that, it was a pickup with a canopy on the back, and another five minutes brought a battered van.

Owen and Tom found seats in the van. As it rolled away from the Innsmouth town square, heading south toward the Ipswich road, Tom said, "I bet this is old hat to you."

Owen laughed, short and sharp. "It's never old hat."

Tom nodded. "I've mixed it up with the Radiance a few times, most of us have, but nothing like this. Still, if the stars are really coming 'round right—"

"I hope," one of the others in the van said. "Oh, Father Dagon, I hope."

They drove through the darkness for a couple of hours, rattling over backroads that had seen many better nights, and finally pulled up a long driveway to a farmhouse, dark except for a single pale light in an upstairs window.

They spilled out of the van, and the driver backed, turned, and headed back down the driveway. As he followed the others to the farmhouse door, Owen looked up, saw light glowing dully off the clouds not far away. Arkham? He guessed so.

Inside were dim lights, tattered furniture, and an old man in farmer's clothes, who got them sorted out into the available sleeping spaces with a minimum of words. Owen got a little room of his own on the ground floor, not much bigger than a good-sized closet, with a frayed quilt on a narrow bed and cross-stitch samplers on the walls; it reminded him somehow of the guestroom for humans in Dhu-shai. Most of the others stayed up talking, but Owen went to bed as quickly as he could, knowing it might be a while before he'd next see a good night's sleep.

The sun was well up before he woke, and the old man was down in the kitchen cooking breakfast for them all. "Tonight," Tom said when Owen came out from his room. "Got a message. We're supposed to be ready by full dark. That's all so far."

The day took its time passing. After lunch, they all went to their rooms to try to get more rest. Owen found that he couldn't sleep, and after a while he got dressed again and went back downstairs. The living room was empty; he flopped down on the couch, looked at nothing in particular, tried to get his mind to think about anything other than what might happen once night came, and failed completely.

After a quarter hour or so, tires set the gravel driveway outside crackling. A car door opened and shut, and the car drove away. A moment later the front door rattled and opened, and to his amazement, Laura came through it.

"Hi," Owen said.

She blinked in surprise, then laughed. "Hi. You're staying here?"

"Just till nightfall."

She looked at the clock on the wall, then at him. "I didn't think I'd see you again until all this is over." Then, after a moment's uncertainty: "Can we talk?"

"Sure." He gestured toward the other side of the couch, saw her hesitation. "Someplace a little more private?"

"Please," she said, with a grateful look.

* * *

There was nowhere to sit in the little room he'd been assigned but the bed; she settled on the quilt up near the headboard as he closed the door, then motioned for him to sit by the footboard when he hesitated. He sat, gestured for her to go ahead.

She opened her mouth, but didn't speak.

After a moment, he said, "I know. Words get pretty clumsy sometimes, don't they?"

That got a smile, fragile and uncertain. "True enough."

"I'm guessing," he said, "I know what you wanted to talk about." He reached for her hands, took them, felt them curl around his.

"When did you figure out that I—" She stopped, again at a loss for words.

"Getting invited to dinner with your folks was kind of a broad hint," he pointed out.

"I suppose so. We're pretty old-fashioned in Innsmouth."

"I'm not complaining. When did you guess about me?"

"I'd been hoping for, I don't know, days," she admitted. "And then when we talked, before you went north with Nyarlathotep, it wasn't just hoping. I wasn't sure, though, until you saw me in the lodge hall, and lit up like a light bulb." She laughed. "Bee's going to tease you about that for years, I hope you know."

"I'll look forward to it," Owen said.

A silence came and went. "When you say you're old-fashioned," he asked then, "how far does that go?"

Her expression was all the invitation he needed. He took her by the arms and gently drew her toward him. She tensed for the briefest of moments, and then slid across the bed and clung to him. Owen thought at first that she was about to cry, she was so tense and trembling. He held her and stroked her hair, trying to silence the babble of thoughts in his mind and simply be present. After a few minutes, he bent down and kissed the top of her head.

He hadn't meant to do anything further, not just then, but she drew back a little and looked up at him, and he couldn't stop himself from bending again and kissing her on the lips. Her eyes went wide as he stopped, and then she slid a hand up behind his head and drew him down into another kiss. This time their lips opened.

All at once she pulled away, got up from the bed. "Owen," she said, and when he moved to follow her: "Wait." She pulled her sweater off over her head, took off her bra, pushed down skirt and panties and shook them off. "Look at me."

Naked, she was no less beautiful: small round breasts tipped with nipples like little strawberries, soft curves of belly and flank, rounded hips, and then the two tentacles descending to either side of her cleft, wide and firm as thighs at first but tapering smoothly to the floor, where they curved in tense arcs to support her.

Owen slid off the bed, knelt before her, took the end of one tentacle, raised it to his mouth and kissed it. Then he got up, took her in his arms and brought her back to the bed.

His clothes joined hers in a pile on the floor. "Owen," she said. "Oh, Owen—"

She cried out twice, clutching him with arms and tentacles, before he found his own release. Afterwards, they lay there tangled together for what seemed like a long time. Owen felt her heartbeat close against him, smelled the familiar salt smell.

"I was so frightened," she whispered then. "That when it came to—this—you'd look at me and see—well, a monster."

"Silly," he said, and stroked her hair again. Then: "No, that's not really fair, is it? A lot of humans probably would."

"But not you."

"No. Remember when I told you I'd gotten used to tentacles?"

"Yes."

"At this point I'm really fond of them."

She laughed, nestled against him.

Time passed, but finally she raised her head from his shoulder. "I hate to say this. I'd rather stay here, but I need to get ready for the working tonight, and you'd probably better get some rest. It's going to be a long night."

"You're probably right." He got up from the bed, helped her up. The two of them got their clothes back on, tried to look a little less disheveled, and then both started laughing at the futility of the attempt.

"Laura," Owen said then, and sat down next to her on the bed. "Once this business is over, there's a question I'm going to want to ask you."

"The answer is yes," she said at once, meeting his gaze squarely. She kissed him again; her lips opened to his like a promise. Then she pulled away, went to the door, glanced back at him with an unsteady smile, and left.

CHAPTER 12

THE GUARDIAN OF THE GATE

As evening faded into night, the young men from Innsmouth left the farmhouse and stood in the driveway, waiting. Owen glanced up at a lit window on the top floor. Laura was there, preparing whatever magic she'd been assigned. He tried not to think of that, forced his mind back to getting ready for whatever he'd have to do before sunrise.

Footsteps crunched on the gravel: a dozen more of the Innsmouth folk, armed with *k'renthwe* and other devices of Deep One make. A few minutes later, another group showed up, equipped the same way. Owen gathered from their talk that the others stayed in three farmhouses further along the same road.

"Okay," said an older man named Carl Eliot, who seemed to be leading the group. "As soon as everyone's ready, we're going to take the footpath there." He gestured past the farmhouse toward a gap under the oaks beyond it. "There's a standing stone up that way about a quarter of a mile. From there, one of the old straight tracks runs to the white stone of Arkham. We'll be met there and get final instructions. Ready? Okay, let's get going."

They walked single file along the footpath, silent except for the rustle of fallen leaves under their feet. The night darkened, and stars came out overhead, visible here and there past the black grasping shapes of the trees that flanked the path. The moon rose in the eastern sky behind them. Finally the path led out from under the trees into an open meadow, and the standing stone rose up dim and stark against the sky.

It took Owen only a moment, once he'd reached the stone, to see the faint voorish shimmer of the moon path leading across the fields. Beyond it lay the dark mass of a hill, and beyond that the dim glow of city lights. He drew in a deep breath, made sure his *k'renth* was safe in his pocket and his amulet was against his heart, and went with the others.

As before, once he was on the moon path, everything outside it seemed incalculably distant, and a murmur and a shimmering surrounded him as he let himself move easily along the route. Wild things watched their passage through the night. None of it seemed strange to Owen, though, not after everything he'd seen since he'd last walked the old straight tracks. It felt as normal and natural as the tentacles of the woman he loved, the caverns of green-litten Dhu-shai, the power of Earth's ancient gods.

The path led them through neglected fields and pastures, past the husks of farmhouses abandoned decades earlier, across old roads long since left to the weather and the weeds. After what Owen guessed must have been two hours, maybe more, they passed a pond he recognized, where flagstones carried the path along one side of the water. Past the pond, the land rose gradually and the track rose with it, and then all at once he was standing on the edge of the ravine, looking across it to the black whaleback shape of Meadow Hill and the lights and traffic of Arkham beyond it.

He followed the others down into the ravine. Someone was waiting for them by the white stone; for a moment he wondered if it was Shub-Ne'hurrath, but a second look with the help of the moonlight showed a woman in nondescript outdoor clothing. She had a band of black cloth tied around her head, and embroidered on it was a yellow shape that looked a little like a Chinese character and a little like a word in Arabic. Owen knew at a glance that it was neither of those; he'd picked up enough lore from his studies to recognize the Yellow Sign.

"This is everyone?" said the woman. "Good. There are several groups on our side in tonight's operation. You don't need to know about the others. What you need to know is that there's a Radiance negation team in and around Belbury Hall, at least fifty strong—the Radiance may suspect something is up. You're going in first; your job is to fake an attack on the hall and draw as much of the negation team away from it as possible." Gesturing, she mimed the routes through campus to Belbury Hall, the ways they would withdraw once the guards started chasing them. "You'll wait here by the stone until I get word. Any questions?"

"What are they carrying?" Tom Gilman asked.

"As far as we've been able to spot, just handguns with silencers. The campus is too public a space for them to risk full paramilitary gear."

"That's something," said Carl Eliot. "At handgun range, a k'renth is even odds."

"Anything else?" After a pause: "Fair enough. You can rest for now; this ravine is protected by a power the Radiance can't touch."

Most of the group from Innsmouth sat down and settled in to wait. Some of them, though, went one by one to the white stone, put one hand on it and bowed their heads in prayer. That struck Owen as a very good idea; he waited until no one else was headed toward the stone, walked up to it, rested one palm flat on the surface and bowed his head. Shub-Ne'hurrath, he thought, Black Goat of the Woods, help us tonight, help us defeat the Radiance. And protect your daughter—that more than anything else. Keep Laura safe.

A rustling in the brush behind the rock broke through his concentration, and he looked up. For a moment he thought he saw the old wise face of the woman who'd been waiting for him at the white stone when he fled the Miskatonic campus, and caught the strong goaty scent he remembered, but a moment later the scent was gone and the face had dissolved into a random pattern of shadows in the brush.

He left the stone, found a dry place to sit, tried to relax. Time passed, the stars wheeled slowly overhead, and the murmur of traffic sounds faded to silence. He managed to doze for a while, despite everything, but woke abruptly to the sound of low voices and movement.

"Time to go," the woman from the Fellowship was saying. "The other teams are in place." Then, making a curious gesture toward them with both hands: "The blessing of the King goes with you, whether you live or die."

* * *

They left the ravine in silence, hurried over the summit of Meadow Hill and down into the trees beyond it. From the crest of the hill, Owen looked past the delirious spires of Wilmarth Hall and the solid mass of Morgan Hall to the tall pale shape of their objective, rising up in a glare of sodium lamps against the distant hills and the pale stars. He checked his *k'renth*, followed the others into the sheltering darkness against the trees.

A car rolled noisily down Garrison Street as they neared the edge of the trees: campus security, from the black and white paint scheme. They waited until it was out of sight, and then hurried across the street into what shadows they could find around Wilmarth Hall's bulbous and rugose walls. Carl Eliot motioned to Owen, who mimed the next part of the route through the campus with one hand. Following his lead, they moved up to the gap between Wilmarth Hall and the parking garage and walked as casually as they could through the deserted campus, past the south end of Pickman Hall, toward the bastion of the Radiance.

Then the mist came flowing in like a tide.

Cold, clammy, and silent, it swept in from the Miskatonic a few blocks to the south, muffling every sound and turning the sodium lamps that dotted the campus into little islands of orange glare in an ocean of the unseen. As it thickened, Owen noticed shapes moving near him that seemed to be more than mist: shapes that slid and writhed along the ground, shapes that flapped and soared overhead, shapes that hurried past him with more or less than the usual number of feet and eyes. The kingdom of Voor, the place where the light goes when it's put out and the water goes when the sun dries it up, pressed close around them.

By the time they reached the edge of the open square that separated Wilmarth Hall from Belbury Hall, all Owen could see of their objective was a dim sense of presence, marked here and there with patches of blurred light that had to be lamps and windows. Eliot gestured again, and they fanned out and started across the square at a steady walk. Around them, the coiling and flapping and crawling shapes gathered, and so did scores of figures walking alongside them that looked human but were empty shadows—meant, he guessed, to draw gunfire.

Everything depended, Owen knew, on how soon the Radiant negation team figured out what was happening. They wouldn't risk taking out students or street people wandering across campus, but once they figured out that Belbury Hall was under attack, it was a safe bet that they'd shoot at anything that moved, and might well hit something other than the shadows in the mist. His mouth went dry as the adrenaline rush cut in. Any minute now, he thought.

Step by step, as he and the others advanced, the vague smears of light ahead drew together into recognizable shapes of lamps and windows. Not quite straight ahead, dark uncertain shapes moved against the lowest bank of windows; a few more steps, and they became the mist-blurred silhouettes of men.

A moment later the muffled crack of silenced gunfire rang through the mist. Owen dropped to the brick pavement by sheer reflex, aimed his *k'renth* and let the rush of panic surging through his veins flow into it. With a shriek of raw terror, one of the figures dropped. More shots sounded. Owen took aim at another of the dim figures, and then another; one crumpled to the ground, the other screamed and ran out of sight. Others dropped or fled as more *k'renthwe* went into action; a muffled cry from the mist warned that at least one of the bullets had found its mark; and then a sudden howl rang out from something Owen didn't recognize—some other piece of Deep Ones weaponry, he guessed—and half a dozen of the figures clutched their heads at the same moment and toppled to the ground.

A trick of the drifting mist gave Owen a brief blurred glimpse of Belbury Hall's main doors, with gunmen in gray urban-camo paramilitary uniforms crouched in front, guns leveled and blazing. Behind them, up against the door, someone who was probably an officer was yelling into a cell phone, "Get me backup, goddammit! We're under—" The howling thing sounded again, and the officer and half the others dropped whatever they had in their hands, clutched their heads in evident agony, and slumped to the ground. Before the mist closed in again, Owen aimed at one of those who hadn't fallen and dropped him, then rolled fast to one side in case he'd been spotted. A moment later, the crack of a bullet ricocheting off the bricks where he'd been lying told him he'd been just quick enough.

The main doors hissed open, then, and more of the men in paramilitary uniforms surged out. A moment later Owen heard a whipporwill's cry behind him—the signal to retreat. He scrambled back into the mist, heard bullets whine over his head. When he was far enough back to be out of sight, he rose to a crouch and sprinted toward Wilmarth Hall. Dim shapes ran in the middle distance around him, not all of them shadows cast by magic, but Owen made sure to angle away from them; their job now was to spread out, drawing the negation team away from Belbury Hall in as many directions as possible. Shouts and drumming boots behind warned him that they'd gotten their wish.

The corner of Wilmarth Hall loomed ahead of him out of the mist, and he angled toward the walkway that separated it from one end of Pickman Hall, kept running. The south end of the parking garage was in front of him—he could just make out the alternating bars of pale concrete and shadow through the blurred gray air. He could run around either side of it, scramble up Meadow Hill, and get back to the ravine, where the force from Innsmouth was supposed to reassemble. Or—

Through the parking garage. The thought pressed itself on him. He could dash up the stairway right ahead of him, run through the garage, go out the other side and be in among the trees in a moment. Impulsively, he decided on that route.

The stairway into the garage loomed up out of the mist. He swerved toward it, bounded up the stairs two at a time. Inside the mist was little more than a haze blurring the glare of sodium lamps. He spotted the exit on the far side, started for it, and stopped in his tracks.

"Precisely," said Shelby, in the cool bland voice that was so different from her own. She had stepped out from behind one of the big concrete pillars that held up the garage, with a pistol in both hands, aimed straight at him. Behind her, half a dozen men in paramilitary uniforms took up shooting stances, with their guns pointed the same direction.

"You should have known we would find you eventually," she said then. "Don't try to use that weapon of yours; if you raise that arm I'll shoot your hand off. I can, you know." Without looking away from him or changing the angle of her gun, she took a cell phone from a pocket, pressed something on the screen, and said into it, "Greg, you can redirect. We've got him."

Mist flowed through the gaps in the side of the parking garage as Owen stared at her.

"Now you're going to tell us what all this is about, Owen," Shelby went on. "What your nonhuman masters are trying to do."

Owen found his voice. "Dream on."

"Oh, you'll tell us," she repeated calmly, and motioned with her head.

Four more armed men came out from behind the concrete pillar. All but one of them trained their handguns on him, but he barely noticed them, because Laura was with them. She was gagged, and one of the men had her arm twisted behind her back and the muzzle of a pistol pressed against her head.

* * *

"We followed your psychonoetic trace," Shelby said then, "and found it on her—no accounting for taste, I suppose. But you have a very simple choice to make at this point. You'll tell me everything I want to know, or you'll watch these men kill her, slowly, in front of you. If you try to interfere, they'll shoot your legs out from under you and you can watch from the floor. It's entirely up to you."

Owen held his face rigid. After a long moment, he drew in a ragged breath. "All right," he said. "I'll tell you. But you have to let her go."

"Hardly," Shelby said.

Owen tried not to see the horror and betrayal in Laura's eyes. "You want to know, you have to deal. Let her go."

Shelby considered him with no change in her expression, then gestured to the man holding Laura. He flung her to the concrete. She landed hard, tried to stand, crumpled back to the garage floor and crawled toward the nearest of the pillars.

"Lower your guns," Owen said then.

Shelby paused again. After a moment, she gestured again and the guns went down. "You've got thirty seconds," she said then. "Talk."

"Sure thing," said Owen. He drew in another breath, opened his mouth, and let the seed Jeff Marsh had placed in him blossom into manifestation. He did not have to speak the Word; it spoke itself, and set the murky air shuddering.

Shelby said something in response and started shooting, and the uniformed men whipped their guns back up and did the same. The bullets went off at strange angles, missing him, missing Laura. The light of the sodium lamps curved and flowed around Owen, and a rushing sound like distant surf rose from every side. Shelby said something else in a louder voice, and the handguns blazed, but the sounds seemed distant and unreal, and the stark concrete lines of the parking garage bent impossibly. Owen blinked, tried to process what his senses showed him, and finally understood: what was twisting and folding around him was space itself.

Only when the first pale globe of iridescence blinked into being, somewhere between him and the men in uniform, did he realize what—or, rather, whom—he had summoned.

Movement that was not the twisting of space drew his attention: Laura, struggling toward him across a floor that stretched and rippled like water. He reached for her, but space spun around them with increasing speed, and their hands missed each other. As she fell away from him, swept to one side of him by the ever-faster movement of space, one of her tentacles brushed against his arm, wrapped tight about his wrist with frantic strength. He grasped it as firmly as he could. A moment later her flailing hand caught his sleeve; he managed to get hold of her arm, and all at once she flung herself against him and they clung to each other in a tangle of limbs and tentacles.

Were they falling? Something flat and hard struck his side and stayed there: floor, wall, ceiling, he could not tell, for it seemed to change from one to another with each moment that passed. Off at an angle that made no sense, he could see the tiny forms of Shelby and the uniformed men. The muzzles of their guns were still flashing, and she seemed to be waving her arms and shouting something in a language he didn't think he knew, but the pale iridescent globes were everywhere, and space twisted and bent more and more tightly around them.

A moment later, space *tore*.

Owen had read about the fourth dimension in von Junzt, but that did nothing to prepare him for the reality of it. A gap, or something like one, ripped across the world of three dimensions, opened onto a direction ninety degrees from height and length and breadth, a direction with no name but Away. Through the gap lay something that might have been a night sky without stars, except that it was alive, and moving, and—

Hungry.

Over the rushing of space, Owen thought he heard the high keening of distant flutes, the tumbling rhythms of muffled drums. The gap widened, and streamers of three-dimensional space flowed in from its edges, for all the world like teeth edging vast jaws. The tiny figures tried to run, then, but space warped around them until every direction led straight into the void. One by one, Owen saw them fall flailing through the fanged gap into unguessable distance, tumbling out of sight into the lightless space beyond.

When the last of them was gone, the gap closed, and the three dimensions knit themselves back together. Space settled slowly back into its usual shape

As the whirling slowed and stopped, Owen found himself lying on the bare concrete floor of the parking garage, holding Laura as tightly as she clung to him. He got the gag off her with one hand, helped her spit out the wad of cloth they'd forced into her mouth, and touched her face; she kissed his hand.

"Are you hurt?"

"Some bruises," she said. "They weren't gentle, but I'll heal. Owen, Owen—"

Her voice stopped suddenly; he saw that she was staring past his shoulder. He looked that way and saw one of the pale globes of iridescence, hovering in the unquiet air. At that same instant, there came whispering through his mind a summons that could not be refused.

He helped Laura roll away from him, got to his knees facing the globe as she sat up. Her hand, soft and cool, slipped into his. All at once she bent forward, murmuring; the words were in the elder speech and unknown to him, but her tone was that of grateful adoration.

That was not for him, not yet, he knew that much at once. Instead, he raised his eyes, and looked straight into the presence of Yog-Sothoth, the Gate and the Guardian of the Gate.

* * *

At first all he saw was himself, Laura, the parking garage, as though mirrored somehow in the surface of the iridescent globe. The reflection opened up slowly, until that whole floor of the garage was included in it. He could see the concrete pillars marching in long rows, cars crouched in their sleeping places, orange lamplight glinting off brass cartridge cases on the floor, two figures like dolls who knelt before a shining globe. It seemed the most natural thing in the world to Owen that he could see pillars and cars and kneeling figures and the rest of it from all sides at once, and that he could hear, feel, touch, taste it all as well: the fading heat in the cartridge cases, the acrid tang of old tailpipe fumes in the concrete of the ceiling, the cool salt-scented shapes of Laura's bare arms, the sound of her voice as she murmured her prayer. He could sense the voor, too, blazing around the iridescent spheres, glowing around the two kneeling figures, curling and flowing through and around and between everything else.

Then he became aware of the floors of the garage above and below him, the mist and voorish currents swirling around and above it, the choked lifeless soil below it, the grass and concrete that surrounded it, the whole Miskatonic University campus as it huddled in the still and shrouded night. Something was happening inside Belbury Hall; he noticed tiny figures running down corridors, flashes of light, surges of voor, and then a sustained flash that set the building atremble and plunged it into darkness. His awareness swept out further, embracing more of the cosmos, and whatever was happening in that little corner of space faded into insignificance.

All Arkham, all Essex County, all Massachusetts opened up around him, and then his awareness stretched further, enfolding time as well as space. Through the currents of dancing voor, he could see Arkham as a forest clearing, a farming settlement, a thriving industrial town, a decaying urban center, a ruin buried beneath mud and semitropical vines, a forest clearing again. He stood watching on the day the Pilgrims landed at Plymouth Rock and the day their last descendants fled to a distant land far to the north. He hunted with the tribes that dwelt on that land before the Pilgrims came and the tribes that would dwell there when the last memory of their presence was gone forever; he looked up at the crannied faces of the glaciers that had covered the land thousands of years in the past and the glaciers that would retrace the same slow movements down from the north thousands of years in the future. He saw drowned R'lyeh when it was still above water, and drowned Boston when millennia of seaweed and coral had settled over its long-forgotten ruins.

The Earth curved away on every side, and his awareness flowed with it, joined in the solemn dance of continents and oceans as they swirled ponderously about one another, moved with the waves of life as they surged out of the ocean and returned to it again. He knew the sentient beings who dwelt on forgotten continents millions of years before the first human ancestor came down from the trees, and the others who would dwell on continents not yet born million of years after the last human beings were no more. He touched the primal stardust that drew together to form Earth in the beginning, felt the impact of the helium flash from the dying Sun that flung the remains of Earth toward the distant stars in the end.

Further out his awareness soared, passing stars, clusters, galaxies, out to the uttermost boundaries of existence, where curved time gives way to angular time and dark hungry shapes course through the surrounding void. Then, just as he glimpsed the whole cosmos as a single arc of space and time, wrapped in the embrace of the kingdom of Voor, the realm of the forever unseen, he began to fall back: toward one glittering cluster of galaxies, toward one great spiral galaxy within the cluster, toward the blazing glory of one galactic arm, toward one group of stars in that curving arm, toward one nondescript yellow-white star in the midst of the group, toward a tiny point of bluish light wheeling around that star, toward the edge of one continent, toward a little patch of light that marked the location of a town, toward the buildings on its northern edge, and in a single gray concrete building there…

Himself.

He had fallen over, and Laura had his head cradled in her lap. A sound brushed against him once, again, and it was not until the third time that the sound took shape in his dazzled mind and he realized she was repeating his name.

Indistinct sounds in the middle distance turned into the pounding of running feet. Laura looked toward the nearest entrance. Owen tried to pull himself up to a kneeling position, swayed, nearly fell forward on his face. Laura caught him and then called out, though he could not tell what she was saying. Dark figures loomed up out of the night, many of them, with one in their midst who towered over them all. A face bent over his, dark, familiar: Nyarlathotep's.

Owen tried to speak, but the words wouldn't take shape. He felt Laura's hand on his arm, heard her voice again. Nyarlathotep nodded once, said something in response, motioned to one of the others, a burly young man Owen thought he recognized.

Then strong tentacles wrapped around Owen and lifted him up.

CHAPTER 13

THE ROAD TO DUNWICH

All lights off, the car wove through back roads at racing speed. Now and then it passed a lone streetlamp or the lights of an isolated house, and the rings on Nyarlathotep's fingers glinted as he turned the wheel. The rest of him was wrapped in shadow.

In the back seat, Owen tried to get his mind clear enough to follow Laura's story.

"Poor Roland met them at the door with a shotgun, but he wasn't quick enough," she was saying. "They shot him dead right through the door—I saw his body when they dragged me downstairs. I heard the gunshots, and locked the door of the room I was in, but of course they just kicked that down. I was sure they were going to shoot me, too, but they didn't. They got my ritual dagger away from me after I cut a couple of them with it, and then they tied and gagged me, and hit me any time I tried to move. The woman with them—"

"Shelby," Owen managed to say.

"Yes. She stood there staring at me for a while after they got me tied. I think she was trying to decide whether to have me killed right there, or to use me to try to trap you. Then they hauled me downstairs and threw me into the trunk of one of their cars and drove for a while. They pulled me out of the trunk in a parking lot just outside campus—you know the rest."

The car slowed, pulled into a rutted driveway, stopped in a thicker darkness. The engine died. "We'll wait here," Nyarlathotep said.

"Is anything wrong?" Laura asked him.

"Quite the contrary." The Old One turned in his seat, or so Owen guessed from the sound. "Friends of ours will be here shortly, with good news—how good remains to be seen."

"Did—" Owen said, and stopped, trying to force the words to come together. "Belbury Hall. Did you—"

"We succeeded," said Nyarlathotep. "They guessed something was up, I think, but they weren't ready for anything like the scale of our attack, and they threw too much of their negation team against your decoy force before we broke through into the basement."

He tried to make sense of that. "How did—" The rest of the words would not come.

"How did we get there? The ground under Arkham is riddled with tunnels—some of them from the days of the rum-runners, some from colonial times, some much older—and we have access to those from a couple of places outside of town. The heptads of the Yellow Sign and the voormis came that way, and the voormis brought shoggoths with them to do the digging—they can dig very fast when they want to. And then—"

He laughed a soft dry laugh. "Then you spoke a Word of Summoning just as we broke into the basement of Belbury Hall. Whoever was commanding the Radiant force seems to have decided that Yog-Sothoth's manifestation must be the main attack, and sent most of their remaining force against it—those men will never be seen again. Still, that let us get in unnoticed, blow up the building's electrical system, and head straight up the back stairs to the ninth floor without running into any opposition at all. By the time the Radiance figured out what was happening, we had shoggoths blocking the stairwells and voormis swarming all through the building in the darkness. I don't envy what was left of the negation team—the voormis had their hooked war-knives out. They have very old grudges against the Radiance."

"There was—an explosion," said Owen. "I saw it." His mind was clearing.

"Good. That was the Fellowship at work; the King's soldiers use human weapons, and explosives are a specialty of theirs. You probably saw the blast that took out the electrical system. They laced the ninth floor with charges once we made sure that's where their machines were, and set them off as we retreated. That started quite a few fires; I don't expect that there will be much left of Belbury Hall by daybreak."

"Good," said Owen.

"Until now," said Nyarlathotep, "we haven't been able to be quite so open. I won't pretend that I didn't enjoy seeing that change."

Laura laughed, then fell silent abruptly. Another car was slowing on the road. It turned up the driveway, its tires audible on the gravel and its headlights glowing like eyes.

"Stay here," said Nyarlathotep. He got out of the car, closed the door.

The other car stopped. In the silence, Laura put her arms around Owen and pressed her face against his shoulder. He returned the embrace and bent to kiss her hair.

A long moment, and then the door opened again. The other car backed out of the driveway, onto the road, and then drove away at high speed. What sounded like a heavy bundle made the springs of the front passenger seat creak. Something else, lighter, went atop it, and then Nyarlathotep got in and closed the door.

"I mentioned good news," the Old One said. "An understatement. We sent a third force onto the Miskatonic campus tonight, and it broke into Orne Library."

"The restricted collection?" Owen guessed.

"Exactly. It was almost completely unguarded, and we got everything of real value: Prinn, Mulder, the Greek and English *Pnakotica*, all three versions of the *Book of Eibon*, and every bit of the *Necronomicon* they had—not just the Olaus Wormius translation but the Whateley manuscript and the other fragments as well." Nyarlathotep patted the bundle on the seat next to him. "All intact, and out of the hands of the Radiance."

"I hope Dr. Whipple wasn't there," Owen said.

"No, fortunately. He'll be informed in a few hours that the books are unharmed and will be safe until they can be returned."

"That should slow the Radiance down more than a bit," said Laura.

"Exactly. They have access to other copies, but not here, and few of them are as complete as these." The lighter package rustled. "Meanwhile, this is for the two of you. Not as important in the greater pattern of things, maybe, but I think it might be welcome. Here."

Laura reached for it, took it and set it on their laps: a plastic shopping bag with something inside. When she untied the top, the smell of fried fish rose from it.

"Father Dagon," Laura said, laughing. "This has to be from Innsmouth."

"It's from Barney's," Nyarlathotep said. "I had one of our drivers pick it up before he went to meet the third team outside of Arkham." He started the engine.

"Thank you, thank you, thank you." Then, a little sadly: "I imagine it's going to be a while before we get to taste Innsmouth cooking again."

* * *

The car pulled back out onto the road, hurtled through the night. In the back seat, Owen and Laura shared fish and chips, and sipped bottled water—fresh for him, salt for her. Neither spoke much. There would be time for that later.

After the bag was empty, she nestled her head onto his shoulder, and a moment later her breathing changed. In a glint of light from a distant farmhouse, Owen could see her closed eyes, and smiled. It was the last thing he remembered for many hours.

He blinked awake to find pale daylight spilling in through the car's back window. They were still moving, though not quite so fast. Along the roadsides, old stone fences half overgrown with brier loomed up, and now and again the car slowed to cross a bridge over a narrow ravine. Great rounded mountains rose up dark to either side of the road, clothed with trees and brush that even in winter seemed larger and lusher than elsewhere. Now and then a crown of standing stones could just be seen atop one of the summits, with a voorish shimmer hovering in the sky over the megaliths.

Laura was still asleep in the seat next to him. Her tentacles had spilled out from under her skirt and wrapped themselves loosely around his ankles. He sat still and watched her breathe, wondering at the feelings she stirred in him.

The car slowed at a fork in the road, turned up a steep and winding road to the right. Laura blinked awake, saw him, smiled, and then looked out the window at the rugged landscape. "Where are we?" she asked.

"In the hill country around the upper Miskatonic," said Nyarlathotep. "The Radiance will probably try to find the two of you, but this is a haven of ours, and far enough out of the way that you'll be safe. We'll reach our stopping place in a quarter hour or so."

"I guess we kicked the beehive good and proper," Laura said.

"True." He took a hairpin turn at improbable speed, brought the car straight again. "A good part of that was your doing, Owen. Summoning the Guardian of the Gate in a Miskatonic University parking garage." The Old One shook his head, amused. "Not a tactic I would have thought of, but it certainly worked—for you, for us, and for the longer term. It'll be years before they can get the gate you opened entirely sealed, and that'll keep them distracted. Jeff Marsh was wise to give you the Word."

"I owe him everything," Owen said simply. "I hope I have the chance to thank him soon."

"In due time. He's been very busy since the evacuation of Innsmouth began."

"I hope everyone got out safely," Laura said. "I've been worried about that since this whole thing started."

"The last message I got said that everyone was safely away," said Nyarlathotep. "Those who could live in Y'ha-nthlei went there, of course, with the Deep Ones' help. The others left by land or sea—the Boston lodge of the Order sent one of their freighters, and all the children and many of the others are on their way to a haven of ours in Brittany, where they'll be quite safe. Some of the others have gone to stay with the voormis for a while, and some will be following you here in due time. A repeat of 1928; the Radiance will vent its rage on empty buildings and go away, and your people can slip back afterwards."

"Like always," said Laura. "Hide, wait, rebuild."

"Until the stars are right," said Nyarlathotep.

The road straightened, ran between tall oaks for most of a mile, and then came around the flank of a mountain and wound toward a round peak in the middle distance. Up ahead, mist tangled in the trees, and here and there among the tendrils of mist rose gambrel roofs.

"Your new home, for now," said the Old One.

The car swept past an abandoned barn to an intersection of sorts. The main road swerved off to the west and away from the roofs, but a narrow lane paved in brick in the old-fashioned way went to the right, across a covered bridge toward the little town. Nyarlathotep eased back on the pedal while the car rattled over the bricks. On the far side of the bridge, the first houses came into sight; they reminded Owen of the houses of Innsmouth, old and deliberately shabby, turning blank unwelcoming faces toward those who didn't share their secret.

The lane turned into a street that ran down the middle of town, with two short cross streets that became unpaved grassy lanes after a block or so. The car passed a few stores, a tavern, a little public library, and a clapboard church with peeling paint, the much-repaired stump of a steeple, and unexpected lettering over the door: UPPER MISKATONIC STARRY WISDOM CHURCH.

The church was on one side of one of the short cross streets, and on the other was a cinderblock structure two stories high with an unhallowed and unwelcoming air. The windows stared out at the morning like baleful eyes, while two tapering pillars flanking the front door resembled yellowing fangs far too closely for the casual viewer's comfort. A neon sign in the first floor window next to the door glared NO VACANCY, and above it was a larger sign with stark letters in blue paint: DUNWICH INN MOTEL.

Laura clapped her hands together. "Lovely! It looks just like home."

"It should," said the Old One. "This has been a haven of ours for a very long time."

"Dunwich," Owen said. "The same one?"

"Of course," said Nyarlathotep, as he pulled the car up in front of the hotel. "We can talk sometime about the farrago of nonsense Lovecraft made out of that business in 1928." He gestured: "I'll see to the car. Go on inside; they're expecting you."

Owen got out, shut the door behind him, and went around the trunk to Laura's side, averting his eyes from the license plate. The bricks of the street and the cracked and crumbling sidewalk didn't look well suited to tentacles, and there were also three rickety-looking steps on the way in. He opened the car door, and once she'd slid over and taken in the terrain, he gestured. "May I?"

She broke into a smile as he bent over, put her arms around his neck, pressed against him as he lifted her up. Before he could close the door, she reached for the handle with a tentacle, pulled the door shut, and then wrapped the tentacle around his waist, half support and half caress.

Nyarlathotep drove away. Owen carried Laura to the door of the hotel, laughed as she deftly reached out with her other tentacle to turn the knob. The lobby inside reminded him forcefully of the Gilman House Hotel: the same carefully shabby look, the same deliberately outdated fittings and wallpaper. He set her down, smiled as she kissed his cheek.

Footsteps sounded in the hall, and a plump gray-haired woman in a blue and white dress and an apron stepped into the lobby. "And you'd be Miss Marsh and Mr. Merrill, I'm thinking," she said.

"That's right," Owen said.

"Oh, good." The woman beamed. "I'm Sarah Bishop; me and my husband Eli run the motel here. From what we heard, you two weren't going to have anything with you but the clothes on your backs. Let's get that taken care of, and then I'll show you to your room."

Laura started laughing. "After all the times I said just that to other people."

"Well now," said Sarah, "I know how you feel. It's been just twenty-two years now since Eli and I had to do that same thing, when we last had trouble here in Dunwich. We had to go all the way to Chorazin, away over in New York State. Good people, the Chorazin folk; my Cassie's husband Ben's from there." She got a pad of paper and a pen from the front desk, started peppering them with questions about everything they'd need.

"There," she said, finishing the list. She turned, then, and called: "Annie!"

A girl in her teens came out from the entrance to the hall: an albino, with crinkled white hair and red-pink eyes. "Yes, ma'am?"

"You'll need to run down to the general store and fetch some things. These two just got here with nothing at all, like that poor child from Providence last year. Here you go." Sarah handed her the list. "Give that to Jemmy Coles at the general store, and he'll give you what's needed. If it's too much for you to carry, and it probably will be, you see if his boys'll help."

"Yes, ma'am," Annie said. She curtseyed and then slipped out the door.

"Annie's a Whateley," said Sarah. "They come that way, with the white hair and all, now and again. She's a good little thing. If you need help and I'm not close by, you just ask her."

She stopped, then, and tilted her head to one side, for all the world like a sparrow eyeing something in the grass. "There's one other thing, if you don't mind my asking. Are you by any chance the same Laura Marsh that wrote *A Princess of Y'ha-nthlei*?"

"Yes, she is," Owen said, while Laura was still blushing and fumbling for words.

"Oh, my Cassie's girls are going to be so excited!" said Sarah. "They adore that book. Have you written any others?"

Laura bit her lip and then managed to say, "Not yet."

"Well now, if you do, you'll have three of the sweetest little things you ever met sitting at your feet waiting for every single word. I reckon—"

The front door opened. Sarah glanced that way casually, then started, turned to face the door and curtseyed. "Old One," she said in an awed voice.

The tall dark figure nodded a greeting, set down a canvas shopping bag he was carrying, and then placed one hand on Sarah's head and spoke a blessing in the Elder Tongue.

Sarah rose from the curtsey, beaming. "I was just about to show these two to their room, Old One, but if—"

"That will be fine," Nyarlathotep said, picking up the bag. "I'll want to speak to them privately, and then I'll be on my way. There will be others coming in a day or two." He allowed a smile. "They don't drive quite the way I do."

* * *

The room was large and comfortable, though the furnishings didn't look any newer than those in the Gilman House Hotel. Sarah Bishop showed them in, told Laura and Owen to let her know right away if they needed anything else, and then made off. Nyarlathotep glanced after her with a smile and closed the door. He settled into a chair against the nearest wall, put down the shopping bag, stretched out his long legs, and waved for them to sit down. They settled side by side on the bed, facing him.

"In ordinary times," the Old One said, "you'd need to stay here or in some other refuge for a year or two at most, and then slip back into Innsmouth—but these aren't ordinary times, and I have no way of knowing how long you'll be here. The Weird of Hali is waking, and one way or another, for good or ill, nothing will ever be the same again."

He turned to Laura. "The initiates here belong to the Starry Wisdom tradition, as you probably saw. Once the others from Innsmouth settle in here, I don't doubt they'll start a lodge of the Esoteric Order of Dagon, and you'll be able to continue your studies there. If you're willing, though, I'd encourage you to seek the Starry Wisdom initiations also. If you can master the mysteries of the stars as well as those of the sea, you'll be far better prepared for the struggle ahead of us."

Laura nodded. "I can do that."

"I know. Joyce Gilman's told me of your progress so far. She thinks you may have the potential to be one of the Order's truly great priestesses."

Laura blushed and looked away.

Nyarlathotep turned to Owen then. "I also have some advice for you, if you'll take it, but I have a question first. You looked into the eyes and mind of Yog-Sothoth, I believe."

Owen blinked. "Was that what happened? I knew it was the Guardian of the Gate who came, but—" His voice trailed off.

The Old One nodded. "Tell me this. What did you see there?"

Owen's mouth opened, but he stopped, at a total loss for words.

"Good," said Nyarlathotep. "Tell me this, then: is man the measure of all things?"

Owen stared at him, and then started laughing. "Here's a child's six inch ruler," he said. "Go measure a galaxy with it."

A slow smile spread across the Old One's lean dark face. "Good," he repeated. "Go on."

"I'm not sure whether or not all things have a measure," Owen said after a moment. "If they do, it's certainly not me." He gestured at Nyarlathotep. "I don't know—are you the measure of all things, Old One?"

"I? No." Nyarlathotep's smile broadened. "Not I, not Shub-Ne'hurrath, not Cthulhu, not Yog-Sothoth, not even blind Azathoth, the ancestor of us all. We're part of the pattern, not the measure of it."

"Then we humans certainly aren't the measure either."

"How does that make you feel?"

"Relieved," Owen admitted. "The measure of all things, the lord of creation, the conqueror of nature, all that pompous nonsense—what a ghastly burden it would be if we were actually supposed to be any of those things. And since we're not, pretending to be them—" He shuddered. "That's madness. I mean that literally. The people who threw Justin Geoffrey into an asylum were the ones who belonged there."

Nyarlathotep was nodding as he finished. "Excellent," he said. He glanced down at his hands, pulled an ornate ring off one finger, handed it to Owen. "When you feel you're ready, give this to the magister of the Starry Wisdom church here. He'll know by that token that you're prepared to enter the outermost circle of initiation."

Owen took the ring, looked at it, and then at the Old One. "Thank you."

"You've earned that much, at least." Nyarlathotep leaned forward in the chair. "You've also been trained in the traditions of human scholarship, though, and that's something our side has rarely had the chance to work with. For that reason I've got something else to place in your keeping." He pushed the canvas shopping bag across the floor. "These are the books we got from Orne Library."

Owen gave him an astonished look, tried to say something, failed.

"You're to keep them safe," the Old One said, "but you're also to study them, and do your best to master the lore in them. There are plenty of others doing the same thing in their own way—witches, initiates, sorcerers and sorceresses of the elder races—and Laura can certainly study them as well, along with the other initiates here; in fact, I'd encourage that. You come to the work with a background that's very different from theirs, though, and you may see things they miss. That might be important as the Weird wakens.

"There's something else in the bag for you, though."

Owen reached into the bag, found something small and familiar on top, and pulled it out: a photo in a cheap standing frame, showing a younger version of himself and five other young men in desert fatigues and buzzcuts, with their arms around each other's shoulders. He looked up from it, swallowed visibly. "Thank you."

"That's what the Radiance was using to track you," Nyarlathotep said. "It was in one of their machines on the ninth floor of Belbury Hall. I spotted it there, and—" He shrugged. "No doubt one of their people stole it from the place you lived in Arkham. I thought it might have some value to you."

"Yes," Owen said. "Yes, it does. Thank you." He handed the photo to Laura, who looked at it, at him, and smiled.

The Old One got to his feet. "I'll leave you now," he said. "You know what you need to do, or as much of that as anyone can know in advance. There's much to do; it may be months or years before you see me again—or it may not. We'll see.

"We've won a battle, but there'll be more battles ahead, some open, some subtle. We'll have to face the full strength of the Radiance, and not even the Great Old Ones can know for sure what that may be. Even if we do our best, we could still fail, and watch the Earth die around us, but there's still hope as long as we can hold on—until the stars are right."

He stepped forward, placed his hands on their heads, and spoke a blessing in the elder tongue; Owen felt the voor shimmer through him, for all the world like moonlight along the old straight track to Innsmouth. Then the Old One was gone, and the door closed behind him. His long swinging stride faded to silence in the hallway outside.

ACKNOWLEDGMENTS

No author writes in a vacuum, but this fantasia on a theme by H.P. Lovecraft depends, even more than most works of fiction, on the labors of others. The most important of these debts is of course to Lovecraft himself, whose stories and essays were a constant source of inspiration for me, as well as a well-stocked warehouse of props and scenery. Fans of the weird tale already know that I have also borrowed plenty of local color from stories by Robert E. Howard, Arthur Machen, and Clark Ashton Smith.

I also owe thanks to two modern scholars of Lovecraft's writings. S.T. Joshi's writings on the old gentleman of Providence were invaluable in helping me grasp the world of ideas that structured Lovecraft's fiction and gives it an enduring relevance. On a different plane, Daniel Harms' *Encyclopedia Cthulhiana* was a constant help in keeping the details straight, and more than once sent me chasing after some detail that turned out crucial to the unfolding story. I am also grateful to Donovan K. Loucks and Boyd Pearson, whose websites—*The H.P. Lovecraft Archive* (http://www.hplovecraft.com) and *The Eldritch Dark* (http://www.eldritchdark.com) respectively—made finding even the most obscure writings by Lovecraft and Clark both easy and enjoyable. In addition,

I would like to thank Sara Greer and Dana Driscoll for reading the manuscript and offering an abundance of useful comments.

Finally, I don't think it's out of place to mention certain intellectual debts that reach well beyond the obvious boundaries of Cthulhudom. Though science fiction has been praised as a literature of ideas, it seems to me that the weird tale, as told by Lovecraft and his peers and successors, has at least as much right to the title, if not more. Where the ideas explored by science fiction stories too often amount to little more than extrapolating current trends in a conveniently straight line, the weird tale at its best poses questions of shattering profundity about the meaning of human existence, the nature of history, and the vexed relationship between reason and reality.

Mortimer Adler used to say that all the works of human learning and culture are part of one Great Conversation winding down through the centuries. H.P. Lovecraft listened closely to that conversation, and of course contributed to it as well; two of the voices that shaped his thinking and storytelling—Arthur Schopenhauer and Friedrich Nietzsche—have also had much to do with this tale. Of the writers since Lovecraft's time who have had a similar influence on this story, one who deserves mention here is Theodore Roszak, whose *Where the Wasteland Ends* whispered a word or two in a Great Old One's ear. None of the above, it goes without saying, should be held responsible for anything in *The Weird of Hall: Innsmouth*.

Printed in the USA
CPSIA information can be obtained
at www.ICGtesting.com
JSHW021346031023
49524JS00011B/7

9 781912 573875